MAINE

&*Mia*

FEELINGS ON SAFETY

3

A NOVEL BY

JOI MINER

Royalty Publishing House is now accepting manuscripts from aspiring or experienced urban romance authors!

WHAT MAY PLACE YOU ABOVE THE REST:

Heroes who are the ultimate book bae: strong-willed, maybe a little rough around the edges but willing to risk it all for the woman he loves.

Heroines who are the ultimate match: the girl next door type, not perfect - has her faults but is still a decent person. One who is willing to risk it all for the man she loves.

The rest is up to you! Just be creative, think out of the box, keep it sexy and intriguing!

If you'd like to join the Royal family, send us the first 15K words (60 pages) of your completed manuscript to submissions@royaltypublishing-house.com

SYNOPSIS

nd that's a whole lotta love, ain't tryna waste it... Like we be runnin' a mile to never make it

Maine and Mia have lost everything that matters to them. Mia losing more, though, with her not knowing who she is or having any memory of anyone in her life. That doesn't stop life from taking them for an even bumpier ride when the man that held it all together is no longer there. It seems like everything and everyone is against them being together, and their love might just fold under the pressure.

Trouble is trying to decide if his coming to Dallas was a mistake. All the drama that he's found himself in the middle of may be too much for him to handle, and he's starting to think that it may be better for everyone if he just goes back to where he came from. But before he can make his final decision, he finds himself facing life and death decisions that could cost him the family that he's just getting to know, or worse, himself.

With their entire empire and their legacy at stake, the King family finds that no one is safe from harm, or karma. Find out who comes out on top and who ends up six feet under in the roller coaster finale of *Maine and Mia: Feelings on Safety.*

ACKNOWLEDGMENTS

ruhhhhhh! This series was something else. But I made it through and can't wait for y'all to, too. I have to give credit where it's due, because without my crew, my fam, my ridahs, my folks, I would've lost my mind with this one.

To my Family: Thank you for giving me the time to write my dreams into reality. Thank you for being the best, most supportive team a girl could ever wish for. I love y'all!

To the Royals: Y'all are the best, most accepting, most encouraging and helpful team any writer could ever wish for. When I wanna quit, y'all push me. I am so grateful.

To my Readers: Thank y'all for your patience and forever rockin' with me, across genres, and up and down the emotional roller coasters that I love to take y'all on. Y'all's reviews and inboxes mean the world to me. Without y'all, there would be no Joi Miner.

To Myself: Chile, stop worrying about the little shit and keep going. You love this more than breathing. You need this to remain sane. You did it! Just finished another series. Now, let's take a nap and do it again… and again… and again!

DEDICATION

*D*edicated to all those who love again, despite their hearts being traumatized in the past. To all the lovers of love. This one is for you.

PREVIOUSLY IN MAINE & MIA: FEELINGS ON SAFETY...

Sa'Mia King

"Sa'Mia? How are you feeling?"

I opened my eyes when I heard a woman speaking, but I didn't know who she was talking to. I looked around, and I was in a hospital bed, hooked to all kinds of machines. I wanted to ask where I was, but I was tired of asking that shit at this point. I was just gonna accept the fact that I was in a damn hospital somewhere.

"I'm hungry as hell. This IV shit y'all feedin' me ain't working," I said, and she smiled broadly. I didn't think that shit I said was funny, but apparently, she did. I wondered if it would be funny if I busted her in her shit with this damn old-fashioned 1950's ass phone that was on the stand right here beside my bed.

She kept that smile plastered on her face while she checked my chart, put that tight ass blood pressure cuff on my arm, listened to my chest, checked the monitor that was on my stomach, and pulled out this long ass needle.

"Yo! Aye lady, what's that? Yeen just gon' be pullin' out long ass needles and stickin' me wit' them shits! Ayeeee! Heeeellllllppp!"

She was coming at me from her cart in what looked like slow motion.

5

She was crazy if she thought she was about to stick me with that shit. I was beating the call button with my hand and screaming like she was killing me.

"Yeen sticking me with that shit, lady!" I hollered and kicked the arm that was holding the needle, making it fly out of her hand and across the room.

She looked like she wanted to say or do something, and I was ready to turn with her old ass. She wasn't about to stick me with some government created shit, smiling at me like a damn Cheshire cat and shit. She let out a deep breath and grabbed another needle from the cart, coming back toward me. Apparently, she ain't get the memo the first time. I was about to resend that shit if she took one more ghatdamned step.

"What's going on in here?" A man in a lab coat ran in like his ass was on fire. It took his ass long enough.

"This Super Smiley Ass Nurse Friendly Bitch tryna stick me with a hot needle. I'on know where I'm at, who the fuck I am, and if I don't know, then my folks don't neither. I ain't 'bout to be one of y'all test subjects to some shit y'all gon' recall in six months wit' one of them commercials. Tell me what the fuck is goin' on, and then we can talk about that needle and shit. *Talk* about it," I seethed, looking at her and then at him.

"I don't make enough money to deal with this shit," she snapped, throwing her hands in the air, needle still held tightly.

"Maybe you shoulda had higher ambitions than wipin' the next bitch's ass, then. Not my problem. But yeen finna stick me with no shit and not tell me what the fuck it is. I'on care how much they damn pay you."

"Sa'Mia! No need to be nasty," the man said sternly, and I looked at him to let him know that he wasn't scaring anything around here. "She was about to put the medicine in your IV for you and the baby. That's all."

"Baby? What baby? Y'all better start makin' sense in this damn place!"

"I can sedate her. Knock her lil' ass right on out, then we can give her the care that she needs, even though I ain't so sure she deserves it at this point," Nurse Smiley-Face said to the man, and he cut his eyes at her.

"See! See! Take that bitch off my rounds. She got a vendetta and shit. All 'cause she got her ass kung-fu kicked. If she'd just told me what the hell she was doin', which is part of proper provision of care—" I looked at the nurse who looked stunned. "Yeah, bitch, I done read a book or two, too. I don't remember who I am, but my mind still sharp as a fuckin' Ginsu in this bitch. Now," I turned back to the doctor. "Tell me what the fuck is going on, and we can go from there," I demanded emphatically, crossing my arms under my titties and waiting for them to start talking.

Instead, the doctor made a call on his phone and motioned for the nurse to walk out of the room with him. He'd better know not to leave that bitch in here with me. Come back and she have that needle sticking outta her damn neck. But I was mad as hell that they didn't feel the need to tell me what the hell was going on. Instead, they just left the room. I was about to get up and walk up outta here. I ain't know where I was going, but I wasn't about to stay here where they didn't follow protocol. Didn't they know the patient was always right? Wait, or was that the customer? Well, a patient *is* a customer, so the shit is right either way. They'd better come correct when they come their asses back in here, that's all I'm saying.

I laid my head back and tried to relax, but I wasn't about to go to sleep, because I ain't trust these folks like that. I would be a sleep-deprived ass before I let Nurse Smiley-Face catch me slipping. I heard the door and kept my eyes closed. I was gonna play sleep, so I could catch their asses trying some slick shit. Then, no mercy.

I heard someone walk close to the bed and then heard a chair being pulled up to my bedside. When my hand was enveloped into a much larger hand and I felt lips at the back of it, I softened up a little bit.

"Mia, I know yeen sleep, mane, so open ya eyes, mama. You used to do that same shit when yeen wanna get up or wanted to hear some shit we was discussing that we ain't want ya ass to hear. I know all ya tricks, baby girl. So cut that shit out," the deep baritone voice that was whispering into my ear made my pussy thump. That's when I realized that shit was hurting. *What the hell happened to me? Maybe Barry White Throat could tell me somethin'.*

When I opened my eyes, I jumped back. I remembered him. He was the one in the hotel room. Who the hell was this man, and why was he in my hospital room? He was in here to finish me off; that's what he was gonna do. I couldn't go down without a fight.

7

"Nigga, what the fuck? You shot somebody in front of me. I'on remember much, but I remember that shit. So you here to kill me, huh?"

"Mia, calm yo' lil' ass down. I swear, you worse without a memory than when you had one." He sighed, sitting back in the chair.

He was sexy as hell. I had to say that. I ain't know what my type was, but he could get it. But from the sounds of shit, he might've already got it. At least, I hoped he was the nigga who got me pregnant. I ain't wanna believe I was out there passin' out pussy like that. Then again, though, this nigga was huge. I was sure I wasn't gon' be able to push his big ass baby the hell up outta my pussy and that snapback be an option.

"Tell me why I should calm down. All I saw was you and that light-skinned nigga shoot each other. And why ain't you got no bandages? I know he hit ya ass. I saw that shit. And the man on the floor. Did you say he was my daddy? Then these folks come in here and tell me I'm pregnant and shit, but I don't remember makin' no baby—"

"They say you're pregnant?" he asked, his face lighting up.

"Outta all I said, that's all you heard, nigga?"

"No, I just thought—"

"Maine, thank you for getting here so quickly. Mia was about to be sedated and restrained if she attacked another one of my nurses," the doctor came back in saying, patting the man in the chair on the back with a laugh.

"That bitch was tryna stick me and not tell me what was in that needle. You know that shit ain't right, man." I huffed and pouted. I felt like a kid in trouble, and I knew I was grown as hell, at least I thought I was.

"I get it, Mia. But you can't go fighting and insulting the nurses. They're the ones who can help or hurt you, real shit," the Maine nigga said. He wasn't nobody to me, so I ain't like his tone, and I was about to let him know, too.

"I don't appreciate your tone, my nigga. I don't know who you is that the doc thought you was gon' come here and get some straightening in a bitch, but you don't put no fear in my hea—"

He stood up and grabbed me by the back of my neck, pressing his lips against mine with so much force that it made me swallow all that shit I was talking. All I wanted was his tongue to keep dancing with mine and to breathe his breath in through my nose as he breathed it out, even though it smelled and tasted like he'd just finished a bag of Cool Ranch Doritos. And a grape soda. The way he was kissing me, I was about to be able to tell you what he had for breakfast.

I melted into the bed, and my heartrate picked up. The way I responded to him let me know that he was somebody important to me. That maybe I was in love with him. But I couldn't remember him, and that made the tears begin to pour from my eyes. I wanted to know this man and what he meant to me. Wanted to know what my life was like with him. Who I was. How was I gonna raise a baby and not know myself?

He let go of me and sat back down with the biggest smirk on his face. "Now, Doc, tell me what's good. I been worried about her but had some shit to take care of."

They shared a look that meant something, but it was lost on me, and I had enough swimming through my head. I didn't even wanna know what they were talking about.

"Well, we got to her right on time. One of the babies didn't make it, but the other one we were able to save. She's gonna have to be on careful, though, but we all know that she ain't gonna listen," he said about me like I was a child and I wasn't standing right there. "I'll send her home with you, if that's ok with you, Sa'Mia—" He addressed me for the first time since he'd started talking. I nodded, and he continued. "Good deal, I'll get the paperwork together. How's your wound?" he asked, and when Maine pulled his shirt up to show the bandage in his gut, I closed my eyes tight.

Not because it was gruesome. But because all them tattoos on him had my ass leaking, and I would feel like a perv if I'd stared at his ass like I wanted to.

"Ahhhhhh! Maine! Right therrrrreeee! I love you! I love you! I love you!"

Maine stopped mid-bounce with me halfway off his dick and stared into my eyes. My eyes, that were squeezed shut in utter pleasure, popped open. I looked at him like he was crazy as hell. I was almost at my nut, and this nigga was fuckin' up the flow.

"I love you, too, Sa'Mia King. I always have and always will. Remember that," he said with a flash of sadness crossing his face…

I let out a heavy sigh, shifting underneath the covers of the bed. My eyes opened so fast the light blinded me, but they landed on Maine, and he smiled. Leave it to me to remember how we made the baby, well the twins, first. So my name was Sa'Mia, and this was my baby daddy. Okay. We could start there.

"Let me get someone to rebandage you, and then y'all can be on your way. Mia, I'm gonna send a nurse to help you, okay?" he asked me apprehensively. I had to laugh. "I'll make sure she lets you know every step of your treatment."

"Thank you, Doctorrrr—"

"Smith. Girl, I been taking care of you since you were in pampers. Hopefully, you'll remember it all soon enough. You have a lot of people in your life who love you. It would be a shame for you to forget us."

I didn't like the way he said 'hopefully' like there was a chance I would never get my memory back. I wanted to tell him that I remembered Maine fucking me so hard and deep that he planted two seeds in me, but I bit my tongue. I would keep that shit to myself for a little while to see if I could remember anything else.

Nurse Smiley-Face brought her ass back in to patch up my man, and I watched her ass like a hawk to make sure she ain't get too loose with them old ass hands. She wasn't 'bout to get her groove back with mine, ol' cougar ass. I saw how she was looking at him.

"Mia, it's good. This is all you, ma," Maine said, calling me out on how hard I was craning my neck to watch her every move.

"I hear you, but she don't know no boundaries. So I'd rather keep my eye on her ass, if you don't mind."

Nurse Smiley-Face said something under her breath that made Maine laugh, but I ain't see shit funny. I was about to get up out this bed and Yabba Dabba Do her ass back to the Stone Ages. She had one more snicker or side eye, and I was gon' Bed Rock her ass like Lloyd. She pulled out a needle and stuck it into Maine's stomach. He grimaced but took that shit like a G. She looked back at me with a smirk, and I knew it was time for me to get out this hospital before I replaced her in the bed that I was laying in.

"I'll go tell Doctor Smith you're all patched up and get Miss King's discharge papers," she said to Maine, her back completely to me.

Walking off, I stuck my tongue out at her wide ass back with the extra fat rolls hanging out her bra and the ass that looked like she had two midgets mud wrestling in her scrubs. *Ol' Majin Boo* looking bitch.

"Mia! Mia!" Maine called my name over and over to bring my attention back to him.

"What, bruh?" I mugged him, because he was too friendly with her ass, too, in my opinion.

"First off, fix your fuckin' tone when you talkin' to me. Memory loss or not, you gon' get some ack right in ya, if I gotta shake ya lil' ass to put it there. Or, beat that shit up in ya," he said, grabbing a handful of his big ass dick through his jeans. His print was showing like sweatpants in jeans. Who the fuck is hung like that? My nigga, that's who.

"My bad. I just ain't like the way that bitch was touchin' on you," I admitted, surprising myself with my reaction.

"You startin' to sound more and more like yaself, mane," he said with a chuckle before scooting back over to the bed and taking my hand into his. "Look at me," he commanded, and I obliged.

"Yes, sir," I said obediently.

"I'm yours. I know it's been some shit that may have made you doubt that shit—" He paused, looking in my eyes like he was hoping to get a reaction or for something to register. "Hell, some of the shit, I hope you don't remember."

There was an honesty in his tone that made me wonder what the fuck he'd been into that he wouldn't want me to remember. I hoped I remembered that shit, just so I could give him hell for whatever it was.

"You know you could tell me and try to jog my memory," I tried.

"You funny, mane. I'm a lotta thangs but dumb ain't one of them muhfuckas. I can tell you some other shit, though, if you want. We got the rest of our lives, and I'll spend every free moment reminding you who you are and why you're so fuckin' special."

I felt my face getting wet. He loved me. I didn't know why he loved me like he did and what I did to deserve a man like this, but I was grateful. "Wha-what if I can't remember?" I asked sadly, because that was becoming more and more of a possibility.

"Then we'll have the rest of our lives to make new memories with you and our seed," he said, wiping the tears from my face with one hand and resting the other on my stomach. *If I wasn't in love with this man before, I could for real see myself falling for him now.*

"Well, you're all ready to go, Mia," Doctor Smith said, coming in with paperwork that he handed to Maine. "I already had her prescriptions filled, and a nurse will meet y'all at your house in about an hour to help you get washed up and in bed. That'll give you the chance to get there and get settled in."

"I'm gonna remove the IV and take these monitors off of you, sugar," another nurse said. I liked her better than Nurse Smiley-Face already. "Are you in any pain? Can you stand and walk, or do you want a wheelchair to get you to the lobby?"

"I think I'm good, but I'll still take the wheelchair. I already lost one baby, I don't wanna do anything to put this fighter inside of me at risk." I smiled, and she nodded and left the room.

"I'll be to check on you in the morning, Mia. Be good until then, okay?" Doctor Smith said, and Maine stood with him.

"I'mma go get the truck so we can get outta here, bae." He kissed my forehead, and my shit started to pound immediately. "You aight?" he asked me, and I didn't know I had closed my eyes.

"Yeah, I'm fine. Just a little tired."

"We gon' get you home so you can rest," he said, kissing my forehead again, and it seemed like every time he did that, he sent a jolt to my brain.

"Okay, I'm just gonna close my eyes."

As soon as I was in the room alone, I couldn't help crying. I was getting tired of crying, but this time was different. I was flooded with images and they weren't coming together to make sense. I wanted them to make sense. I needed to remember.

"You're all good, Mia. Come on, let's get you downstairs," the nurse said, waking me up. "Are you strong enough to change into your clothes that Maine brought you?"

I shook my head 'no' groggily. I didn't know that I was asleep, and damn sure didn't feel her take all the tubes and monitors off of me. She helped me out of the bed and into the wheelchair, letting me keep that ugly ass open-backed hospital gown on. When we got to the lobby, Maine picked me up from the chair, and I wrapped my arms around his neck tightly. He carried me to the truck and put me in the passenger seat where I drifted back off to sleep.

That didn't last long because his phone kept ringing on the way to his house, and I wanted to get upset, but still wasn't sure if I could. He looked down at the screen and finally answered it, and all I could hear was a frantic female's voice on the other end of the line. I wasn't trying to listen, but the bitch was loud and sounded like she was crying.

"Mane, you gotta be shittin' me! I just—stay there, Marissa! I'll be there as soon as I get Mia settled," he said, pulling up to the gated community that I assumed was his home and punching in a code really aggressively.

This nigga had anger issues, and I wasn't about to be on the receiving end of that shit. He could save that for whoever the Marissa bitch was that had been calling him all crazy. He whipped into the driveway of a beautiful house, and I could tell that this nigga had bank. Made me wonder what kinda shit he was into. Especially getting frantic ass calls at one in the morning and shit.

"Fuck! Fuck! Fuuuuckkkk, mane!" he hollered, tears racing down his cheeks and punching the steering wheel.

I reached over to comfort him, and he looked at me with the saddest eyes. It almost hurt to look back. I rubbed his back, and he kept crying, looking like there was something that he needed to tell me.

"Ar-are you aight?" I asked, my brow furrowed, feeling his pain in my chest.

"No, Mia. I'm sorry. King is dead," he told me, pausing and waiting for a reaction.

I turned my head to the side, trying to process what he was saying and trying to connect that name to someone or something that meant something to me. His face told me that I should. That I needed to. That I was supposed to. But I came back blank. Finally, I looked him in the eyes and reached over to wipe the tears from his cheeks before speaking.

"I'm sorry. Who? Do I know him?"

ARKINO "MAINE" SHANE

"*D*amn, mane! This shit can't be real!"

      I paced the space in the safe house where King's body was, in complete shock. I felt like I was stuck in some kinda damn nightmare, and I couldn't wake up from the shit. My mentor, my father figure was dead. I was filled with a saddened rage that had my chest heaving.

I wanted to punch holes in walls, put bullets through skulls, and cry 'til my heart stopped bleeding all at once. But I couldn't do any of that. I still didn't know if Trouble was alive and lurking in the shadows ready to murk a nigga. And without King and with Mia having amnesia, I was in this shit alone. I had to play it smart. Smarter than I felt like right now.

"They're gonna come get him and take him to be cremated. That's his request," Doc Smith said, coming out the back looking like he'd been crying. "There's a reading of the will in five days. Make sure you and Mia are present."

"Get me the details, and we'll be there," I promised, turning to leave. I couldn't stay in this space any longer.

"Maine," Doc Smith called behind me.

"Yeah?"

"Mia still doesn't have her memory back. I don't know what something like this would do to her. Try not to upset her more than you have to, okay?"

"That's the plan," I called over my shoulder, leaving out the door and getting in my truck.

I needed to be close to Mia. I didn't know how close she would let me be, still not knowing who I was, but I would take anything right now. Even just being in the same house on different floors, in different rooms. I just needed to know she was close.

Walking in the house, I heard music blasting from the kitchen. I was shocked when I walked in there and saw Mia dancing to Beyoncé, who she hated, singing her ass off and cooking.

"We like to partayyyy! Ayyyyeee! Ayyyyeee! Ahhhhhhh!" She screamed when she did a spin singing into the wooden spoon she was holding in her hand and saw me standing there. "Make some damn noise when you come in a room. Damn. You'd think your big ass would walk like Sasquatch."

I laughed because the "pop the fuck off" region of her brain wasn't damaged at all. Sitting at the counter, I looked at her, loving and hating that she didn't know who she was or who I was and what we had. If she remembered that I was fuckin' Neisha, or the video of us getting leaked, or me shooting her brother, she may never want to see me again. I couldn't let her find out before I made her mine. Permanently. I couldn't live without Mia.

"Aye! Did you hear me?" she yelled, popping the back of my hand with the wooden spoon.

"Be careful with that shit, girl. I like it rough."

"You nasty." She giggled, walking back over to the stove. "I said whoever this bitch Beyoncé is, she got them hits! Did I like her before?"

"No," I said with a laugh. "You hated her, actually, because she was from Houston and got her fame 'on the backs of other heauxs' was how you used to put it eeeeeeevery time she came on the radio."

"Well damn. New me, new taste in music I guess," she said with a shrug. "Did you know I could burn in the kitchen?"

"You mean burn down a kitchen?" I joked.

"Yeen funny, lil' nigga. Ain't shit burnin' up in here," she said, moving

15

her arm over the pots that were boiling over the stove that had it smelling heavenly in here.

"Ain't shit lil' 'bout this nigga here," I boasted, grabbing my dick and making her eyes bulge. She blushed and turned around, busying herself at the stove.

I just sat there, watching her, my eyes glazing over. I loved her more than life. I owed my loyalty to her and her father, and since he was no longer here, I would protect her like I knew he would want me to.

"What's wrong with you?" she asked, and I didn't realize she'd walked over.

"Nuh-Nothin', mane. Nothin' to worry your pretty lil' head about. Worry 'bout not scorchin' my pots," I said, wiping my face. My hands were drenched with tears that wouldn't stop falling.

"You upset about the King man dying?"

Something about hearing her speak of her own father in such an unfamiliar way broke the dam.

"Oh noooo, what did I say?"

"Listen, mane, get dinner ready, and I'mma take a shower, aight?" I told her, not wanting to break all the way down in front of her.

"Oh, okay. Don't be takin' no long ass showers, though. Dinner's almost—*ding*—done," she said, rushing to the oven to take what looked and smelled like garlic crescent rolls out of my stainless-steel oven.

This had to be the most action my kitchen had seen in a hot minute. I watched her and knew this was the life I wanted. Just me and Sa'Mia. Her making dinner, carrying my seed. Yeah, just me and her for the rest of our lives. But with the way shit had been going, I couldn't say how long my life—hell, our lives—might be.

Walking to the bathroom, I took off my clothes with lightning speed, hitting the button to turn the water on. I used the touchpad to set the temperature like I liked it before stepping in. I let the water fall onto my head and down my body, breaking down as it cascaded down. Images of King laying there lifeless kept flashing before my eyes. I still couldn't believe he was gone.

I rested my palms against the tile of the shower, feeling the water beat my tense muscles. I had to get all this shit out before I faced Kong or

Kellz or even Neisha's ass. I wanted to kill all them muhfuckas with my bare hands.

"Fuck, mane!" I hollered, punching the wall and busting my knuckles.

The blood and water washed down the drain, but I wasn't feeling the pain that I should've been feeling. The only pain I felt was the loss of my father. My pops. The only one I knew. Alonzo King. Then I felt something that took all my pain away.

"I'm sorry you're sad," Mia's voice permeated the beating of the water. "Is there anything I can do to help?" she asked, stroking my back with her hands.

I couldn't think of shit but one thing and didn't want to push her to that. Not right now. Not while she was still unsure of so many things.

"I love you, Sa'Mia," I said, turning to face her. She was everything to me. And right now with the water falling onto her, making her locs stick to her beautifully crafted body, she looked like everything a nigga like me could imagine having. Mia was *my wet dream.*

"You know, staring is rude," she sassed, making me smile.

"My apologies, Miss Mia. You're just so beautiful to me."

"Awwww, you tryna sweet talk me outta my drawls? But I ain't got none on." She flirted, and my will power was now washing down the drain with the blood and pain that were pouring from my hand and my eyes at the same time.

"Mia, maybe we shouldn't—"

"Shouldn't what? Ain't I already pregnant with your baby? So, we've already done the shit before, right?"

"What about dinner?"

"You got a microwave, don't you?"

"Yeah." I chuckled. "Yeah, I do."

I couldn't argue with her logic. But I still didn't feel right about it. Felt like I would be taking advantage of her. She took my wash cloth and washed my entire body up, focusing especially on my dick and balls. Her hands on me felt better than anything I'd felt in a while. She couldn't hold the lil' nigga in her hands completely, but she still handled that thang like a pro.

She put more soap on the washcloth and cleaned herself as well. Her body, under that water, had me on rock and lightheaded. I had to get outta here and either the hell away from her or the hell up in her before I passed the fuck out.

"You seem to still be on the fence. Let me fix that for you," her soft voice permeated my thoughts, as she squatted down in the shower. "Some things you never forget."

She took my dick in her mouth and my knees buckled. Mia sucked me like she was trying to take the pain away. Like she wanted to make it better. Like she remembered us. Our love. What we once had. She sucked me with so much force that I came in a matter of seconds. That shit had to be a record. And I was gonna return the favor and make love to her like we'd just met, and I wanted her to be mine. She'd taken the pain of the past away from me, and I was going to inject my hope for our future into her.

Picking Mia up, I walked out of the shower, dripping all over the floor. I ain't care. I had one thing in mind, and that was tasting Sa'Mia. Standing her up, I turned her around and bent her over the edge of the bed. Jiggling her ass cheeks in my hands, I squeezed them both in my massive hands before getting down on one knee and spreading them apart. Mia looked over her shoulder at me, and I slapped her left cheek before biting her on the right one.

"Who told you to look? Assume the fuckin' position," I barked, my tone full of bass. She smiled before turning back around and slid up onto the bed on her knees to give me better access.

Not wasting anymore time, because I knew that it was of the essence, I straightened my tongue and slid it in and out of her hole, feeling the tightness of her walls around it. That shit made my dick rock up harder than it already was, and I had to massage it to make the lil' nigga simmer down and wait his turn. I had been missing Mia since our first time, and fuckin' Neisha only made it worse. She didn't feel like Mia, and I wasn't in love with her, so I could never get into it. I didn't know how niggas fucked different bitches all the time, because I'd have to think of Mia just to get my shit to stay hard. Maybe I was just wired different.

"Ahhh, Kino, yesssss!" I paused, because she called me by my name. Well, the nickname that she and only another select few used. It gave me hope that maybe she was starting to remember.

"Say my name again, Mia!" I mumbled with a face full of her ass and a mouth full of her pussy.

"What you say? Boy, stop talkin' witcha mouth full," she joked, twerking her ass on my face. *Oh, she think this shit funny,* I thought, lifting her up off the bed and taking her clit in my mouth. I went to work on her little ass like I wasn't gon' fuck her again in my life! "Wait! Shit! Baeeeee! Shit. I'm sorry. I'm sorry. I swe-eeeearrrrr!" she begged, shaking and cumming all in my mouth.

I ain't give her the chance to catch her breath, I flipped her over on her back and slid into her wetness.

"Unhhhh fuck, girl. This shit still feel brand-new. But wetter than I remember," I moaned, leaning on top of her, my mouth on her ear. Once I was all the way in, we both let out a sigh that made me pause and just rest in heaven for a hot ten seconds.

I started moving my hips real slow, letting me stretch her back out. She dug her nails into my back and bit my chest, before licking the same spot, sending a jolt through my dick. See, shit like that was why Mia was pregnant now. Leaning back out of the reach of her mouth, I looked down at her, and she was so gorgeous. Her round face was scrunched up, and she was biting her bottom lip so hard she was about to split her shit.

Grabbing two handfuls of my sheets, I picked up the pace with deep hard strokes, leaving my mark all on her shit. I was grateful that she hadn't been with anybody but me, even though I couldn't say the same. But I knew I would kill her and that nigga if I felt even the slightest curve in her shit.

"Mia! Shit, girl! I love yo' lil' ass, you know that?"

"Mmmm hmmmm," was all she could get out. Her eyes were rolling back in her head and slipped shut in pleasure.

"You love me, Mia?"

Her eyes opened and she looked at me with a confused expression. I won't lie and say that shit ain't hurt my feelings, but I had to remember what was going on. I needed to hear her say it, though. Losing King, I couldn't lose the bond I had with Mia, too. She *had* to remember.

"Mia!" I yelled, grabbing the sheets and looking at her with hurt in my eyes. "Do you love me?"

She still didn't answer, but I was gonna jog her memory. I leaned back on my heels, picking her up, and started slamming her on my dick. She was holding on like she thought if she let go, I would bounce her ass up off my shit and through the ceiling.

"Shit! Baby! Oh... my... God!"

"Shut the fuck up! If you can't say you love me, don't say shit! Just take this dick!" I snapped, gripping her ass and holding her down on my waist.

She had tears in her eyes but didn't tell me to stop. She was enjoying the shit, but I knew she could tell I was hurt. Her tears were of frustration because she wanted to remember as badly as I wanted her to. But she didn't want to say something that she didn't mean.

I kept fucking her like I loved her, tears streaming down my face, too. I loved Mia, I missed King, and he had just left this world. I was happy that we were having a child to continue his legacy, made from the love that Mia and I shared. A love she didn't remember. I kissed her deeply, tasting our tears in both our mouths. I tasted our pain while exchanging passion in the tangling of our tongues.

I let her mouth go, pulling back and taking in her face before laying her back down and slow grinding her passionately. I felt my nut rising and wanted to pull out so I could prolong the session. But Mia grabbed me and held me in place, not wanting me to stop. She bit my neck, my chest, tracing my tattoos with her tongue. Her moans filled the room and made my nut come even faster. She got wetter. And wetter. And wetter. Then clenched around my dick in a convulsing series of orgasmic contractions. Sucking the nut right outta me.

"Kino," she gasped. "I lo-lo-love youuuuuu!"

Whether that nut brought it outta her or she meant that shit, I'd take it. I kissed her and fed my baby, collapsing on top of her with heavy breaths.

"I love you, too, Mia. More than life. More than me. More than—"

Bzzzzzzzzz!

My phone rang on the nightstand, and I wanted to ignore it, but it could've been about King, or something else serious. Looking at Mia, her eyes were getting low, but her face said that she didn't want me to answer the call.

Bzzzzzzzzz!

The phone went off again, making it harder not to answer. Kissing her forehead, I sat up and grabbed the phone, seeing that it was Kong calling. The last nigga I wanted to hear from right now.

"Yeah," I answered, trying to hide my frustration.

"Meeting in a half hour," he said, hanging up the phone.

Looking over my shoulder, Mia had sat all the way up, and was staring a hole in the back of my head. I turned to her and saw a tear fall from her eye. I reached to wipe it away, thinking that she was going to turn away, but she didn't. Instead, she leaned into my hand like she needed me. I knew she did. But right now, I had to do what was necessary to protect her.

"I gotta go to this me—"

"It's cool. The less I know, the better. Just—" She paused and reached out to touch my face, looking lovingly into my eyes. "be careful. Please."

"I will," I promised. "I won't be long."

"Okay."

I got up and got dressed in some gray joggers and a white tee. Putting on some socks and slides, I was ready to see what the fuck Kong had to say. I was sure that he knew by now that King was dead, not that he gave a fuck.

"Ummmm, where you think you goin' wit' my shit on display like that? You better put on some jeans, nigga. Not that it makes a difference." Mia eyed me and the print in my joggers.

"Mannn, you for real right now?" I asked her.

"Does a bitch look like she playin'?" she asked, sounding like the old Mia.

"Gone on, mane. Ain't no bitches even gon' be there," I lied.

"You know, you're a terrible fuckin' liar. I hope you never get caught up." She folded her arms across her chest, her nice ass titties sitting just right on top of them.

"Aight, Mia. I gotchu," I conceded, taking off the joggers and grabbing a pair of jeans off the floor.

"And drawls, nigga. Dafuq you think this is?"

I laughed and went to the drawer of my dresser obediently, pulling out some camo Hanes boxer briefs and putting them on. I turned around and adjusted my dick in the upright position in front of her, loving the way her eyes bulged at the sight.

"Does *this* meet your approval, Miss King," I asked, grabbing my dick again.

A frown flashed across her face briefly, not the reaction I expected at all. Like something I said made her think of something else. Maybe a piece of the scattered puzzle of her memory coming into place. It disappeared quickly, though, and I didn't have time to dig into it.

"You good, Mr. Shane," she said, and that made me smile. She *was* remembering.

"I love you, Sa'Mia. See you soon." I smiled at her, pulling on my jeans and putting my slides back on. I walked over to her, and she crawled across the bed on all fours, meeting me halfway. I kissed her deep and hard, and she grabbed my dick, making me hate having to leave her instead of being able to lay up in that tight ass pussy all night.

Pulling away, I stepped back and took her in, in all her beauty. Shuddering under my gaze, she bit her lip, and her body reacted with hardened nipples and a glistening wet pussy. She blew me a kiss and I caught it, putting it in my pocket for later. She smiled and blushed, blowing me another kiss for me to have for now. Call it corny, but we had that goofy made for TV love. The kind they don't tell 'bout young black kids like us. Until now.

"Wait, you didn't eat!" she shouted at my back as I walked toward the door.

"Yeah. Yeah, I did." I smiled and looked over my shoulder at her.

I paused, looking at her like it was the last time I would see her in my life. She smiled and looked at me, but her smile didn't go up to her eyes. I couldn't tell if it was worry or sadness that was there, but I hated that I made her feel anything other than happiness. This was the last time that I would ever make her feel that. On my life.

MARISSA HERVEY

I got back to that fucking warehouse so fast, you would've thought I teleported. I was fueled by nothing but anger. It was like I wasn't walking, I was floating off the ground to the spawn of Satan I gave birth to. She had been nothing but hell to me. Here I was feeling like a bad parent, and I'll admit there are some places that I could've improved with her. But Neisha was just a bad seed. The more I thought about it objectively, no longer making excuses for her and blaming myself for her decisions, like most parents do, I saw that shit. She was gonna pay with her life for what she did to King. What she'd done to all of them.

BOOM!

"Where you got the little bitch?" I asked a startled Chica, who was cuddled up with Twon's little brother DeRico on the couch in the sitting area of the warehouse. I thought it was strange that they were together, but right now, I couldn't muster up a single fuck to give. I was focused on one thing and one thing only.

"She's in the back. Neicey is watching her. Is it time?" she asked, rubbing her hands together like this was the moment she'd been waiting for.

I didn't respond, just pulled the gun that she'd given me when we left the police department from behind my back and made my way to the back of the massive building. When I heard talking, I slowed my pace, and then realized that it wasn't a conversation being had.

"Right there, Neisha. Yessss, that's it! You wanna get outta here? Huh? Show me how bad you wanna get—" *Pop! Pop!*

I didn't even announce my entry, just handled the disloyal bitch that was in here *not* doing her job. Neicey's body fell to the floor, and Neisha looked at me, licking her lips with a smirk on her face. This girl cared about nothing and no one but herself. She'd probably planned to kill Neicey herself as soon as she let her go. I saved her the trouble.

"Damn. Nasty bitch was in here 'bout to give this heaux freedom for a lil' head, huh? Can't trust nobody nowadays." Chica spoke truth then. I didn't really believe I could trust her, but again, that wasn't my concern.

"Mother, you seem upset. Did something happen? Did someone diii-ieeee?" she taunted, making me angrier with every word. *WHACK!*

"You don't value *shit*, do you?" I asked, stepping back after slapping her across the face with the gun. "You take life like it ain't nothin'! You ain't loyal to nobody! All for what? A lil' clout and money? You think you cut out for this shit? Huh, Ray'Neisha? Where the fuck did I go wrong with you?" I was yelling so loud that my words were bouncing off the walls and high ceilings and echoing through the empty room.

"Don't come with that caring mama 'where did I go wrong' shit. You never gave a damn about me! You were too busy running behind the nigga with the biggest name in the fuckin' streets. Yeah, you got a degree and acted like you cared about the kids at Lincoln. But you were more worried about PTA meetings and the athletes and your precious Math Club geeks than you were about me. Where did you go wrong? Knowing that ya nigga was fuckin' me and not caring 'cause he wasn't makin' enough bank for you. You don't give a damn about King. You mad 'cause he won't be able to save ya ass now that he's dead!" She paused, studying my reaction to her words and then bust out laughing. "Oh shit. He issssss dead, huh? Welp, guess you gon' be on ya knees suckin' off Kong or Kellz, whoever gets the throne now, huh?" She laughed, stabbing me in the chest with her words.

"Untie her," I said to Chica.

"Say what now?" Chica asked me, like she was hard of hearing.

24

"I said untie her. She got all that mouth and a chin made of fuckin' porcelain. I'mma beat her ass like I should've all her damn life."

I walked to the corner of the room and took off my heels. I sat my gun down while Chica reluctantly cut Neisha loose. I had just taken off my earrings and started walking toward my child. My only child. We circled for a minute, Chica stepping back to watch the fight that was about to go down. When I saw that Neisha wasn't gonna throw the first punch, I reached out and touched her ass with a jab to that fat ass mouth of hers. She touched her lips and saw that they were bleeding, knowing that she was about to have to fight for her life.

Shooting another jab at her, she ducked it, only to run right into the right hook that was coming for her as a follow-up. It made her stagger to the side and into the wall. A look filled her eyes that I had never seen before, and she rushed me with force, picking me up and slamming me on the floor. My head hit the floor, stunning me for a second, and she took advantage, beating my head into the concrete floor.

"You—" *Bam!* "You made me who I am. I hated you from the day I knew what love should have been!" *Bam!* "I told Rylo to keep you drugged the fuck up!" *Bam!* "I hated you and hoped you would die!" *Bam! Bam!* "But you were taking too long! So when I caught Tank giving you head in your sleep, I knew it was a gift from Rylo and took the chance to take everything from you! Blowing his head off was worth it to ruin your fuckin' life! Hahaha!" *Bam!* "I'm glad King is de—"

Pop! Pop! Pop!

I was dizzy but felt Neisha's body fall forward on top of me. I used what energy I had left and pushed her off of me onto the floor. Looking up, Chica was holding the smoking pistol in her hand with tears in her eyes.

"I just needed to hear it from the bitch's mouth," she said, shaking her head and walking out of the room.

I said a prayer, asking forgiveness for my failure as a parent, looking at the blood coming from the three holes Chica had put in my child. One through her forehead, one in her chest, and the other through her middle. Every shot was a kill shot, but I knew it still didn't give her any peace. I wish I could at least give her that. But hell, I needed to find some of my own before I worried about giving any out. I stood up and looked down at the lifeless eyes of my daughter, realizing that they weren't much different from the way they looked when she was living. Leaning down, I closed her eyes with my hand before turning and walking out of the room. Chica and DeRico were gone from where they were when I arrived, and I didn't bother looking for them. Instead, something told me to get out of that warehouse, and fast.

Running to my new BMW, I hopped in, cranking it up and speeding away from the building. I didn't look back but couldn't stop the tears from pouring from my eyes, blinding me and making it almost impossible to see. Pulling over on the expressway, I got out of the car and walked around to the grassy area on the side of the median. I felt nauseous and couldn't hold it in. Soon, I was throwing up everything on my stomach. I didn't stop until I was dry heaving and even then, I felt like I could've puked my insides out.

Ka-Boom!

The sound of an explosion behind me caught my attention, and I realized why my instincts told me to leave the warehouse. All I saw was a ball of flames and debris before billows of smoke filled the air. More tears filled my eyes as I calculated the losses I'd taken in such a short time. I shed tears for my child. For Neicey's mother who would soon get a call that she'd never see her daughter again. I hoped they ended on better terms than I did with mine. I cried for King and his children who had just lost their father. For Chica and the loss of her brother. For my career. Hell, I even shed a tear for Rylo, and for my sister JaRhonda, forgiving her for the hurt place she must've been in to sell me out like she did. But that wasn't gonna save her life. Nope. She would be my final "stop" before I left this fucked up city. And I knew just how to do it.

KELLEN "KONG" KING

*L*et the weak niggas handle themselves, that's my motto. Dafuq I look like getting my hands dirty when I can just set the stage and watch the shit play out? Sitting in my office, yeah, you read right, *my office*, I smoked a fat ass cigar, thinking about how easy this shit had been. Trouble and Maine tried to take each other out, and as far as I knew, Maine was the last one standing in that shit. I ain't expect for Mia to be a casualty, but that's how this war shit went. I would rather her little ass be murked now than have her come back on some revenge shit.

This shit fell right in place. I ain't know why Pops thought I couldn't handle this shit. It was easy peasy. Maybe it was too easy. I had to watch my back, because just like a bitch, the same way you get the kingdom was the same way you'd lose that shit. Especially when you had so many cutthroat ass people around you. The only person I knew that I could count on was Maine. He was in his feelings right now, but I'd known him my whole life, and the nigga was solid. He was in love with Sa'Mia, but that hadn't trumped his loyalty yet, so I wasn't too worried about it happening now.

Kicking my feet down, I smiled when Chica and DeRico came through the door. They'd been given a mission, and I was waiting on them before I started the meeting I'd called. I needed some shit handled.

"How'd it go?" I asked, smiling from ear-to-ear.

"Yeah, it's handled," DeRico said, avoiding eye contact.

When Chica came to sit on my lap, I thought I saw his jaw tightened, but I knew I had to be seeing shit. Gripping her ass, I took in her scent snuggling into her neck. Chica was the kinda bitch I wanted on my team. She was down as fuck, fine, and still hood enough to finesse any nigga or bitch if I needed her to. I wasn't planning to fall for her, but aye, shit happens. And with the way shit had been going lately, I needed to settle down and have me a down ass bitch to put some babies in and keep me grounded while I ran this empire I wasn't sure I wanted anymore.

"Aye Rico, go set up for the meeting I just called. Need to get some shit in order," I said to him, kissing Chica's shoulder. She was looking fine as hell in her off-the-shoulder hi-lo sundress, and I could tell by the heat in my lap that she wasn't wearing any drawls. I wanted to speak on that shit because she'd been with DeRico all day, but she knew a boss nigga when she had one, so she wasn't gon' fuck this up for a rookie.

"Gotcha boss," he said, gritting his teeth.

"You got somethin' you wanna say, my nigga?" I asked, not letting the shit get past me this time.

"Naw, I'm good, man. Just ready for all this war shit to be over so we can get back to business. You stopped supplying with all the heat Neisha was bringin' our way. So now that she's out the way, I hope you ready to meet with the connect so we can flood these streets and get to this money," he said, and I nodded, knowing there was more to his demeanor but not pressing the shit. If he ain't bring the shit up, then it was a non-issue in my eyes, 'cause only cowards and bitches don't speak their minds.

"What you need me to do, baby?" Chica asked with a smile, running her fingers through my locs.

I slid my hand up her dress and into her pussy. I wanted to feel her before I had to handle some shit. She let out a sigh and threw her head back into my chest, moving her hips back and forth with my stroking her wet ass pussy, and making my dick hard at the same time. She turned her head and kissed me, making me stand up and bend her over my desk, pulling her dress up over her ass. I was about to pull my dick out when I realized DeRico's perverted ass was still standing in the doorway watching.

"My nigga, I don't know if you want my bitch or you want my dick, but you better get the fuck on, and handle what the hell I just told you. Dafuq wrong witchu?"

He didn't say shit, just looked at Chica in a way that made me wanna know what the fuck happened when they went to kill Neisha's ass. But I had one better for they asses as soon as I got up out this pussy. DeRico finally walked away, and I drove my shit so deep in Chica that she hollered out. DeRico left the door open, so I knew he was standing right outside out of my sight, listening. I planned to give his ass something to listen to, too.

"You fuckin' the help, Chica? That's what you on?" *Whap!*

"Ahhhh! N-n-noooooo, baby! I would never do that shit to you. What the fuck I want wit' his ass when I got youuuuu?" she stuttered while I drilled her ass, holding her by the back of the neck, her left cheek pressed down against the desk.

"Who pussy is this, bitch?" I was getting madder and madder the more I thought about her fuckin' DeRico. She didn't reply fast enough for me, pissing me off all over again. I wrapped my hand around her neck and saw tears pooling in her eyes. Since she ain't wanna answer, I was gonna make her suffer, then decide whether or not to kill her.

"Yo mane, what's DeRico doin' standin' his ass out—oh shit, my bad," Maine came in the door asking and unknowingly snitching on DeRico at the same time. I was two strokes from a nut, so I wasn't about to miss my shit for nobody.

"Hold that thought, my nigga—*unh ughhhhhh*—" I grunted my way into a nut, not giving a damn if Chica got hers or not. "Go clean up, Chica. I need to talk to my nigga before we kick this shit off," I said, sliding out of her and tucking my dick back in my pants.

"Nigga, you gon' wash that shit off?" Maine asked me with his face all balled up while Chica stood up, adjusted her dress, gave me a mean mug that could kill, and stomped out the room. "Dafuq been goin' on in here since I been gone, mane?"

I didn't answer Maine's question. Instead, I eased toward the door. I motioned for him to keep talking so they wouldn't know that I could hear them, and he did just that.

"Man, just chill out, bae. That nigga 'bout to make you second in command, I still got the info for the accounts from Neisha's triflin' ass, and we gon' rob this nigga blind, you gon' meet the connect and build a rapport with him and kill his ass. That nigga ain't got no loyalty, so we gotta get him before he get us. Shit, look how he did his fam and shit. Come on, bae. Don't be like that," Chica said, and I could tell that DeRico was all in his feelings about me fuckin' his—my—*our* bitch.

"Bitch, getcho hands the fuck off me, and don't put ya fuckin' mouth on me, either. You just fucked *that* nigga. Go bathe, douche with some bleach or some shit, and I might consider givin' ya ass this dick again. I saw what the fuck he workin' wit' and know why you fuckin' wit' a nigga. Hell, did he even put a dent in that deep sea you got down there?" DeRico snapped.

I felt my head get tight and wanted to blow both they brains out right there in that hall, but I had to play that shit smart. Instead, I walked out and looked at them standing there looking like they'd just got caught fuckin' by their parents.

"Aye, Rico, you got shit set up, man?" I asked, waiting for him to lie.

"Naw, boss. I was comin' in to ask you a question, but you was—ummm, busy."

"Already. What was the question?"

"Uhhh. Ummmm—"

"Man, don't even worry about that shit. You heard from Kellz? I can't get that nigga on the wire." I laughed because that nigga couldn't keep up with his lie.

"Yeah. Just got off the phone with him."

Strike two, I thought, because they were talking, but Kellz had been avoiding me since I sent him to the hotel with King and Mia and Trouble got popped. Knowing his ass, he had King somewhere beatin' his ass to get his rocks off, and ain't want me to stop him from doin' that shit. That nigga was weird. I had a hard time believing he was my real Pops. Maybe a nigga needed to do a DNA test on his ass or some shit. Truth be told, after getting to know him, I ain't want the nigga to be my Pops, and I ain't like that Neisha was my sister. Hell, I thought Sa'Mia was bad, but Neisha made me appreciate her spoiled ass, and Kellz definitely made me appreciate King and all he'd done for me. Maybe I could still reconcile with them. At least King, since Mia was gone now.

"Make sure he at the meeting, then. And gone get that shit set up. If you remember what you was gon' ask a nigga, lemme know," I instructed before turning to Chica. "You wash that shit up? You know daddy like his pussy fresh and clean when he up in it. And I plan to celebrate in dem guts all night long after this meeting," I said, before kissing her and walking to the bathroom to wash my dick off. I needed to talk to Maine before the meeting because some shit was about to change. Literally, in a matter of minutes.

I left them both there with their mouths hanging open and went to clean my nuts. Looking in the mirror, I saw that nigga Kellz all over me. I mean, I was his damn namesake. That shit was eating me alive from the inside out. If I ain't make a change, and soon, I was gon' fuck around and turn around and be fucked up out here. When I was done cleaning myself up, I opened the bathroom door and heard feet moving fast as hell. I had to laugh, because they scattered like roaches. But I had to wonder what they were still doing out there, but I would handle that shit soon enough.

"Mane, you need to watch them two," Maine said, as soon as I walked back into the room. He had a look on his face that let me know he'd heard something.

"I got it under control," I said, sitting at the desk, leaning forward with my hands in front of me.

"Already."

"But listen, it's a lotta shit 'bout to go down. I just need to know if you still fuckin' wit' a nigga. As soon as I locate Kellz ass and get King back here, I'mma try to fix this shit. I mean, I know I can't do shit about that Trouble nigga or Mia bein' dead. I'm sorry about that, by the way, my dude." I paused, looking him in the eyes so that he knew I meant that shit. I knew my nigga was hurtin' behind that loss. But I was glad he handled that nigga Trouble for me. And even though I was about to have to get rid of Chica and DeRico's asses, I was glad to have Neisha out the way first, too.

"Wait, what you talkin' 'bout, mane?"

"What part?" I was confused.

"About King. Yeen hear?"

The look he was giving me was one of complete shock. I didn't know

31

what he was talking about, but I had a feeling I wasn't gon' like that shit at all.

"Hear what, Maine? Spit that shit out!" I yelled, slamming my fist on the desk. "My bad, man. It's just been too many surprises for me for one day."

"Naw, I get it," he said, his brow furrowing like he was thinking about what to tell me. Or maybe he was considering *how* to tell me what he had to tell me.

"King's dead. Got the call last night when I was taking—when I was leaving the hospital and shit," he caught himself, but I ain't miss that slip. *Did my nigga just tell me King was dead? This had to be some shit like they be writing in them books or puttin' in dem movies. 'Cause King's ass is invincible. He can't be dead behind some shit I did. Naw, this ain't what I just heard.*

"Yeen know," he said sullenly. "My bad, mane. I thought—"

"Naw, it's good," I said, pressing the bridge of my nose, refusing to let the tears fall. "So, him and Mia go—*mmm mmmmmm*," I tried to clear the knot in my throat. "Gone?"

"Naw, Mia made it. King saved her life," he told me, refusing to look me in the face. But the way he was tightening and loosening his jaw, I knew he blamed me for this shit and hated to tell me that Mia was still alive. He didn't want me to go after her ass again.

"Listen, Maine, I ain't gon' come for Mia no more. I hated that the shit went down the way it did. And the loss of my pops—" I froze, my words catching in my throat with the look he shot at me when I called King "my pops" was one that said he could murder me with his bare hands. "The loss of King is sobering than a muhfucka. So let me offer *you* my condolences, for the loss of your mentor and father figure. You valued him and respected what he had goin'. I didn't—"

I let my words fall off, but the meaning was there. The room was heavy with silence, and the pain he felt—we felt, was deafening. King didn't deserve that shit. Not like that. If he was gon' die, it shouldn't have been at the hands of that jealous ass brother of his. Jealousy is a dangerous thing. And my ego blinded me to the shit 'til it was too late, and the wrong ones were able to get close enough to end him.

"Boss, everyone is present and accounted for," I heard DeRico's voice come over the intercom. I stood up without a word, and Maine stood with me. Leaving the office together, we walked silently, side by side, looking like the bad ass niggas we were. Well, the bad ass nigga he was, and I wanted to be.

We entered the conference room, and all eyes fell on me. I decided to do shit a little differently and pay homage to Alonzo King, the man who raised me.

"Lemme tell y'all a story," I said, walking to the front of the table. There were fifty men there, all parts of King's empire. All mugging me like they wanted to take my last breath. All but Maine. *My nigga gets me*, I thought with a smile in his direction before continuing.

"There was once a man. A real humble type nigga, who was blessed to get the come-up of a lifetime. And the type that he was, he brought all his niggas wit' him. Some were appreciative and held that nigga down. But some were jealous and let that shit consume them, making them want what he'd gained. But they weren't willing to learn at his feet or do the work he did to get what he had. That man lost everything and everyone he loved. Everything, but his kids. He gave it all up to save their lives but ended up having to revert to old habits to provide them the life he felt they deserved."

I looked around the room, and the men who had been with King since day one were nodding. They knew this story all too well. They, too, had given up a lot to fuck with the man who had fed their families and made them some very rich men. Seeing that I had their approval, validated something for me. Add the fact Kellz, who knew this story real well his damn self, was moving around in his seat like he had crabs on his dick, my power and position was definitely confirmed.

"One of the kids was disrespectful as hell and let that shit go to his head, letting snakes in the camp that ended the life of the man who'd built it all from the ground up. That great man died—" I paused, letting what I'd just said sink in. "Protecting his kids and his kingdom. For those of y'all who ain't caught on yet. That Trap God was my pops, Alonzo King. And the ungrateful ass kid—*sniff-sniff*—was me. I would put a bullet through my own head, but I'm the only surviving heir capable of continuing my father's legacy. I know I gotta prove myself and gain y'all's trust.

33

But I'm willing to learn from y'all. Something I wasn't man enough to do with my pops."

I felt the tears running down my face, but I didn't try to stop them. King deserved every guilty, salty tear that streamed down my cheeks.

"That nigga ain't yo' pops, lil' nigga! I am!" Kellz stood up screaming, making every gun in the room draw and aim in his direction.

"Nah, y'all, I got this one," I said, holding my hands up to let them know they could lower their heat.

Boomp... Boom-Boomp... Boom-Boomp-Boomp-Boomp

All you heard was guns being laid aggressively on the table. I knew it wouldn't take but one wrong move from Kellz *or me*, for there to be bloodshed.

"It takes more than nuttin' in my moms to make you my pops, nigga. But that's all you did. Yeen raise me. Hell, I ain't know who you was 'til Marissa and Neisha's ass brought me to you. You ain't shown me shit but what I can become if I don't humble my fuckin' self, my nigga. All them years in hiding. All them years you ducked off like a coward, fuckin' King's bitch on the slick, just like you did with my mama. All them years, you couldn't do what the fuck you just did. You had to use his love for his children. His love for *me*." I hit my chest. "To get close to him. Yeen no pops of mine, my nigga. Yeen even a man in my eyes. You a bitch!"

Clack-Clack Pow!

Without another word, I blew Kellz's brains out all over DeRico's face and clothes. The nigga was sitting there with his mouth open, so I'm sure he got some blood and brain matter in his mouth.

"Bae! What the fuck!" Chica shouted, standing up from her seat beside me.

"Sitcho heaux ass down!" I yelled, aiming the gun at him. "Matter of fact, nah. Come here, *bae*."

She got up reluctantly, walking over to me and standing there like she didn't know what I was about to do or say next. She kept looking around the table, but her eyes fell on DeRico more than anyone else. Maine looked at me, letting me know that he caught that shit, and all I had to do was say a word.

"See, one thing I've learned through all this shit was who you can trust. And that a bitch will fuck a nigga that's on a lower level if she can handle his ass like a puppet and run his ass and the empire. Ain't that right, *bae?*"

"Wha-what are you—"

"You gon' play wit' me, Chica? You know what? If yeen fuckin' DeRico's disloyal ass, then show me. Show me who you belong to. Who your loyalty belongs to."

I reached into my pocket and pulled out a pocket knife. Handing it to Chica, she looked at it, and then at me like she was torn. DeRico looked scared shitless, and he should've been, because he was dying today. Whether by her hands or mine.

She took the knife from my hand and walked over to DeRico at a snail's pace.

"Hurry the fuck up, Chica! Yeen hesitate when you was fuckin' that nigga behind my back. You willing to lose your life for this nigga?"

"Man, fuck you, Kong! You don't deserve this shit! How you get it, huh? Yeen earn it! You killed ya own po—*gurrrrgleeee.*"

Chica hurried up and got to him, slitting his throat. I was sure that shit was more so he couldn't tell me something about her ass than because she was suddenly so eager to prove her loyalty to me. Blood sprayed across the room. A mess was being made, and Chica would have the honor of cleaning it up as soon as I finished this meeting.

Everybody was still seated, nobody flinching at the blood spill or running away to keep it from getting on their clothes. See, this was the kinda team that you knew was solid. Young niggas tryna be dealers nowadays, myself included, would've been in thousands of dollars' worth of clothes and would've been having a bitch fit about getting a droplet of blood on their shoes. But these old heads were waiting to see what I was gonna say or do next. So I continued as not to waste any more of their time.

"He's right, y'all. A nigga killed his own to get to the top. I ain't no better than the muhfuckas that just died in this bitch. And if y'all wanna take a young nigga out, then so be it," I offered, putting my piece on the table and standing back with my arms outstretched. I was ready to die and felt it would be my karma after everything that I'd done.

"Nah, youngblood, you don't get outta this shit that easy. You say you the only suitable heir, huh? Where's Tywan?" one of the old heads, Nate asked, sitting there with a stern look on his face.

"Who?" I asked before realizing who he was talking about. Before I could answer, Chica collapsed into a ball on the floor, crying like she loved that nigga DeRico. "Man, Maine, get this bitch the fuck outta here before I kill her ass. Crying over that nigga right in front of me. Dafuq wrong with her!" I yelled, pissed the hell off.

Maine almost had to scrape Chica off the floor, and she fought being pulled away from DeRico's dead body like a baby mama laid across the casket at a funeral. She even pulled the chair from under the body, making it fall on the floor, his neck opening all the way up. *Damn, she 'bout took that nigga's whole head off*, I thought, looking at the scene happening in front of me.

"I gotcha Pops' will, and Tywan is supposed to take over this shit if King died. You, well, you still get to learn the ropes. He left you West Dallas," Nate said, and I wondered how he knew all that shit.

"Where the fuck is this will you talkin' about? And how a dead man gon' run some shit?" I asked proudly with my chest poked out.

"Dead?" Nate laughed. "Well, damn, you really outta the loop, huh? And you thought you were ready to run some shit? You ain't even third in line, Kong."

Nate shook his head with a disgusted look on his face. The rest of them laughed with him, and I felt dumb as fuck. So Trouble wasn't dead. And he was the prodigal son. The nigga was right under my nose the whole time.

"Reading of the will is in two days, *boss*. Enjoy your rule until then," Nate taunted, standing and tucking his guns into his chest holster. The other old heads did the same, and they turned their backs and walked out of the room. That was some disrespectful shit, but what was I gon' do about it? I couldn't kill all of them, and even if I could, that would be stupid. The way they were treating me, I deserved.

Leaving the bloody ass conference room, I went into the office, surprised to see Maine in there alone.

"Where the fuck is Chica, nigga?" I asked.

"She went to clean herself up," he said with a shrug.

"Mannnnn!" I hollered, going from room-to-room and bathroom-to-bathroom until I had searched all of them. Going back to the office, Maine was sitting on the couch like he was unbothered. I ain't say shit to him, just stormed over to the desk, turned on the TV, and rewound the camera feed. Just like I thought, Chica's ass was running out the back and had hopped in DeRico's Chevy, peeling away from the warehouse.

"Well damn," Maine said with a laugh.

"You let that bitch get away, my nigga. Who side you on?"

"Question me the fuck again!" he yelled, getting up from the couch and standing toe-to-toe with me. "I done lost everybody I loved bein' down witcho flaw ass. You mad at me 'bout a bitch that you was fuckin' that was fuckin' another nigga? Really, my nigga? Like yeen know Chica was a 'round the way play ass heaux. You mad? Make some shit move, mane. Dafuq I look like babysitting ya bitch when you tried to kill mine, gotcha pops, naw, *my pops* killed, and sat here while that shit went down. You was so pussy drunk, yeen even see the shit that was happening, and muhfuckas lost they lives, mane. *They lives!*"

He had me up by my collar, yelling so hard spit was flying from his mouth. I pushed him back, and he laughed, straightening his clothes and looking me up and down in a way that I'd never seen him look at anybody before.

"You know what, though? It's cool. You gon' get what's meant for you, my nigga. And prolly at the hands of that bitch you all fucked up for." He smirked and backed out of the room, not breaking eye contact until he'd gotten to the door. "Karma is a bitch, my nigga. And usually comes at the hands of a bitch."

With that, he left. I had never felt so alone before in my life. Probably because, for the first time in my life, I *was alone*. I had no family. No bitch. No team. No Pops to go to for guidance. It's lonely at the top, they say. So why a nigga feel like he'd just hit rock fuckin' bottom?

MIA

I laid in the bed, loneliness consuming me. I didn't know what Maine did for a living, but it'd had him gone for eight to twelve hours at a time. I was alone in his house unless my nurse came to visit me. I would give anything to remember who I was. I wondered if I had friends. I hoped I did. I needed one now, for sure.

Bzzzzzzzz!

I looked down at my phone, and it was ringing for the first time with a name and number that wasn't Maine's. It said Chica, and I was hesitant to answer it, but I wanted it to be somebody who would come spend time with me. Just to sit with me, hell.

"Hello?"

"Hey, girl! How you been? Long time no hear from. You good over there? A bitch thought you was dead," she said, and I pulled the phone away, looking at it and hoping to remember who she was.

"Yeah, I'm okay. Why would you think I was dead?"

That was a strange thing to say, in my opinion. But at the same time, maybe that's how we talked to each other. I mean, how was I supposed to know?

"Girl, 'cause we don't go this long without talkin' to each other. And then that shit at the mall with Neisha. I thought you were hurt bad or some shit."

I didn't know what she was talking about, but I knew how to find out. Nowadays, everything was on social media. I remembered enough to know that shit.

"I'm good, girl. You know it's gon' take more than that shit to take me out."

I had no idea what I was even talking about. But she was buying it, so I was gon' keep right on selling it.

"True. True." There was an awkward silence, and I had to think fast. What does a chatty bitch love to do more than spill tea and talk about themselves?

"So, what's been up with you?" I asked to get her to talking.

"Girl, not much. I mean, a bitch on a come-up and shit—"

While she was talking about shit that didn't matter to me, I zoned out. Putting her on speaker, I went to Facebook and looked at my page, checking for tags. It didn't take me long to find one of Chica, and lots of pics of us together from the past. But then, they got sparse. Wondering why, I went to her profile and saw her with a girl that looked familiar to me for some reason. A Ray'Neisha "Tru Boss Bitch" Brown. Clicking on her profile, I saw a lot of Live videos. This bitch loved her some attention. Before I watched them, I saw she had recently posted a lot of pictures with Maine.

"Mia! Girl! You listenin' to me?" Chica yelled before I clicked on them to read the captions.

"My bad, girl. What you say? You went out on me. You drivin' or some shit? You must've hit a dead spot," I lied. *Well, the finesse part of my brain is working just fine.*

"I am driving, actually. I asked you where you was at. I miss you, boo. I wanted to come see you."

"I'm at Maine's house."

"Oh, for real," she said hesitantly. "That's what's up. Which one, 'cause you know that nigga gotta million of them bitches with how long his money is." She tried to recover, but that shit ain't work like she thought it did. Or like I let her think it did.

"I'll send you my location. I need somebody to chill with. Maine gone all the time—"

"He gone now?" she asked too quickly.

"Nah. He said he was gon' be out late. Something about handling business. I don't know what he be talkin' about. He been keepin' me outta the loop a lot lately," I half-lied. I hadn't heard from Maine since he fucked the shit outta me and left hours ago. But him keeping me out of the loop was the truth, and I didn't like that shit.

"Well, maybe it's better that you don't know a lot. When it comes to this street shit, the less you know, the better. You ain't gotta lie if you're forced to testify and shit," she said. "I got ya destination. I'm coming through."

"Aight. Call me when you get to the gate."

"Ok boo. See you soon."

As soon as I hung up the phone, I went back to Facebook and looked at the pictures of the Neisha bitch and Maine. The last one was of them at prom. I was confused. Were they a couple or some shit? Clicking out of the pictures, I went back to her Live videos. There were so many of them. She really liked herself and thought people gave a fuck about what she had going on. Some of them had a couple hundred views, and some were in the thousands. Those were the ones I wanted to see. Scrolling back to a couple of weeks ago, I saw a caption that caught my attention. It had over a million views. *Dallas Dope Princess Got Dat Deep Throat…*

Bzzzzzzzzz

The phone vibrated in my hand, and I almost threw it across the room. I was on my third Live on this bitch's page, starring me. And this one included Chica. It was the one from the mall that she'd referenced in our conversation. Chica's name covered my screen, saving me from the torture I was putting myself through. I didn't remember shit still, but those videos were enough to make me wanna kill the Neisha bitch, Maine, and Chica's ass for the company she kept. Now I wasn't so sure that Maine loved me or was the father of my child. Maybe he worked with Neisha and she sent him to get me and bring me here so that they could get me out of the way or something. Or kill me. Maybe that's why Maine is gone and Chica hit me up all of a sudden.

Bzzzzzzzzz

She was calling back, and I needed to answer. I had already told her she could come, so if I didn't then she might suspect something. I went into the closet and got on my tiptoes, reaching in the top of the closet where I'd seen Maine put a bag that was full of guns. I had to protect myself.

Bzzzzzzzzzz

I ran back to the bed where I'd thrown my phone in my mad dash to the closet and answered it.

"Bitch, I thought you'd changed your mind or some shit," Chica snapped. "Tell this nigga you invited me here so he can open this fuckin' gate! Here!" There was some shuffling, and then a male voice came on the line. "Miss King, this is Officer Miles. Mr. Shane told me that I wasn't to let anybody in this gate saying that they were coming to see you."

"That's my homegirl. You can let her through," I said, reaching for the bag of guns again. I felt a strap and pulled on it.

"You sure?" he asked, sounding like he knew something I didn't. That was all the confirmation I needed. I started snatching at the bag now, because I knew that it wasn't a damn game.

"Yeah, she's fuckin' sure! Open the ghatdamned gate!" I heard Chica yelling in the background.

"Miss King, are… you… sure?"

"Yeah, I'm sure. Ahhhh!"

With one hard ass snatch, the bag jumped off the shelf. Of course Maine didn't have the shit zipped up, and guns rained down on me like money on a stripper bitch on a Friday night. A couple of them hit me upside the head, making me stumble back and fall on my ass.

"You alright, Miss King?" Officer Miles asked, sounding concerned.

"Yeah, just slipped on Maine's shoe. You can let her in. I've got it covered. But I'll definitely call you if I need you," I told him, meaning it.

"10-4," he said, letting me know he read me loud and clear.

I didn't even bother cleaning up the mess. I knew I didn't have to worry about Chica coming in and seeing them. She wouldn't make it that far into this house. Not with me alive, anyway. And I wasn't dying today. She was gonna answer some questions for a bitch, and the first time she said or did something that I didn't like, I was gonna blow her shit open and look for the answers myself.

41

Walking toward the front of the house, I closed the door to the bedroom and headed to the front of the house. My head was thumping where the guns hit me, and I was gonna need some pain meds. That's when I realized I hadn't eaten. All that food I cooked, and Maine's ass left without eating. And I was so fucked up behind his ass that I hadn't ate shit either.

Ding doooong

I guessed me eating was gonna have to wait. Walking to the door, I made sure that my guns were hidden by the oversized tee that I had on. I'd put two in the waistband of my PINK sweatpants and one in my sports bra.

Dinnnnng Dooonnnnnggggg Ding-Dong Ding-Dong Ding-Dong

This bitch was impatient as hell and on my nerves already. When I opened the door, she was looking over her shoulder like somebody was chasing her ass. Looking at her made my head hurt even more.

"Girl! What the hell is up with you?" she asked, giving me a one-armed half-hug. "You tell a bitch to come over and then don't answer the phone or the door. Treating me like a groupie or some shit." She fake laughed.

"My bad, girl. This baby got my bladder on go. All I do is eat and pee. Speaking of eating, come on in and I'll fix you a plate."

"Baby?" Chica asked, exposing herself. If we were besties, then why wouldn't she know I was pregnant. "Girlllll, congratulations! Now I see why Maine got you on lockdown. Gotta protect his seed. Move around so I can come on in, though. You know I never pass up a chance to get some of that Mama Mia's Gourmet Cookin'," she said excitedly. I reluctantly stepped to the side to let her in.

"Thank you, girl," I said, when she walked past me, looking around.

"Damnnnnn, this spot is nice! Gone fix me a plate while I sit on this comfy lookin' leather sectional. I could get used to visiting you here, boo. Oooooh yeahhhh, this is the life!" She punctuated the last part with dramatic hand claps, making my head hurt even more. She sat on the couch, kicking her feet up on the table. *Oh, this bitch is real disrespectful*, I thought, ready for her to go, and she'd just got here.

"Lemme go fix the plates."

Walking toward the kitchen, my vision got blurry. *Maybe I should call* the nurse. *One of them guns might've given me a concussion*, I thought, holding onto the counter for support.

I looked at the stove and all the food and shook my head. This was supposed to be me and my man's meal, and now I was sharing that shit with a bitch who had been playing both sides against the middle. Taking slow steps, my vision cleared up, and I opened a pot, the smell hitting my nose and making me hungrier than I already was. I reached into the cupboard to take down a couple of plates and set them on the counter. When I started spooning food onto them, a pain shot from my forehead to the back of my head like a lightning strike.

"Mmmmm, Mia. I think you got it. You're gonna be a better cook than your man one day."

I heard a voice in my head but couldn't see a face.

"One day, Daddy? I already am. But it wasn't hard to surpass somebody who burns toast."

Blinking fast, I felt another pain, and then another until they were coming back to back. Then, they stopped just as suddenly as they'd started. Picking up both plates, I started walking to the living room.

"What the fuck you doin' here, Chica?" I heard a man's voice say.

I knew it couldn't be nobody but Maine. I didn't hear him come in, but then again, I couldn't hear or see shit with my head acting like a damn plasma ball. Static shocks going on in my dome and shit.

"I caaaaaame to see my best friend," she said loudly, trying to make sure I heard her. "And to take what's mine," she said that part as a whisper.

"What the fuck are you talkin' about, mane?" He gritted. I stopped right on the other side of the wall, leaning in so that I could hear them.

"I seen the way you look at me. Let's handle this bitch and Kong so we can be together."

"You delusional as hell, bitch. Why the fuck would I want your community pussy havin' ass?"

"Don't try that shit, Maine. Mia told me she pregnant. How you even know the damn baby yours? She was with that nigga Trouble at the prom," she said, and my face balled up.

"You mean her *brother* Tywan? Her *twin brother*?" Maine let out a laugh that told me exactly what Chica's face must've looked like. "Yeah, bitch. Now, like I was sayin'."

Clatter-clatter-clatter

The plates fell from my hand when another jolt shot through my head.

"Mia?" I heard Maine's voice coming close.

"Ye-yeah," I said, bending down, picking up the food and putting it back on the plates.

"You aight?" he asked, finally reaching me.

"Yeah. Just been getting these pains and one hit. I dropped the food. My bad, Chica. I'll make us some mo—"

Pop! Pop!

Before I could finish my statement, my reflexes kicked in, and I fired twice.

"Mia!" Maine hollered, falling over to the side. He looked at me and then at himself like he thought I'd shot him. *I should've shot your ass with all the shit you done put me through,* I thought, shocking myself.

When he realized that I hadn't shot him, he looked behind himself to see Chica on the floor, bleeding out on his Persian rug, a gun in her hand. I didn't know if she was aiming for Maine or me, but I wasn't about to take any chances.

"That's my favorite fuckin' rug. Shit, mane!" he cussed.

Whap! Whap! Whap!

I knocked his ass in the head with my gun, knocking him over. Before he could react, I was on top of his big ass, beating the shit outta him with my gun.

"I just saved your life—*whack-whack*—and you worried 'bout a fuckin' rug!" *Whack!*

"Ahhhh! Dafuq you on, Sa'Mia?" he yelled, throwing his arm up to block the blows I was raining on his head.

"I should beat yo' ass for all the shit you done took me through. Fuckin' that snake bitch—*whack-whack*—Us fuckin' all over the ghat-damned internet! I'm on WorldStar and shit!—*Whack-whack-whack!*—Now my daddy's dead! And my brother! Not Kong's bitch ass, but Trouble! Did you kill him?" I asked, no longer swinging, but pointing the shit at his head, ready to end his ass, too, if he said the wrong thing.

"No. He's alive. And I'm sorry about your pops, Mia. He was like a father to me, too," he said, sitting up and looking in my eyes so he could show me that he was sincere.

"How can I trust you? After all of this shit? How can I—"

I fell over on the floor and balled up in the fetal position. I wished I hadn't got my memory back now. All this pain. All the shit I'd been through. I was better off not knowing. Not remembering. I felt a pair of arms wrap around me, and then a body press against me from behind. I wanted to fight him off, but I needed his comfort at the same time. I was so torn. I felt so lost. And the one person who could help me was dead. And I didn't even get to see him before he died.

Crying even harder, Maine's arms wrapped tighter around me while mine wrapped around my stomach. Holding my unborn child. I knew they could feel my pain, and I was sorry for that. I cried in the arms of the man I loved more than life. The only person I had left, other than my brother. But he wasn't here. I was losing everyone I loved, and Maine might have been next. I was gonna protect him and Trouble with my last breath. Just like they had me.

"Aye, Mia Mayweather." Maine spoke into my hair.

"Hmmm," I answered, feeling him tighten his arms around me. I didn't know if it was more to restrain me or to console me.

"You know that wasn't the first time you was on WorldStar, right? Yo' ass got so many fight videos on that bitch they gave you your own fuckin' page and hashtag," he said with a laugh.

In that moment, something snapped. But not in a bad way. Instead of shaking loose, the final piece snapped into place. Opening my swollen eyes, I looked at a dead Chica, the first best friend I had, realizing that bitches will betray their own mama for a come-up and bust out laughing with him. But it wasn't as much at what he said, even though the shit was funny.

I laughed until tears came from my eyes. But this time, they weren't tears of sadness, or pain. They weren't tears of joy, though, either. This laughter, these tears, were that of a beast being born. A beast the likes of which Dallas had never seen.

TYWAN "TROUBLE" NOBLES

"*W*ell, look what the cat dragged in," Mama Pearlie said with a broad smile on her face, hugging Doe and Eli long and hard. "I can't remember the last time I had all three of my sons together without having to call a contractor to replaster my walls," she joked, and they both kissed her on a cheek before brushing past her and walking into the house.

I met eyes with her, and it felt like she was looking through my soul. Against my brothers' wishes, we'd left the wheelchair in the trunk of the car, and I was using my cane to help me walk. I just didn't want to scare her. She knew I'd been shot and could see my arm in a sling, but if I didn't have to worry her, I wouldn't. The way she was looking at me, though, I couldn't hold it together any longer.

"I fucked it all up, Mama! I shoulda just stayed here." I fell into Mama Pearlie's arms in tears. Her sturdy body held me up, but Eli and Doe came to both our rescue before we fell backward into the living room.

"Come on, T. It's gon' be aight, man." Eli tried to soothe me, but it only made things worse because I knew he was lying. He didn't see what I saw when I went into that room my pops was being held in. Losing two parents in a such a short time was enough to break a nigga.

"Listen, man, I know you feel like you lost all the family you had, but you ain't know them. We been ya family your whole life, son. Don't forget that shit," Doe snapped, and I could tell he had some shit on his chest.

"You got somethin' else you wanna say, my nigga?" I asked, poking my chest out, the tears stopping immediately. He was talking with a lot of bass in his voice, and there wasn't no bitch in my blood. Thugs cry too, my nigga. But the tears were gone, and if he said the wrong damn thing, I was ready to make his slick mouth ass bleed. He'd let the NYC air go to his head.

"Man, sit yo' Pokémon chest ass back in that seat before I deflate that lil' bitch. You still the smallest muhfucka in the room, Ty. Don't get beat the hell up behind folks who ain't gon' miss you when you gone."

"And you did? You just up and left, Doe. So fuck you and all that shit you talkin'. You don't know what the fuck I been through since you ran up North like a slave tryna get free. Miss me with that rah-rah shit, bruh," I said, waving him off dismissively.

Eli was laying over on the dining room table laughing until Mama Pearlie shot him a look that made him shut up. She looked back and forth between me and Doe like she knew this day would come. It needed to. He'd left me because of some beef with Eli. That ain't have shit to do with me. Now, he got the nerve to be acting like a jealous bitch because I went looking for someone to fill the void. Doe had always been like a dad to me. Eli was more like a big brother, teaching me about the hustle and hoes. But Doe, he was the one who kept my ass in line and outta dumb shit. Well, as much as he could. So when he left, he left me without that guidance, and I went searching for it. All the way to Dallas.

"Rah-rah shit, huh?" Doe asked, and I didn't even look in his direction.

"Yeah, nigga, you heard what I said," I snapped, and felt myself get snatched up.

"See, you done went out there and lost your fuckin' mind. You forgot who the fuck I am, lil' nigga, huh? You got some hair on ya chest and talkin' like ya balls done dropped. Like you wasn't just over here cryin' like a lil' bitch behind muhfuckas who ain't called to check on ya ass since you got on that plane."

"Doe! Put that boy down!" Mama Pearlie yelled, grabbing at his arms, trying to get him to put me down.

"Naw, Mama. This nigga need to know what's really good. Takin' responsibility for shit that ain't on you. That nigga's shit was fallin' the fuck apart *long* before you got there, ain't no way that shit happened just 'cause you showed up. That shit been brewin' since before you was shot out ya pops' sac, and you can blame ya heaux ass mama for that shit!"

"Come on, bruh! You goin' too far now," I heard Eli say, his voice getting closer. But Doe's words had already hit their mark. That shit hurt like a bitch to hear.

Whop! Crack!

I hit his ass so hard over the head with my cane the wood splintered. He dropped me and grabbed his head with his right hand and snatched the gun from his waist with his left.

Pow!

I was barely balancing on my legs but when I heard that gunshot, I laid on the floor on my belly. Looking up, I realized that the shot didn't come from where I thought it had. The only person still standing was Mama Pearlie, and she was holding a .380 that I had no idea where she'd got it from. Not that I was paying attention.

"Y'all gon' fight? That's what happened the last time I lost y'all. Blood all on my couch plastic and shit, holes in my walls from bullets and heads. Y'all won't never disrespect me like that again. I got this gun just for when y'all was all home at the same time again. I knew it would happen someday. It's four bullets in here. One for a warning shot, and one for each one uh y'all hardheaded ass boys. I'll kill y'all before I let y'all hurt each other like that again. My heart can't take that shit again."

Mama sat in her worn-down La-Z-Boy. We'd bought her a nice leather recliner, but she still chose that old raggedy ass chair no matter what. She smoothed the fabric of her orange floral polyester house dress with the big pink Hawaiian flowers all over it and sat the gun tight in her lap. Motioning with her head, all three of us made our way to the plastic covered couch, the plastic squeaking underneath our asses when we sat down. Eli sat between me and Doe, like I wouldn't reach around and touch Doe's stubborn ass.

"Y'all more like y'all mamas than ya daddies, I swear. They stayed bickering about nothin'. From men to money to hair and clothes and makeup to men to money."

We all noticed she said 'men and money' twice, but none of us corrected her. We knew better.

"Donte…" She called Doe by his first name. "You left this boy in a crucial time in his life, and he needed you. You can't fault him for looking for what you took away from him."

Doe looked down, and I could tell that he was thinking about what she'd just said. She spoke my truth for me, but I never felt like Doe would hear me, understand, or give a fuck if I did say it. But he was listening now. Because it was Mama Pearlie talking, and because her ass had a gun. None of us doubted that she would use it either.

"Elijah, you out here in these streets and ain't step up like he needed you to. You was wrong for that. But it wasn't your responsibility to do that when his daddy was still breathing. That's why I let him go to Dallas. He needed to know his daddy. You ain't been the same since Rachelle got killed, but you coulda been here for Trouble more."

Eli's jaw tightened at the mention of his sister's name. Nobody spoke about that shit. It seemed like forever since I'd heard her name. It was then that I realized how much E and I had in common. I was gon' go to him about that shit, too. But later. Not right now while we had a gun on display and bullets with our names on 'em.

"And, Tywan. Baby, I know ya mama fucked you up. Finding her like you did, her never really being around. I get it. And I'm sorry. I did the best I could with those girls, but just like with y'all, I had to let them find their own way after a while. And then for Earline to be the one who put y'all, you and your sister, in the middle of this path of destruction," she said. I hadn't heard my mama called by her middle name in months. Pops called her Dani, but maybe that was his pet name for her. I'd ask him about that shit as soon as I got healed and went back to Dallas. Yeah, I was goin' back. I had to.

Bzzzzz! Bzzzzzzzzzzzzzzz!

Mama Pearlie reached into the pocket of her house dress and pulled out her cell phone. She wiped the tears from her eyes, and all three of us sat there silently, studying her and feeling guilty for being the reason for her tears.

"Mmmm hmmmm. This is her. Whatchu say now? You certain,

Nathaniel? My gawd. Lawd hammercy. No. No, I'll tell him. Okay. Thank you. Mmm hmmm. Bye bye."

Fresh tears fell down her face, and a chill ran down my spine. When she put the phone back in her pocket and looked up at me, it confirmed what I feared more than anything. He was gone. I could feel that shit. Him or Mia. One of them was dead. Or both. I just needed Mama Pearlie to confirm it.

Mama Pearlie just stared at me crying, the words seeming to be caught in her throat. I needed her to tell me what the fuck was said on that call because my mind was going crazy. I had just met that side of my family, and so much had gone down. We were all beat the fuck up, but nobody had been killed yet. None of us, anyway. But that didn't look like it was the case anymore.

"Mama, what's up? Just tell me. Please." I heard my voice crack, and that seemed to make her sadder.

"King is dead."

The words came from her mouth, and I saw her lips moving. I read the words that her lips were shaping, but I didn't hear her voice. I didn't hear shit but the screams inside of my head. Then everything went black.

"Can you believe this nigga passed out?"

"Man, gone. That was some heavy shit to hear. He just met his pops and lost him just like that. I mean, he just saw the nigga. You can't say what you'd do if you was in his shoes. He been shot, got stitches and shit in his head. Then you add in all that drama that they just went through, and what you think? Hell, yo' ass would pass the fuck out, too."

"Naw the fuck I wouldn't. 'Cause I ain't no bitch," Doe said aggressively.

"You ain't, huh? You shole sound like one to me right now talkin' shit 'bout my lil' nigga like that."

"Oh, now he yo' lil' nigga? When I raised his ass where the fuck was you at?"

"You gon' stay pullin' the surrogate daddy card, huh? When you left his ass where the fuck was I at?"

My eyes eased open just in time to see them square up.

"Aye, take that shit to the ring. I ain't 'bout to get shot 'cause y'all wanna bicker like two heauxs over a rich trick's dick. A nigga just lost his pops, got shot, and y'all in here fighting over nothin'. Over the past. Oh, and Doe, fuck you, nigga. Yeah, you raised me, but yeen the same nigga that raised me. If you want me to owe you for that shit, gimme the ticket so I can pay that bitch and send you on ya way witcha 'I gave up my teenage years to be a daddy' receipt. I'on owe you for that shit. That's what the fuck family do. Period."

I closed my eyes, not giving a fuck how he felt about that shit at all. I hated a nigga that held your circumstances against you. And brother, cousin, stand-in pops, or whatever the fuck, if he couldn't love me enough to be here for me when I just lost my real pops, then I ain't owe him shit.

"I thought I heard your voice. How you feeling, baby?" Mama Pearlie asked, walking into the room and looking from me to Doe to Eli to Doe and back at me.

"I'll be aight. I'm hungry, though," I admitted. I was more than hungry, I was starving.

"Doe, come help me fix Tywan something to eat," she said in a tone that told us she wanted to have a word with him. "Oh, and I know it's not something you might wanna think about now, but they're reading your daddy's will day after tomorrow, and I think you should go to that and his funeral."

"Yes, ma'am," I said simply.

As soon as they were outta the room, Eli leaned in like he had some kinda government secret to tell me. "Don't be mad at Doe, man. He wanna protect you and feel helpless as hell. He just handlin' the shit wrong. He mean well, though."

I heard him but didn't respond. Doe needed to learn to watch his damn mouth. Everybody didn't give a damn about his feelings or his opinion, and I was one of the ones who couldn't muster up the fuck I needed to give. Not right now. I sat up, moving slow and easing my feet to the floor. I needed to get out of this bed and move around. I could feel myself losing the feeling in my legs.

"Where's my cane?" I asked Eli, looking around.

"You broke that shit over Doe's head, bruh. I knew that nigga head was hard, but damn. He took that fuckin' lick, 'cause you reached back to all them ass whoopins he'd gave you when you was a lil' runt ass nigga and swung tryna take his shit off."

"Damn. That cane was flyy as hell," I said sadly, planning to get a few more when I got back to Dallas. "Y'all get up that plaster from the ceiling when Mama shot that Dirty Harry ass gun in the air?" I asked, changing the subject. Mama Pearlie was a gangsta. I woulda hated to see her in her day.

"Ain't need to." Eli chuckled and shook his head. I stopped trying to stand up and looked at him like he was crazy. I knew I was upset, and me and Doe were into it, but she shot up in the air. I heard that shit. "Blanks. She said she had bullets in her shit and that there were four of them slugs. She ain't lie. Just ain't tell us they wasn't live bullets."

"She hell, man," I said, joining Eli in his laughter.

"No lie heard," he shook his head saying right when she came back in without Doe with a wooden tray.

I looked on the tray, and there was a plate piled high with fried chicken, collards, mac-n-cheese, cornbread, and I saw a bowl that I knew had her famous bread pudding in it. I could smell it.

"Mama, all that looks good," I complimented, rubbing my hands together and sitting back in the bed.

She sat the tray in my lap and sat in the chair in the corner of the room to watch me eat. She always did that, watching us eat. I think she enjoyed watching us enjoy our food. That, or she wanted to make sure our asses ate all our food. Knowing Mama Pearlie, it was probably a little bit of both.

I looked around, noticing that Doe hadn't come back in the room, and figured whatever she'd said to him had him in his feelings. I wasn't about to ask, because I wasn't in the mood for his bullshit. Might ruin a nigga appetite with all them damn he-motions. I was eating good.

"Mama—*smack-smack-smack*—I shole missed yo' cookin'—*smack-pop*—They don't know how to cook—*smack-smack*—in Dallas! You put yo' foot in this!" Smacking my mouth and sucking all this good ass seasoning off my fingers, I realized that my eating noises were the only sound in the room. All eyes were on me, and I had to wonder why.

"Boy, ain't I raise you better than that? You eating like you ain't gotta lick of manners."

"Mama, he done everything but lick that damn—I mean doggone plate," Eli joked.

"It's hard to find a woman who can cook nowadays." Doe walked in the room chiming in. "Listen, bruh, I'm sorry. Aight? I feel like shit for what I did to you. How I treated you. You ain't deserve that shit, especially now with everything that you went through and are going through. Anything you need, you know me and E got you."

I looked at him and smiled with a mouth full of food. Doe never apologized for anything. Like, anything. So I knew that shit was as hard as chewing nails for that nigga. I would take what I could get and how I could get it.

"And what am I, chopped liver? Y'all better not count me out. I still got some pop in this here pistol," Mama Pearlie added in.

"The only thing you got poppin' is them knees and your shoulder when you sleep wrong," Eli joked.

Sssssss

Me and Doe both hissed when she popped him in the head. His head slung to the side so hard we thought he'd broke his neck. He asked for that shit, though. He'd lost his mind talkin' to Mama Pearlie like that. Like she hadn't just shot in the air and would square up with our asses when we were younger. We all laughed, even Eli while he rubbed the spot on his head where her hand connected.

We shared a laugh like we hadn't in forever, before it died down, and the silence hit again. A deafening silence. I knew they were all worried about me and trying to keep me in good spirits, but I had to address what was really hanging like a fog in the room.

"Look," I said, looking at Eli, then Doe, then Mama Pearlie. "Mama, you said the reading of the will is coming up. I'mma go back. But I wanna go by myself. I don't want y'all in this shi—mess. My bad, Mama." I apologized for almost cussing in her house.

"Okay, one you ain't goin' alone. Eli will go with you. And before you open your mouth, Donte, Elijah is the calmer of the two of you. We don't need no more bloodshed. So you'll sit this one out." Mama Pearlie gave me a look that dared me to say something other than 'yes, ma'am'. Remembering her hitting Eli, I decided I'd had enough head shots fuckin' with Mia to last me a lifetime. *Mia...* As bad as that girl got on my nerves, I missed her, and I hoped she was okay.

"Yes, ma'am," I agreed, digging into the bread pudding. Until I found a bitch I loved as much as I loved my sister or Mama Pearlie's cooking, I would never be in love. That's word.

"Booking the flights now," Eli said, pulling out his phone. I savored this bread pudding and looked at the only family I'd known my whole life like I might never see them again. Going back to Dallas, that might just be the case. Now, I was glad that Eli was coming with me. With the muhfuckas that were gon' be at that will reading, I had a feeling I'd need backup.

MAINE

"Come on, baeeeee," Sa'Mia whined.

I ain't know why she even had me out here this time of night. I shoulda been sleep, or better yet, diggin' deep up in her guts. But nah, not Sa'Mia's ass. She had a nigga out here in these streets at three in the damn morning luggin' this shit.

"Mane, ma, what the fuck you doin'? You gon' start out gettin' ya hands dirty and shit?" I tried to reason with her, but it was fallin' on deaf ears.

This kill, her first kill, this shit was personal, and she wanted to make a point. I knew that already, and honestly, Chica's fence-straddling ass deserved exactly what she got. She was two-faced and grimy as hell. One of them bitches that fucked her way to the top. She'd tried to take advantage of Mia's situation and memory loss and came to my crib to kill Mia tryna get me. Not that she ever had a fuckin' shot. And when she found that out, she tried to take a shot… at a nigga's head… literally.

See, my woman was set to be the new boss in these Dallas streets. We'd got word that her daddy had given the throne to her and her twin brother, Trouble. It would be confirmed at the hearing in the morning. All the more reason we needed to be asleep instead of at this damn bridge, disposing of a damn body.

"Arkino LaKeith Shane, if you don't get ya ass outta that damn truck so we can get this shit over and done wit', I know somethin'," she fussed.

"What you know, Mia?" I asked her flirtatiously, batting my eyes at her and blowing her a kiss. She blushed for half a second, and then, just like that, it was gone.

"I know this bitch body ain't gon' be the only one they find floatin' in the damn Trinity River. Howboutdat?"

"Aight, ma, damn. But you owe a nigga some head or some shit when we get back to the crib, 'cause this some bullshit here," I snapped, getting out of the driver's side of the car and walking around to the trunk.

Lifting it, I pulled the bitch Chica, who was wrapped in my favorite Persian rug, out of the truck and threw the body over my shoulder like she was a sack of potatoes. Mia was already standing at the edge of the bridge, anxiously awaiting my arrival. I had to laugh because her lil' ass was no more than five feet tall, and even though she was thicker than a Snicker, she still couldn't have done this job alone. I shoulda let her, though. Something just ain't feel right about bein' out here. I mean, there was no traffic. And, granted it was a Tuesday night, there was always, and I mean always, somebody headed somewhere on these Expressways.

"Next time, ya lil' ass betta get a dolly and drank some Powerade, 'cause this shit here for the birds, Mia." I continued to fuss. I knew, though, that the man in me would never in my life, send my woman to do no shit like this on her own. Now, that would be some lazy, kept nigga type shit.

"Yeah, yeah, yeah. Put the bitch ova the edge so I can push her fuck ass on over, and we can get back to the house. I got a surprise for you." She smirked, letting me know what time it was by the devilish grin on her face.

My dick got hard. Shit like this was why I loved Mia. Now, when I met her, I never woulda thought she was wit' all this. I thought she was the good girl. Daddy's princess, and her brother, and my then best friend, was the one who was the mastermind. That's why I hollered at her. But I soon found out that she was more than met the eye. She was smart, sexy, and fun-sized. I used to daydream about puttin' my babies in her lil' ass.

Now, she was pregnant with our first son, Arkino, Jr. No, she wasn't far enough along for us to know the gender yet, but that was my little nigga in there. I just knew it. Hence, the reason I was out here doing all the heavy lifting. We were too young and in these streets to be having a baby, but with pussy like Mia got, my pullout game was weak as fuck. Man, who was I tryna fool? There was no pullout game where she was concerned. Hell, I wanted to sleep in that shit like you did beneath the covers every night I could. Pussy was a nigga's weakness, mane. Ain't nothin' wrong wit' it, and if you say it is, it's 'cause you ain't had none this good-good like I got. Have a nigga toting dead bodies at three somethin' in the morning to dip up in it.

"The hell you over there fantasizing about, Arkino?" she asked, breaking me from my fantasies of her pretty heart-shaped ass bent over in front of me.

"Yo' sexy ass," I smiled and said, leaning down to give her a kiss and put the body on the bridge's edge.

I knew she wanted to be the one to push her over. Like I said before, she had a point to prove. She was about to start some shit, and I wasn't in the mood for it, but I knew that it was necessary. She was bringin' all the snakes on out so she could cut they heads off, and then we could rule this empire in peace. Both she and I knew that there were some people who weren't happy about the way things had turned out. Mostly because they weren't gon' be too keen on takin' orders from a bitch, even with Trouble running shit right beside her. You know how niggas be. It does something to their egos when a woman was in charge of some shit. Well, they were about to learn that Sa'Mia wasn't the average woman, just like I did.

"One, two, thrrreeeeee!" Mia shouted and pushed the body on over the edge.

Woo-woo-woo-woo-woo

We heard the sound of it tumbling toward the water, flipping in the wind.

Splash

When I heard her hit the water, I was ready to go. My granny always taught me to trust my intuition, and mine was screaming for us to get the fuck outta dodge. I started to turn to leave, and Mia squatted down, snatching her gloves off and my pants down in what seemed like one motion. For my woman, my baggy pants weren't a fashion statement, they meant easy access. I wanted to stop her, but she'd already pulled my dick out, and even though the chill in the air had him limp, the moment her warm mouth wrapped around him, he was ready for business, growing and snaking his way down her throat. I grabbed the back of her head and fucked her in the mouth, fast and hard. She was sucking and slurpin' so good, I was 'bout to nut already. *I swear to God, I'mma marry this woman!*

"Ahhhh shit, Mia! I'm finna cuuuuuu—"

"Freeze!" I heard behind me, and the sensation that was overcoming me left as quickly as it had come. Mia ain't stop, though. She never did until I was finished. With one motion of her tongue, the shit I called her 'Mama Mia Magic Trick', she had my nut rising again and my knees getting weak. "I said freeze!" the police officer behind us shouted again.

I put my hands behind my head, and so did Mia, but I kept fuckin' her mouth, and she kept suckin' 'til I bust. We was both doin' that shit wit' no hands. When she finished, she licked her lips, winked at me, and stood up slowly with her hands still behind her head. We were bum-rushed by cops and cuffed. They picked Mia up off the ground, and she ain't say a word to them as they read her her Miranda Rights. I wasn't even listenin' to the cop read me mine; my eyes were locked on my woman's. Before they lowered her head into the patrol car, she yelled out to me.

"Aye, baby daddy, put that thang away before you put one of these cops' eyes out and they be tryna claim you was resisting," she said, laughing so loudly I could still hear her after they closed the door on her.

They drove off with my baby before putting me in the car. A friendly ass female detective, 'bout five-nine, stacked in all the right places, with too much makeup on and thirst gleaming in her eyes, came to the car before they closed me up in the patrol car that was gon' take me downtown. She eyed me then my dick and reached for it. I moved away 'cause I ain't want her touchin' my shit. It belonged to Sa'Mia and Sa'Mia only. She gave me a smile and closed the door before sayin' something to the other cops who were still there. They opened the door, and she pulled me out, taking me to her unmarked and opening the back door.

I gave her a look that said I didn't trust her ass to get in her car. The more I looked at her, the more familiar she looked. I knew her from somewhere; I just couldn't put my finger on it. She pushed my head down, leaning in to whisper in my ear.

"You either gon' make this easy or hard for yourself. Mmmmmmm," she said, reaching around to grab my dick. "I'm hopin' you make it hard. If not, I plan to help you out with that."

"Mannnn, take yo' old ass hands dafuq off my shit," I snapped, wanting to kick her ass.

"Fine. I'll just pay your bitch a special visit when we get to the precinct. I've got some evidence that'll make sure her hands won't touch ya shit again either," she threatened. "But if you cooperate, as often as I like, I'll see what I can do to make all of that go away."

Ducking down, I slid into the back of her ride. "I thought you'd see things my way," she smiled and said before closing the door on me, getting in the car, and pulling off.

As soon as we were far enough away from the bridge for her, she took a turn off the freeway and made a few turns, goin deep into East Dallas. When she got to a street that was littered with abandoned houses and had most of the street lights out, she put the car in park and looked at me in the rearview mirror with a smile that made me wanna snap her damn neck. She turned down the radio and hit a couple other buttons, before speaking.

"That dick must be magic for ya bitch to risk getting her head blown off to finish suckin' that shit. Now, you can make this shit easy, or you can make it hard. Matter fact, I'mma make it hard, so yeen gotta worry 'bout that," she said with a giggle, laughin' at her own lame ass joke. That's when it hit me. *Marissa! This is the cop that took her away at prom. I thought she said this bitch was her sister. Why she lookin' into Mia?* My mind started to race, and I had to think fast.

She got out the car and came to my side, opening the door. She had her hand on her Taser and squatted down, moving her face toward my lap. I scooted away. She wasn't about to do this shit. I just knew it. Her neck rolled, and she popped her mouth before pulling out her Taser.

"Have it your way, then," she said before tasing the fuck outta me.

My body stiffened up as the voltage surged through me. I fell to the side, and she smiled and climbed in the back seat with me. The last things I remembered were thinking of how I was gon' murder her bitch ass when I got outta that cage and feeling her mouth on my shit before passing out.

When I came to, I was in a room sittin' up in a chair. As soon as I opened my eyes, the steel metal door opened, too, and in walked this tall, lanky detective came in followed by the bitch cop who had violated me.

"Mr. Shane, I'm Detective Barnes. Officer Purty here told me that you were quite cooperative. I think we can make you an offer that you won't wanna refuse," he said with a smile, brushing past and up against Officer Purty's hoe ass. *Fuckin' thot cop. I gotta make sure I get tested as soon as I get the fuck outta here,* I thought to myself, looking at her ass with murder on my mind.

"I ain't got shit to say. I want my attorney," I said forcefully. I wasn't about to play wit they asses.

"Mmmhmmm," Detective Barnes said, rubbing his chin like he was thinking. "Well, that's too bad, 'cause your wife, or whoever the fuck she is to you, yeah, her life depends on you, and it saddens me to know that you're so willing to let her down." He gave the indirect threat to Sa'Mia.

Officer Purty smiled and walked toward the door, pulling out her baton. I knew she would kill Mia if I didn't cooperate. Hell, they'd pretty much just told me so. I couldn't let that shit happen. If I had known that was some bluffing bullshit, I woulda told his punk ass to go fuck Purty with that stick, but I didn't... and there was no way in hell I was gon' let nothin' happen to Sa'Mia. I would die protecting her. My shoulders slumped, defeated. They exchanged a look before both sitting down in front of me and pulling out a recorder to get a confession out of me. For what, I had no idea.

"So, here's how this is going to go—" Barnes started to try to coach me before she pressed the record button.

Creeeeaaaaaakkkkk! Slam!

The heavy metal door opened, and an old white man in an ugly ass old-school pinstriped black and green suit with a white collared shirt walked in, accompanied by a black woman in a black pencil skirt, white blouse, and hot pink blazer walked into the room. I couldn't believe my eyes, but I knew I wasn't seeing things.

"Detectives, Randy Abraham, and I'll be representing Mr. Shane *and* Miss King. Purty, didn't expect to see you again, and so soon," the man said, reaching out to shake their hands, which they both rudely declined.

"Well, when you're representing the same pool of criminals, you're bound to cross paths with the law more often than not," Purty snapped.

"By criminal, do you mean your sister Marissa Hervey?" the woman asked in a mousy voice. "Because that would make you more closely linked to her than them, right? They're just her students. Two in five hundred. But you two, you shared a dad, huh? 'Til he decided that he liked her mama more than yours?"

Barnes looked on in shock as the woman checked Purty before sitting on one side of me while the white man, Abraham, sat on the other side. They were face to face with the Detectives, and I felt like I was protected on all sides. Because I was. The expressions on the faces in the room were epic. Purty looked like she'd just been punched in the mouth. Barnes was looking at Purty like 'what the fuck have you got me into', and Abraham was sitting there smugly with his hands folded in front of him, resting on the table. And the woman, well, she was pulling manila folders out of her briefcase. I was loving the shit but had to keep a straight face. I *knew* we were in the clear.

"Now, we have a couple of things to discuss with Mr. Shane. But before you go, let's discuss a couple of things. Liiiiike, the sexual assault of Mr. Shane before he was brought into the precinct. I believe that was you, Detective Purty, right?" the woman asked, her sweet, innocent sounding voice adding insult to injury.

"I didn't touch him!" Purty snapped, but you could tell by the aggression in her tone that she was lying.

"Oh, you touched him. And we can prove it. Gratefully for him, I dispatched a cruiser to your area, and they came around the corner before you could do more than fondle his sausage, if you know what I mean," Tatiana said with a giggle that made me look at her goofy ass with the side eye. She straightened up and flipped open the manila folder on the top of the pile, sliding her glasses to the bridge of her nose dramatically.

"Fuckin' bitch," Purty insulted under her breath, crossing her arms and sitting back in the chair like a spoiled child.

"What was that?" Tatiana asked, but Purty said nothing, just kept grumbling, probably calling Tatiana all kinds of things her mama didn't name her in her head. Tatiana didn't break her gaze with Purty. She was challenging her, waiting for her to respond.

"Nothing," Purty grumbled.

"Oh, okay. Speak up next time you say nothing, mmmmkay?" she taunted with a smile, moving the folder she'd opened to the side before looking at the other detective. "And you, Detective Barnes, where do we start? Pedophiliaaaa. Hmmm, something you and your partner here have in common, huh? Or do you want to talk about your solicitation? How about your ummmmm, recreational habit?"

Bingooooo, I thought.

"Who the fuck are you?" Purty asked.

"My assistant, Tatiana," Abraham offered, but then Tatiana spoke up.

"Your worst nightmare, darlin'. A bitch wit' a brain. And the upper hand. And since you haven't denied anything that I just mentioned, I think we can meet with our client now while we wait for you to make all this mess against him and Miss King disappear. And maybe we'll do the same." Tatiana slid her glasses back up on her face, patted the bun she wore all the time at the back of her head, and smirked.

The detectives looked like they wanted to shit a brick and slap this bitch all at once. Instead, they got up and left out of the room. I sat back and let out a deep breath.

"So, I was right?" I asked.

"Right-a-roonie," she said, and I had to laugh at her corny ass. "Now sit back and chillax. Y'all will be outta here in a jiff."

Laying my head on the cold table, I tried to relax, but that was damn near impossible. This had to have been the hardest fuckin' week of my life. And we still had one more bullshit ass incident to live through. The reading of King's will. The worst part? I didn't know if Mia and I would survive this one. But I had to be her backbone. That was what love was. Having each other's backs. I would forever have Mia's just like I knew she would always have mine. 'Til death do us part. 'Til *death* do us part.

MIA

"What the fuck happened in there?" I asked when Maine walked up to me outside of the police department. I had my hands on my hips and was patting my foot because I was annoyed as hell. I wanted to know how we got out. If he snitched somebody out, I needed to know who. This was just too damn much. My first night on some queenpin shit, and I get arrested. That was almost enough to scare a bitch straight. *Almost.*

"Nothing to talk about out here," Maine said, pulling me into a hug and kissing the top of my head.

I wanted to take his word for it, but I was pissed. Especially when that bitch said she fucked my man when she was out-processing me. Maine's dick had been way too fuckin' friendly, and I was just about tired of that shit. I didn't wanna end up behind bars for killing a bitch for sampling my shit. He and I were gon' have a conversation, and it was the last one we were gonna have. Or next time, he'd be the one being tossed in the river.

A Prius pulled up with a woman in the driver's seat, and I looked at Maine like I wanted to kill him with my bare hands right then. The window rolled down, and the girl leaned over before speaking.

"Hello Sa'Mia. My apologies, Miss King. I'm Tatiana. I thought you might need a ride. Maine, you ready?"

Maine nodded and went to reach for the handle. They both had me fucked up, and I mean allllll the way fucked up.

"Maine, who the fuck is this bitch, and how the hell she know my name? I ain't got all my memories back, but I don't remember this heaux not once."

"Mia, calm yo' ass down, and get in the fuckin' car, mane. Why you gotta turn every damn thang into somethin'? We outside the damn cop station, and you wanna get an assault with a deadly weapon charge?"

"Deadly weapon?" I asked. He threw me off with that one.

"Yeah, that mouth of yours," he said with a smug ass smile that forced me to smile back. He knew how to shut me up.

"Man, shut the hell up."

"Getcha lil' ass in the car," he ordered, opening the back door for me.

"You got me fucked up. You sit in the back, nigga. I'm royalty. I ride in the front. Dafuq you thought this was?"

Shaking his head, Maine opened the passenger side door, and I stepped into the car. He closed the door, then got in the back. The Tatiana bitch pulled away from the curb, and I studied her face, trying to see if I could refresh my memory. Nope, I'd never seen her before.

"Sooooo, Tatiana, is it?"

"Yeppers, and I have to say it's an absolute honor to meet you. Sa'Mia King, in the flesh, in my car. It's like... it's like better than meeting Beyoncé or Taylor Swift!"

Did this bitch just say Taylor Swift? Yoncé, I was ok with. But not Taylor damn Swift. And why was she gushing and shit? Who was this bitch?

"Nice to meet you... too. I think. Wanna tell me who the fuck you are and how you know me? And more importantly, how you know my man?"

"Whooooaaaaa, mamacita," she said with a giggle. She had a voice that I guess some could call cute. But with the corny shit she let come out of her mouth, it was just annoying as fuck to me. "I'm NOBODY."

"What the fuck you mean you nobody? You some damn body. You know me and my nigga. So tell me how, before I pop you in your shit. I done had a long fuckin' night and a longer damn month. I don't have the patience a newborn baby has for the tit. So stop fuckin' playin' wit' me."

"No, really. I'm Noooooooobody," she dragged out, and I wanted to slap her stupid. Hell, she was already sounding stupid, so maybe I need to slap her ass intelligent.

"Bitch, I just told you 'bout playin' wit' me!" I hollered, swinging for her head, but Maine caught my hand. "Nigga, I know you better let me dafuq go."

"Chill out, mane. She really is N0B0DY! She's the tech girl. My hacker and secret weapon. She's the one who can make all this shit disappear."

"Well, why them damn videos still on Facebook of us fuckin' and shit then?" I seethed, feeling like Maine was defending this bitch over me.

"Evidence, sweetie cakes. Neisha and Purty will go down for all the things that have happened to y'all. Neisha is dead, but Purty will lose her career for her part. She was mad at you for shooting her boo thang at the club when he was about to kill Trouble. By the way, your brother fine as wine in the California sunshine. He single?"

I looked upside her head like she couldn't be for real. She was such a square, and she thought she had a chance with Trouble? That would be a fun pair to watch.

"Yeah, he single. But that ain't the matter at hand. You can holla at him later. So, what all will be pinned on them?" I asked curiously as she pulled up to the gate at the house. Officer Miles let us in, and I wondered if that man ever went home.

"Everything. Even Marissa got a pass. Not that I could save her career, but at least she'll get to be present at your graduation. Then she'll bow out gracefully and keep her retirement. Courtesy of moi," she said proudly, and I almost felt bad for nearly popping her ass in her top.

"Well, thank you, I guess."

"Awwww, she thanked me. I'm in there," she said with a broad smile, and I cut an eye at Maine because I couldn't take her serious. He just chuckled and got out to open my door.

"It was nice to meet you, Tatiana," I said over my shoulder.

"No! The pleasure was all mine. Truly, truly all mine!" she shouted as loudly as her tiny voice would allow her to.

"I'll hit you up in a couple of days to make sure everything is good, aight?" Maine said to her, and for the first time, I was glad he was gonna deal with her ass and not me. *She's truly, truly annoyin'*, I laughed to myself as I mocked her in my head.

"I think you got a groupie," Maine said, reaching around me and opening the door.

"Ya thank?" I asked, laughing. That whole encounter was unreal. *Is this what my life is about to be like?* I thought, touching my stomach and worrying if it would impact my child like it had me and my brothers. Pushing that thought out of my head, I accepted my fate and checked myself because I knew my pedigree. I would protect my seed like my father had us. With my life. And I knew that Maine would do the same. "What time is it?" I asked him, turning around and wrapping my arms around his neck.

"Mia, the sun's way up. We 'bout got a couple hours before we gotta be at the reading of Pops' will."

"What if I'on wanna go?" I asked, pouting. I wasn't ready for this shit.

"Yeen got no choice, mane. It's that, then graduation. Them two thangs are non-negotiable, Sa'Mia," he said with bass in his voice. My pouting didn't work. One thing that I was grateful for was that my daddy didn't want a funeral. He didn't think it was safe with everything that had gone on. His body was cremated, and we would get the ashes at the reading today.

Maine removed my arms but held onto my hand, walking back to the bedroom. I followed obediently, wishing that shit coulda been different.

"Make love to me," I asked, fighting back tears. He looked into my eyes, wiping the tears that fell and shook his head 'no'.

"As bad as I wanna feel your super soaker ass pussy right now, we need rest." He reasoned with me.

"Will you at least hold me?" I begged.

"Of course," he said, pulling me into our bed on top of him.

Whommmp! Whomp! Whomp! Whomp!

I looked at my alarm, and it read noon. I felt like I'd just gone to sleep. Hell, I ain't remember falling asleep. Last night was a bitch, and now I had to get outta bed and go hear the reading of my daddy's will. Sitting up, I looked Maine in the face and admired his handsome features. I wondered which of his features our baby girl would have. Maine kept saying the baby was a boy, but I wanted a girl. I wasn't the girliest girl because I didn't have a mama. I wanted to do all the girly stuff with my daughter that I didn't get to do. The time I spent with Marissa getting ready for prom was nice, even though I was laid up all fucked up. I wanted to give that to my child.

Reaching up and touching my stomach, Maine opened his eyes and smiled at me.

"Since the first day I laid eyes on you, I dreamt of makin' you mine. Puttin' my babies up in ya and makin' you my wife. I ain't see shit goin' like this. But to be with you, Mia, that's all a nigga been wantin' for as long as he can remember."

I leaned down and kissed him, and he palmed my ass. "Nope. No time for that shit. We gotta go to this shindig and see what my daddy left his princess."

"You ready for this shit?" Maine asked, studying my face. "'Cause you ain't gotta get into this drug shit, Mia. Your trust fund and the money I have saved, plus the stocks and shit I got is more than enough."

"I get that, and I ain't sure what I want, bae. But right now, we don't have to talk about that. Let's just take this one day at a time."

"Gotcha," he said, kissing me so passionately that it made my pussy thump. He was gon' have to stop that shit or we were gon' be late.

I got up to get dressed, choosing a baby tee and a pair of black PINK joggers. I tied my hair into a top bun, slipped on some slides, and I was ready to go. I sat on the couch, patting my foot nervously, waiting for Maine to bring his slow-moving ass on. I was the girl, but his pretty boy ass had to make sure that every wave on his damn head was perfect.

"Maine!" I yelled, tired of waiting.

"What, Mia?" he asked, coming toward the front.

"Come on witcho slow comin' ass, that's what."

"I'm here now. Damn, I got how many more months of your mouth being on pregnant?"

"Shut up and come on," I fussed, leading the way out the door.

The car ride was silent as hell. Both of us were in our own thoughts. I wanted to know where his head was, but I had my own shit to think about. Not that I didn't care about Maine's mindset right now, but I needed to prepare for this little meet and greet. I had a feeling in my gut that it wasn't gonna go well. Or maybe that was the baby moving. *Is it too early for all that?*

Something on the radio caught my attention, and I turned it up. Smiling, Maine reached over and took my hand. I looked at him lovingly, while he kept his eyes on the road. But at the traffic light he stopped, looking over at me, and did something that I never expected. Singing, and I don't mean playing around, either. My baby had pipes. Hell, I would've took my drawls off and thrown them at his ass, if I was wearing drawls.

"And that's a whole lotta love, ain't tryna waste it. Like we be runnin' a mile to never make it. That's just too bitter for worse, don't wanna taste it. That's just too bitter for worse, don't wanna face it." Maine sang Ella Mai's "Trip" to me, making my eyes water.

More memories flooded my head. The headaches were more a nuisance than a pain now, but the more I remembered, the more I loved Maine. I hated the life that I was thrown into, and that made me think about what he said about us not having to do this dope game shit. Maybe I would take him up on that.

"You know you can't ever go another day in our lives without singing to me. Every... day... Maine."

"I can do that. Every day for the rest of our lives," he promised, pulling up to a huge building in Downtown Dallas. Victory Plaza was a beautiful five-story space that was glass all the way around and fit right into the chic feel of the area.

I let out a deep breath and waited for Maine to open the door for me. Walking into the building hand in hand, he checked his phone and pressed the button on the elevator for the fourth floor. Stopping at the directory, Maine checked his phone again before balling his face up. Holding up a finger, he pressed send and walked away to have a conversation.

Coming back a few moments later, he grabbed both of my hands, turning me to face him. I was concerned, and he had my anxiety at an all-time high. I was already nervous about all of this, and now he was acting strange. He looked over my shoulder, making me look back, and I shook my head at my brother Kong.

I hadn't seen him since I got my memory back, and I couldn't say that seeing his ass here right now gave me any kind of pleasant feeling at all. When I looked back at Maine once Kong was on the elevator and the door had closed, he was wearing a mean mug that I was sure matched mine, but it softened as soon as our eyes met.

"That's what I was about to tell you. Kong is gonna be here. So is that nigga Trouble," he said with a grit of his teeth.

"That's my brother, Maine. Let that shit go. You don't even know what really happened. But y'all been beefin' for a hot minute. He beat ya ass, y'all shot each other, and it was all because y'all love and wanted to protect me."

"I was hoping you wouldn't get back the part of your memory where he beat my ass, mane." He laughed, rubbing his hands over his waves.

"And you fucked the nurse and shit?" I reminded him. His face showed the shock of me remembering more than he thought I had in such a short time. Those guns hitting me in the head had done it, though.

"Aight, we ain't here for alladat." He cut off my oncoming rant. There were some things that I needed to get off my chest and boundaries that needed to be set before we moved forward. Because the shit that I remembered that he did to me, no bitch in her right mind would deal with it and take his ass back. "And don't be lookin' at me like that."

"Like what?"

"Like bein' witchu wasn't hell. You was somethin' serious, Sa'Mia. Still are. But I loved you still, and I love you now. Hell, the way you kicked a nigga in his shit. Lil' AJ you carryin' now might be the only one you get outta me. Glad I dropped that load off in ya before you sterilized a nigga."

"Man, shut the hell up and let's go." I laughed at his stupid ass, but he cut my laughter off with a kiss that took my breath away.

"You ready, Mia?"

"Yeah."

"You sure?"

"Nigga, as sure as a bitch can be about hearing her daddy's will being read and having to sit in the same room as the nigga who's the reason that he's dead. Now stop asking me before I change my fuckin' mind."

"Already, let's go," he said, letting go of only one of my hands and leading the way to the elevator.

He pushed the number nineteen, and we rode to the top floor of the building in total silence. I was praying that nothing popped off and this could be handled with the respect that my daddy deserved. But I knew Maine, and the way he was looking, he was preparing for the exact opposite. *Welp, let's get it.*

Ding.

"Nineteenth Floor."

MARISSA

"*D*amn, I'm gonna be late," I said aloud to myself, parking in the deck of the Victory Plaza Office Building.

It was 11:30, and I wanted to get there so that maybe I could figure out what was going on before the kids arrived. I didn't feel like I belonged at the reading of Alonzo's will. I knew there was nothing in it for me, so when Mr. Abraham called and told me that my presence was requested, I was so confused. I'd even tried to call Nate to get something out of him, but he'd been tight-lipped, and then just stopped answering my calls and texts.

When I exited the elevator on the nineteenth floor of the Victory Plaza building, I walked as quickly as possible to Mr. Abraham's office. There was no receptionist at the desk, so I sat there and waited until someone came. It wasn't but a couple of seconds before a cute black girl with a bun and turtle shell glasses walked over to the desk and sat down with a steaming hot cup of coffee in a pink mug that read "Girl Boss" and had a gun handle as the handle. I had to laugh at how inappropriate that was for the setting that we were in. But if there was one thing that I'd learned from being around Alonzo and his children, it was that nothing was ever what you expected it to be.

She sat down, gulped the coffee so hard that it made *me* cringe, because I just knew that had to burn her throat, and started typing away on her computer's keyboard. She didn't even acknowledge my presence, which I thought was rude. *Ahem*, I cleared my throat to bring attention to me sitting there. Still nothing. *Oh, she's about to get cussed the hell out. I already don't wanna be here, and now she's acting like she don't see me sitting here. We the only two people in the room right now. Maybe the bitch needs a new prescription, because she gotta be Stevie Wonder blind,* I thought, standing up and getting ready to walk over there and knock that mug of scalding ass coffee in her lap. *Bet that bitch'll know I'm here then,* I seethed. One thing I hated was disrespect, and with my nerves already being bad as hell right now, it wouldn't take but one damn thing to send me over the edge. And I think this was that one thing.

"You must be Miss Hervey," she said in a mousy voice.

"I am. But if you knew that, why didn't you say shit when you walked back in here?"

"I thought you were getting your thoughts together. This is a tough time for so many, and I've learned that you have to let people prepare for what they are about to face instead of rushing them and shoving them into a room where they'll hear the last wishes of their loved ones." I looked at her and felt like an ass immediately. Here I was thinking that she was being disrespectful, when in reality, she was being considerate. "And usually, when they're ready, they'll come and let me know. Like you just did." She smiled over the top of her mug, taking another gulp of coffee.

"I'm sorry," I said, and she looked at me with a lost expression on her face.

"Sorry for what?"

"The thoughts I had of you," I told her, and she laughed.

"Ohhhh, you thought. Oh, wowzers, no ma'am. Maybe I should say something like, 'let me know when you're ready' so that people know I see them, huh?"

"That might save you from getting cussed out, yes." I laughed, because that's sure as hell what she was about to get from me.

"Gotcha. Thanks a bunch. Are you ready to go to the room where the reading will be held?"

"Yes, please," I said, breaking eye contact, because I really wasn't ready at all. In all this time, I still hadn't dealt with losing Alonzo. I hadn't been able to say goodbye. Maybe this would be the thing that allowed me to do that. The thing that gave me closure.

Following the mousy woman, she led me to the very back of the office space where there was an enclosed conference room. The only entryway or exit was the door that we came through, and there were chairs and couches scattered all around, angled toward a huge desk against the back wall facing the door.

"Mr. Abraham and Dr. Smith will be in here shortly," she informed me before pulling the door closed and leaving me in the room alone. "Oh," she said, popping her head back in. "If you need anything, there's a button on the desk. Just hit it, and I'll be at your service in a jiff."

I nodded, and she closed the door. I could hear her whistling as she walked away. Sitting in the plaid armchair in the far corner of the room, I leaned back with my eyes closed, waiting for Nate and Mr. Abraham to come in, like she'd said. After what felt like an hour of sitting in there alone with my thoughts, the door opened, and Nate walked in.

"Nate! What's going on? Why am I here?" I asked him, leaping from the chair.

"Because Zo wanted you here, Rissa. Just relax," he offered, walking over and hugging me before kissing my cheek and sitting me back down.

"But why would he—"

"You'll find out soon enough, Miss Hervey. Please don't worry, okay. It's a positive, I promise. But that's all I can say at the moment," Mr. Abraham assured me, entering the room as well.

I looked back and forth from him to Nate, becoming more and more frustrated with the swivel of my head. Seeing that they both wore expressionless faces, I folded my arms under my breasts and laid my head back on the back of the chair. *I don't want shit that he could've left me. I want him*, I thought, tears filling my closed eyes. *All I want is him.*

KONG

"I'm on my way to this will reading. Still ain't heard nothing from Chica?" I asked Nick, one of my newly promoted lieutenants.

"Nah, man, can't find her for shit. Found out she was workin' with a cop, and that bitch won't tell me shit either. Well, other than that Chica was 'bout to sell you out and was wearing a wire and shit. But the bitch ain't gon' be no more help than that. She said all cases concerning the King family are closed."

"Wire?"

"Yep, that bitch was a snake, man," Nick said, sounding disgusted by her disloyalty. All I wanted to do was find her and ask her why. There had to be more to the story, but only she would be able to tell me what it was, and she'd been missing since she ran up out the warehouse that night I killed DeRico and Kellz's asses.

"Aight, man. I just pulled up. I'll hit you when I'm leaving here," I told him, my mind still clouded by confusion of the information that he'd given me. *A snitch? Not Chica. There had to be more to it than that. She just needs to come home and tell me what's really good, so we can work this shit on out*, I thought to myself, pulling into the valet parking and handing them my keys.

"You hear me, Kong?" Nick asked, and I really hadn't.

"Nah, what you say?"

"I said keep ya head on straight in there. Don't be thinkin' 'bout a bitch that might not wanna be found, and don't lose your cool in a room where you're outnumbered and outgunned. Really wish you woulda let a nigga come with you to make sure you was good," he said sincerely.

"I got you, man. Good lookin' out. And nah, this is family business, and it needs to be handled amongst us," I told him and hung up the phone.

Nick had been down with my crew for a while, but I never noticed him, how he thought, looked out, and moved until I had to. He was one of the few that were still fuckin' with a nigga. So when we sat down to talk and he pointed out where I'd made the wrong moves and how not to make the same mistakes again, I realized that I had underestimated him.

Walking into the building, I saw Maine holding Mia's hands and looking at her with so much love in his eyes. She looked over her shoulder and mugged me before looking back at him. His eyes didn't leave until I was on the elevator and he had a look on his face like he wanted to shoot a nigga. I matched that shit, even though I ain't have no bad blood with him.

My only problem was that he was here, with his bitch, and mine was still missing. The fact that she went missing on his watch only made that shit worse. I sucked my teeth, jealousy swelling in my chest just thinking about the shit. Then it hit me. What if Maine and Mia had something to do with Chica being missing? It ain't too many people I know that can spook cops like that. One of them was the man whose will they were about to read, and the other, well, I'd just seen their Bonnie and Clyde wannabe asses in the lobby.

When I walked into the lawyer's office, there was this cute, bubbly bitch typing away at the keyboard.

"Hey, beautiful." I greeted her, walking right up to the desk. She looked at me over her glasses and shot a smile my way.

"OMG," she said in the cutest little voice. I even thought it was adorable that she said the letters instead of the actual words. "You really do look like him!"

"Like him?" I asked, my brow furrowing. I didn't know if the 'him' she was referring to was King or Kellz or somebody else.

"Yeppers, you look just like T-Pain!" She gushed, making me chuckle. I'd heard that more than a few times before. Some bitches thought I was cute because of that shit while others said a nigga was ugly. But I was far from that.

"I hear that a lot. Can I buy you a drank later, and then I'mma take you home with me?" I said, and she laughed at that lame shit.

"No thank you," she said, her face suddenly straightening. It happened so fast that it made me think the bitch may be a little bipolar. *Dodged that bullet*, I thought to myself as she stood up from her chair.

She was small at the top, but her hips and ass made up for it. She was shock you fine, because with that voice and the school teacher look that she had going on, I never would've thought she'd be stacked up the way she was.

"That's cool. Where they reading the will at for Alonzo King? A young nigga got moves to make and no time to waste," I said, not letting her know that her rejection had bothered me.

"Right this way." She motioned, leading me to the back of the office. I watched her ass jiggle in her work slacks and had to tell myself to chillax. I hadn't had no pussy since I last dug up in Chica the night she got ghost on me, and I was feenin' for a hit. And since this bitch wanted to say no, I'd accepted that challenge. She was gon' be mine, just for the night. Or maybe until I found my wife. I planned to knock that bun loose on the back of her head. She ain't know it, but she was officially on my To-Do list.

I heard voices on the other side of the door that she stopped in front of and wondered who else was there. She didn't open it right away, and the way she looked over her shoulder at me nervously, before flashing a fake ass smile had me even more curious.

Bop-Bop-Bop

She knocked on the door with some force, and the voices stopped.

"Come in," I heard someone say, and she opened the door and stepped to the side. I walked into the room past her, intentionally brushing up against her.

"We'll talk some more before I leave here about that drink," I said, letting her know that I wasn't taking no for an answer. She hit me with the eye roll and the lip smack, but that shit didn't move me. "See you in a lil' bit, beautiful." I flirted, ignoring her attitude. It was in that moment that I realized that I hadn't gotten her name in that moment, but she was a nobody anyway, so I wasn't about to waste my time tryna get to know nothing about her but how them guts felt later on.

Seeing Dr. Smith and Marissa in matching armchairs, and a white man sitting behind a big desk made me see red. I wished I'd let Nick come with me now. Apparently, this was less of a family affair than I'd thought. I'd shoot him a text with the address and tell his ass to be on standby.

"I'll go on back up front and wait for the rest of the attendees to arrive," the woman said, before closing the door quick as hell. It was like she knew by the tension in the room that some shit was about to go down.

"Mr. King, thank you for coming. I'm Randy Abraham, your father's counsel. We're waiting for a few others, and then we can get started. Have a seat anywhere you like an—"

"What the fuck is this bitch doin' here?" I asked, looking from Doc Smith to the white man named Abraham. Nobody spoke, but I wasn't sitting no damn where 'til somebody answered me.

"Your father wanted her here, Kong. That's what she's doin' here," Doc Smith said, standing up like he was about to do something. He was on King's payroll, so I ain't really know what the fuck he was doin' here either. Unless he was here as damage control, in case some shit popped off and somebody needed medical attention.

Seeing Marissa's ass sitting in here like she belonged, somebody probably would.

"Please have a seat, Mr. King. Everyone who will be here was requested by the instruction of your—*ahem*—father. When the others arrive, it'll all make sense," Abraham said, his face turning red like he was afraid. And he should've been. History showed that when the King family got together, somebody always ended up either hurt or dead.

I pulled out my phone and shot Nick that text.

Me: *2323 Victory Avenue Dallas, TX 75219 19th Floor Randy Abraham's office. Straight to the back.*

Nick: *Already. U good?*

Me: *No. Need backup*

Nick: *B there in a min.*

After reading his response, I sat down with a smile. I hoped Mr. Abraham knew how to duck and was wearing a bulletproof vest.

TROUBLE

"*L*isten, bruh. I don't wanna have to kill nobody. You gon' be able to keep your shit together?" Eli asked me when we walked up to the elevator and pressed the up button.

"Yeah, I just wanna get this shit over with. Pops ain't want a funeral, and that's what's up. I don't know if I coulda took another one of them," I admitted as we rode to the nineteenth floor of the building.

"Aight. I got ya front, back—"

"And both sides." I finished the saying that me, him, and Doe had when we were walking into a situation where shit could get real.

We followed the directory to The Offices of Randy Abraham, and when we walked in, a bottom thick ass brown-skinned chick with glasses was just walking back up to the office shaking her head.

"This shit is too much. I don't have time to get shot. I'm too much of a cutie pie to get shot," she said to herself under her breath. Well, I thought it was under her breath until she saw Eli and I standing there. Her expression went from worried to shocked, making me look at Eli and him to look at me lost as hell. She threw her hand over her mouth all dramatically, and her eyes got big behind her lenses. "OMG, you're-you're-you're Tywan "Trouble" Nobles," she said, using air quotes when she said my nickname.

What threw me more than anything was that she was screaming, but her voice was still soft as hell. It even squeaked a little bit.

"Do I know you?" I asked her, never getting this reaction from a woman before.

"I'm NOBODY—I mean, I'm somebody—But I'm NOBODY—My-my-my—Geez Louise," she stammered, and Eli's smile made me elbow his ass in the side. He was about to bust out laughing and make ol' girl feel played. And even though I didn't understand her reaction, I couldn't say a nigga wasn't flattered by the shit. "My name is Tatiana. You can call me Tati, though. But I'm NOBODY, and it's soooooo nice to finally meet you," she got out after catching her breath and fanning herself. You would've thought that nigga Hov had walked up in here or something.

"Well, you're somebody. Never call yourself a nobody. But again, do we know each other?" I repeated, because she'd said it was nice to finally meet me.

"We haven't met in person, but I know you. I mean, I've been watching you. I mean— Get it together Tati, what's wrong with you?" She checked herself, and this time I couldn't catch Eli before he started laughing.

"You've been watching him?" he asked in between laughs.

"Yes. But not in a stalkery, creepy, weirdo kinda way. I get paid to. I'm NOBODY."

That time, it clicked. "Ah shit! Hey! C'mere girl," I said, reaching out and pulling her into my arms in a tight hug, and her body went limp like she'd fainted. "Nice to finally meet you, too," I said, turning to Eli, my arm still around her shoulders. "Bruh! This is that genius ass tech girl that Pops and Maine use. She's the best, E. Man, listen."

"I might have a use for her services, then," Eli said seriously, a smirk still on his face. He was eating this meeting between Tati and me up.

"I'd be honored, Elijah," she said his full name, making both of us look at her. "I told you I was paid to watch you. You have to know all the characters in the Trouble Show, and he made an appearance. Of course, the background checks and things were—" She paused when she realized that she may be telling us too much. "Well, never mind. If you ever need me, Trouble knows where to find me."

"Aight, I'll be looking for you soon, I'm sure," Eli said. "And if she has it her way, I'll find her in that nigga's bed."

I hoped that nigga was tryna whisper and failed, but knowing Eli, he said that shit just loud enough for both of us to hear it on purpose. He didn't talk much, but when he opened his mouth, this nigga was a muhfucka. Either that, or he was being goofy as hell.

"Soooooo, the meeting's back here," she said, slipping from under my arm that I hadn't realized was even still around her until then. *That ain't a nigga's usual moves*, I thought to myself. She walked off toward the back, walking like she knew we were watching her. Y'all know how a woman walks when she knows a nigga lookin' at her ass, a little bit harder so her hips swayed, and her ass jiggled more than usual. If her ass was real. And this ass was definitely real.

Knocking on the door, she pushed it open when a man's voice said, "come in". Eli went in first to survey the room, and when I reached the opening, I saw Marissa and Doc Smith. Before I got all the way in, Tati grabbed my arm gently, making me pause.

"I know this might be inappropriate with the time and circumstances of our meeting today and all. And the business and pleasure thing. And the fact that I've seen you naked and fuckin' bitches and shiiiiiitttt," she rambled.

"But?" I urged her to get to the point.

"Do you think you might wanna get a drink or something later? I mean, it doesn't have to be today later. It can be tomorrow later. Or next week later. Or a month from now or so laterrrrr—"

"Yeah, that'd be cool. But let's talk about that later. Like, after this shit is done later. Aight?" I asked, and she smiled and nodded up and down fast as hell. "You got all my info and shit, so just hit my line." I leaned in and kissed her cheek before walking all the way into the room.

"This nigga," Eli said with a laugh, but I didn't join him. Seeing Kong sitting on the couch beside the door had me ready to put a bullet in his fuckin' skull.

"You a on-sight nigga, but outta respects for *my* pops, I won't ack a fool right now. You might wanna beat me out this bitch, though," I threatened, and Kong stood up like he was ready to move something.

"Y'all sit the fuck down, and act like you was raised with some sense.

I know King and Mama Pearlie raised y'all better than that shit there," Doc Smith snapped, and I paused, because I'd never seen this side of him. This nigga had some gutta in him, but what did I expect when he was on King's team?

"I gotcha, Doc. But that nigga heard what the fuck I said." I gritted my teeth, tightening my jaw, never breaking eye contact with Kong.

"Boy! Sitcho ass the hell down," Eli snapped, grabbing my arm and pulling me to the chairs on the opposite side of the room from Doc Smith and Marissa, who looked like she wanted to be anywhere but here. Not that I could blame her, 'cause she was sitting in a powder keg that could blow at any minute.

Bop-Bop-Bop

"Come in," the white man on the other side of the desk said, blowing out a breath like he was ready to get this shit over with.

The door opened, and Sa'Mia walked in and rushed me. I stood up and wrapped her up in a hug, picking her up off the floor.

"Troublllllleeee! I thought you were dead. I missed you! Are you okay?" she asked, looking me up and down.

I just nodded. My legs were feeling better, but I'd refused to come in this room in a wheelchair or on a cane. I had it with me, though, just in case shit got worse. I knew I would pay for that shit later, and the look Doc Smith was giving me told me I was gon' hear it from him, too. But coming in here lookin' like I was at 100 percent was something that a nigga *had* to do for my own ego's sake.

"I missed you, too, lil' hot headed ass. See you still fuckin' wit' dis nigga," I said, nodding my head toward Maine. He was mugging me and hit me with a head nod, which was more than I expected. But I returned the gesture.

"Yes, I'm still fuckin' wit' him. And y'all gon' get this shit together before I drop this damn baby. We already lost Daddy. I ain't losin' y'all too, just because y'all asses can't get over an ass beatin' and a damn gun fight," she snapped with her hands on her hips.

I just smiled and sat back down. She walked over to Maine and sat in his lap.

Clap!

"Well, the gang's all here, so we can get started!" the white man said.

"As I've told some of you, I'm Randy Abraham, Mr. King's counsel and executor of his last will and testament. Y'all are all here because he loved you so much. All of you," Abraham said, looking around the room at each of us. "Before he was kidnapped, he met with me to record his last will and testament," he said, picking up a remote from the desk and pressing a button that dropped a projector screen down and dimmed the lights.

Seeing my pops' face on that big ass screen had me shedding silent tears. *Damn, I ain't know how much I missed my old man 'til just now.*

MAINE

"Mr. King had several properties, businesses, and a great deal of funds that need to be dispersed," Abraham said, looking at all of us one at a time.

I was holding Sa'Mia close to make sure she didn't hop up and put hands on nobody. She was bad before the pregnancy. But now she was worse. I ain't think that was possible, but I was seeing it. And her memory coming back made her a bad bitch with a vendetta. The way she was staring at Kong made me hold her a little tighter, to make sure she stayed in place.

"Ahhh, there you are, Tatiana!" Abraham said, sounding really nervous.

There was no doubt that he knew what King was into and could tell that everyone in the room was probably in the same business. The way that we were looking at one another, if I was the only white man in the room, I'd be nervous as hell, too.

Tatiana came in and stood beside Abraham's desk, taking in the room and the tension between all the parties present. "Wow, this is a tense one, huh? Well, let's get this show on the roadie, so we can get outta here, shall we?" she asked Abraham, and he nodded.

Picking up the pile of manila envelopes that I just noticed were on his desk, she walked to each of us, giving us the sealed folder that had our names on them.

"Don't open these. King wanted you all to open them when you were in the comforts of your homes, so that there is no issue. And if there is one that arises, you can contact me directly, instead of addressing it with one another," he informed us, and I smiled at the fact that King was still trying to keep down the drama in the afterlife.

Mia's hard-headed ass started to open her envelope, and I took it from her. If looks could kill, I would be in a hole next to her father, but I didn't care. She wasn't about to start a domino effect that could end in a fight, or worse, up in this damn office. Too many white folks in these office spaces for us to be able to get away without somebody witnessing something. I wasn't about to get locked the hell up because she wanted to be impatient. She got up out of my lap and sat in the chair a little ways away from me. I just chuckled and shrugged, still holding both envelopes in my hands. Being with Mia was like having a spoiled ass child sometimes, but I would spend the rest of my life spoiling her if that's what it took.

"And now that you all have your envelopes, it's time for the grand performance," Tatiana stated, making us look around curiously.

I didn't know what she was talking about, and the way King did shit, I wouldn't be surprised if he walked his ass through the door on some Machiavelli type shit. Tatiana walking to the door had me ready to get up and dap my nigga, my mentor, my father figure, and future father-in-law up, but I was sadly disappointed when he didn't walk in. Instead, she stopped and had a look on her face like she'd seen a ghost when a nigga walked in, smiling at her and walking over to sit beside Kong.

My instincts kicked in, and I knew some bullshit was about to pop off. Looking at Trouble, even though I wasn't fuckin' wit' that nigga like that, I was glad that he'd peeped game, too. Both of us were sitting here all fucked up because we were into it over Mia. Had squashed the beef and everything just to bring that shit back to life again, and the real problem was sitting there with a smug ass mug on his face. Then had the nerve to call back-up.

"Nick, you're not a party to this reading, so why are you here?" Tatiana asked the nigga that had sat next to Kong, and I wanted to know how she knew him and why seeing him had her so scared.

"That nigga there ain't either, but he sitting his ass up in here," Kong said, pointing to the nigga sitting beside Trouble. I'd wondered who he was and why he was here, too, but I trusted his presence more than this Nick dude. Especially because he was late to the party, was with Kong's ass, and I had never met his ass. On top of that, the nigga with Trouble gave a real chill ass vibe. He ain't seem to be tryna cause a problem. Tatiana being spooked had me concerned, though.

"Mind the business that pays you, my nigga—"

"I am, bruh. You the long-lost son in this shit, just poppin' up and shit. I'm the one runnin' this shit, so this *is the business that pays me*," Kong stated with bass in his chest, cutting Trouble off.

"See, that's where you got it right *and wrong*. You're right, I did just pop up, but I wasn't lost. Pops knew about me all along. How you think I found him... and y'all, my nigga? Then, that son part. That's the part that matters most. 'Cause you ain't Alonzo King's seed, so you being here is a fuckin' courtesy because my old man had a heart and gave a damn about yo' bitch ass. And that runnin' the empire shit you spittin'... You got that shit by pairing wit' yo' fuck ass flunky sperm donor and killin' the man who raised ya punk ass even when he *knew* you wasn't from his sac. Know your place, my nigga, because the situations you got goin' on, including the fact that you still breathing right now, are temporary as fuck," Trouble threatened, and I knew this nigga was the rightful heir. He played no games and showed no fear. I wanted to dap him up, but I ain't like his ass like that.

"Oop!" Mia said and busted out laughing.

I couldn't do shit but shake my head. If Trouble checking his ass wasn't embarrassing enough, that shit with Mia damn sure should've been. They were on some twinning tag team bullshit, and I knew Kong. He wasn't gonna take that shit lying down. What had me more concerned was that Tatiana still had the door open, and her and the Nick nigga were having a whole conversation with their eyes. I ain't like the way he was looking at her, but I couldn't speak on it right now without Mia showing her little ass in here. She looked like she wasn't sure if she wanted to run out of the room and the building or close the door and pray that she got shot if this shit continued to escalate.

Abraham took the initiative and hit a button, making a screen lower from the ceiling and a panel open in the wall, revealing a projector. *Oh, this some new age shit. He makin' real money 'round here*, I thought, and I could tell, once again, that Trouble was sharing my thoughts by the way his bottom lip was poked out, and he was giving an approving nod. That had distracted him from the stare down that he was having with Kong, and even though I would put my money on Trouble if it came down to them two serving up their beef, I ain't want that shit to happen with my woman and my unborn in the room. None of these other not-so-innocent people in here, either.

Tatiana flipped the switch on the wall, turning off the lights, before scurrying back to the desk beside Abraham. She was trying to put as much space between herself and Nick as possible. I was gonna get to the bottom of that ASAP, and I would body his ass if I had to. Tati didn't fuck with anyone, so for her to fear this nigga let me know that they had history, and not good history, either.

When the projector came on, all chatter in the room stopped, and our eyes were glued to the screen. Looking at the man that was loved by *most* of us in the room, sitting up in a hospital bed, all beat the hell up, was fuckin' wit' a nigga. Had me ready to kill Kong with my bare hands. I adjusted in my seat, so I wouldn't have to look at the nigga, and kept my eyes glued on Mia. She was fidgeting in her seat, making me want to hold her close and comfort her. But the way her hormones were set up, on top of the attitude she was born with, I knew that shit wouldn't go well. I'd just watch her and jump if need be.

Looking at King trying to work the recorder had me tickled. I knew he was old, but it wasn't until now that I realized just *how old* he was. Taking a deep breath, I sat back, looking at the envelopes in my lap, waiting for the recording to start. I wondered what King had in store for us, both on the recording, and in the envelopes. Knowing him, we would all be good. But how good and how *some* ungrateful ass folks would receive the shit —*cough cough* Kong—would determine if the shit was about to hit the fan, or if it was about to die down.

ALONZO KING, POSTHUMOUSLY

THE RECORDED READING OF THE LAST WILL & TESTAMENT

"*H*ey, Nate! Come show me how to work this shit, man!" I yelled, because I was waiting for the light to come on. I had a smartphone, but that shit was smarter than me. I missed the old days when your phone was just for talking. And the way Nate had his phone set up, it was like a camcorder, but not. I could see myself, but there wasn't no light. He had left the room to give me some privacy, but he should've stayed his ass in here, because I was never any good with this technology shit.

"You see the time running?" he yelled, and I leaned in real close to see if I did. I needed my reading glasses, but I wasn't about to dull my sexy with them things.

"Yeah," I responded, sitting back with a huff. Maybe I should've just written letters. That would've been easier. But when had I ever taken the easy way out? Guess that's where my kids got the shit from.

"Then it's on, Zo! Just gone and start talking," he hollered back, making me ball my face up. I hoped he was right because I didn't want to do this but one time. Call me One Take Shawty, because I was ready to speak my piece and gone take me a nap. I had been preparing for this day since I got back from visiting Pearlie in Bama. I needed to make sure that my kids heard, from me, in my voice, what my wishes were so there wouldn't be any confusion.

"If y'all watching this, I'm shooting die on High with the real HNIC JC or Jesus Christ," I said, chuckling and rubbing my hand over my bald head. "That was a joke. Lighten up! The worst thing a parent can do is outlive their child, so y'all had to know this was comin'. I just hate it was so soon. It's my hope that y'all can squash all this beef and come together. Y'all family. I raised you together."

I paused, thinking about Trouble and the fact that he wasn't raised with the rest of my kids, and felt bad about that. But I did it for him and hoped he understood.

"Tywan—" I said his name thoughtfully. "You weren't raised with the rest of my kids, Sa'Mia, Kellen, Arkino—" I smiled because I really did consider Arkino to be one of my kids. "But it was for your protection, and ya mama's mama, Pearlie, did an amazing job with you! I was so proud of how you turned out! Kellen… Kong, you're my son, even if not by blood. But you're definitely your mama and daddy's child." I chuckled. "Dani was a piece of work, but I loved her more than I loved myself. Yeah, more than I loved myself."

I felt myself tearing up. I truly loved Danielle with every bit of myself. She was the reason I pushed as hard as I did and the reason I lost every-thing I had—twice now. I mean, I raised the child she had with my brother and left *my* blood, *my son*, behind. But I knew from birth that Tywan was the strong one. And he proved to be just that and came to find me when he was ready.

"So, lemme get to this shit, because it's hard to know that I'm gon' be leaving y'all at some point. But that's how it goes, right? *Sniff-Sniff* —I have millions in disposable income. I knew there was four of y'all, so I got twelve mil in accounts for y'all. Three a piece that y'all can access when you present your diploma to the bank. That's on top of what ya already got in your trusts. They have photos of y'all, and your code words are in the envelopes Abraham handed y'all. Thanks, man," I said, addressing Abraham. "You been loyal as hell and got me and my kids outta plenty of binds. And for that, you can retire with what my accountant will give you once this meeting is done. I know you love what you do, but I know you like fast cars and faster women more, so now you can spoil your women with the bottomless account I got set up for you."

I leaned all the way back and shook my head. This was the hard part. I knew this wasn't gonna go over well, and I knew that Abraham might not survive my reckless, hotheaded ass children to spend a penny that I left for him. But I was hoping they would get it together, for me, because they were gon' need each other.

"Nate, the infamous Dr. Nathaniel Smith. Man, you already know what it is. What's understood don't ever have to be explained. You were there when all my kids got their asses smacked and cried for the first time. This shit been a roller coaster ride, man. And you been there wit' a nigga through it all. And I know that money ain't your motivation, but it don't hurt. So, know that I gotchu. I love you, man. Like my blood. Know that shit." I smiled because Nate had been here through the ups and downs. Even stopped fuckin' wit' me for a minute, but he was there when I needed him. That kinda loyalty is hard to find. Hell, my kids could learn a thing or two from him.

"You done?" Nate came into the room and asked, and I wiped my eyes and looked at him like a nigga caught getting a blow job by the bitch's nigga. He *would* come in when I was talkin' to his ass.

"Naw, I'm gettin' there, though. Man, this shit is eerie as hell. Who woulda thought when we was young niggas, I'd be recording my last will and testament and shit?" I asked, rubbing my hand down my face.

"Man, that's the life you chose, Zo. Hell, some niggas don't get the chance to do *this much*," Nate said, sitting down on the edge of the bed. "You want me to cut this shit off? I can pause it," he offered.

"Nah, you good. They need to hear this. All they see is the money and the street fame. They need to know that ain't all that comes with this shit."

"They should. Hell, you school they asses all the time. But they hard-headed like yo' ass, so yeah. But think about it. Joe Doe locked up on some trumped-up charges. All the other Compass Kingpins dead or locked up. None of them got to distribute they shit before they went in or went down. They kids was lucky they mamas wasn't on no bullshit. You sure you want me to keep this shit on?" he asked again, and I knew what was coming next. *Dani… he never cared for her.*

"Nah, man," I said with a nervous chuckle. I knew he was about to go in on Danielle. But hell, she wasn't the poster child for wives and mothers, that's for damn sure. "Just play nice," I said, nodding at the camera on the tripod.

"Man, in that case—" He paused, rubbing his head and shaking it. "Maybe you should tell 'em. 'Cause you know I was never "Team Dani and King" as the kids say nowadays. She cost me too much. More than she cost you, man."

He got up and walked back out of the room, his shoulders hunched. I was sad thinking about what we all went through. All because of Danielle and Kellz. I had spared the kids the ugly details of the story, but maybe that was my mistake. Thinking about whether or not I wanted to just finish the reading of the will or tell the story of all the drama that we went through, I was torn about which would be the most helpful. There wasn't any point in bringing up dead shit, if it wasn't gonna make anything any better. But at the same time... they needed to know that sometimes love just ain't enough. They needed to know that loyalty to the wrong person could cost them everything they worked for, or worse, their lives. They needed to know that everything I did was for them.

"Listen... before I finish this will shit, I need to tell y'all a story. Sa'Mia, put ya eyes back in your head, and the rest of y'all can take them mugs off ya faces. I know all of y'all like the back of my hand, and unless God himself came down, y'all ain't changed just because I'm dead. Kong, you lookin' up at the ceiling, not wanting to face what you did to cause this. Sa'Mia, if you ain't pissed off at Maine, as usual, then y'all all hugged up. Otherwise, you sitting in a chair alone all mugged up, ready to act up for no reason. You gotta hairline trigger temper, baby girl. That shit gon' do you more harm than it does good."

I cleared my throat, because I didn't know Trouble as much as I knew my other children. *I'll save him for last*, I convinced myself.

"Maine, I'm so sorry. Mia is spoiled rotten, and it's my fault. You love her, but she so much like her mama. So much like her mama," I repeated sadly, staring into the camera, even though my mind went elsewhere again. Coming back, I gave him the only jewels I could since I was sure he was gonna stay with Sa'Mia. "But, if you hang in there with her and do right by her, her lil' Pitbull ass gon' be loyal. And I'm almost certain you're looking at her right now like you'd give her your last breath. Soooo, good luck with that."

I raised my brow, giving the camera a fatherly look. I knew my kids were in their feelings, more because the reality of my death was setting in than because I was calling them on their shit. But I wouldn't be me if I didn't go out with one last hoorah. It was only right.

"Nigga, yo' long-winded ass still goin'?" Nate stuck his head into the room and asked.

"How about you worry about what's your business to handle and bring me something for this pain," I snapped, my chest starting to hurt.

"Marissa, you're biting your nails, or your bottom lip. Or both." I smiled warmly. She was on some fuck shit in the beginning, but that didn't take away from the joy she gave me. And not just when we were wrinkling the sheets. "You and Nate have my blessing. I ain't a selfish man, and we too damn old to be on some you fuckin' the homie kinda shit. Hell, my brother fucked and created life with my wife, *and with you.*" I remembered, in that moment, that Neisha was Kellz's child, too. This nigga had a thing for anybody who wanted me. I was starting to think that he had some unnatural crush on me. *That's some nasty shit.* "Whether you and Nate work out or not, you got something waiting for you. Something that'll make sure that you good. You took care of my kids, and I appreciate that. You don't ever have to work again. Unless you want to. I know it ain't the same as being with a nigga, but I hope you take it as a token of my love and thanks for the times we did share. I love you, girl."

I blew a kiss to the camera and grinned like a nigga who was in love for the first time. She made me feel that way. Just the thought of her gave me butterflies. I had a sweet tooth for trifling ass women, for sure. Because she was on some bullshit and came around. But even if she hadn't, I couldn't say that I would've left her alone. I was a hopeless romantic. And that made me a fool so many times.

"Anyway, that brings me to you, Tywan. If I know you like I think I do, you're sitting there plottin'. You hurtin', but you got a strong pose on. You like me. Wanna take care of your family, and that's gonna be your strength and your weakness. Trust your discernment and your brothers. Not Kong, Eli and Doe. I'm sure one or both of 'em came with you. They

91

some hard asses, but that's 'cause they love you. Trust them. Rely on 'em when you need 'em. Aight. And now, back to the matter at hand."

I grimaced at the pain I was starting to feel. I knew that I wasn't gonna be able to sit up much longer. I had to get this shit out while I was able to talk. While I still had strength.

"Lemme tell y'all a story. There was a man, ya old man. He loved—" I paused, deciding to tell them the real. "Listen y'all, I won't give y'all that fictional bullshit. I loved Danielle so much. She was everything to me. She was spoiled and ungrateful. Sa'Mia, that shit ain't cute. But it was my fault, too. I knew that she wasn't tryna settle down, but I forced my desires for us onto her. Maine, don't be like me, man. If she don't want the shit, let it go. I did everything I could to make Dani happy. I needed her to be happy. Worked all my life for that shit. But it wasn't something I could give her. She wasn't happy with herself. Nate knew that shit, but tellin' a nigga in love something's wrong with the woman he loves is like tryna get a blind man to see something that's right in front of his face."

I was schooling myself and schooling my kids, too. It was never too late to learn, though.

"Trouble, you saw more of your mama's true nature than the rest of them, so you know. Danielle wanted nothing but to party and get high. Kellz got her hooked on that shit, and no matter how many times I had her in rehab, she found a way to get that shit. Even after he was gone. I'm sorry you found ya mama like that, son," I concluded sadly, knowing that it had to fuck him up to find her dead. "But don't let her being fucked up make you think ain't no good women out there. Look at Pearlie. They don't make 'em like her no more, but you can't mistreat women tryna get back at her for choosing the dope over you. She never wanted love. Never wanted kids. Never wanted the happily ever after. So if you gon' blame anybody, blame me. I can carry that weight. But your anger with her would crush her, even in the afterlife." I tried to remind my son of just how powerful he truly was.

My eyes slid shut, and my breathing became weak. I wanted to say so much more, but I didn't think my body would let me. I had to finish, though. I had to. For them.

"Y'all—*ahem*—y'all all have your inher-inheritances spelled ou-ou-out in the envelopes. But I nee-need to go on record as say-saying this," I pushed the call button because I didn't have the strength to call out to Nate this time. "Trouble, you get the em-pire. You and Sa'Mia. But-but you're the o-o-oldest, so youuuuuu run that shit—*ahem* —" I leaned over and took a sip of water, but that didn't help like I hoped it would. "Kong, you-you get the West. You'd do best to learn from your bro-brother and earn his re-respect. Maine, you-you're his right hand. Kong is gonna need you. And may-maybe one d-d-day, I'll look down and smile 'cause-cause all my children runnin' this shit to-to-together. The King Trilogy. Try to ge-get there? For me?"

I stopped talking and laid my head back. I was getting weak and needed to rest. Forcing my eyes open, I smiled at the camera. At my kids. At the fact that all the shit I'd done had afforded me the ability to give them a comfortable life without having to be in the drug game. But, I also knew my kids. And Sa'Mia might walk away from it, but the rest of them needed to be in the streets like they needed to breathe. My eyes shut again, and this time, I couldn't open them. I had a pained expression on my face, because a nigga was in some real pain.

"You good, Zo?" Nate's voice was full of worry.

"I'm tired, Nate. I just wanna sleep…"

"Aight, man. But don't go dyin' on me," he joked, and I cracked a smile, but didn't respond, because I couldn't make any promises. He injected some pain meds into my IV. I flashed him a smile and looked at him when the pain meds kicked in just long enough for me to lift my lids. I watched him walk over and stop the recording on the camera.

"An hour, Zo? Ain't that much damn talkin' in the world," he said, shaking his head, laughing.

"And you bet-ter not edit that shit," I stated weakly. He flipped me off with a laugh. That was the last thing I saw before my eyes fluttered shut… again.

MIA

*M*y face was wet with tears. I couldn't believe he was really gone. I mean, we know that we were meant to outlive our parents, but this shit here was too much. I wish I had never gotten my memory back because then maybe it wouldn't hurt so bad. I missed my daddy, and there was nothing I could do about it. I stood up and ran to Maine, who held his arms out to me. He held me close and let me weep in his arms. I could barely breathe for the bear hug he had me in, but the tightness made me feel safe.

"So, that's it? This nigga and this bitch takin' the empire, and I get the West? That's all? I should be runnin' this shit! Not y'all asses!" Kong snapped, jumping up and throwing a tantrum.

"Simmer down, lil' nigga. He said what he said. Respect that shit. You might've had a chance to run some shit if ya ungrateful ass hadn't abducted him and shit. You might've been given more. You better sitcha ass down, 'cause if I was Pops, I wouldn't have gave you shit. But because I wanna respect his dying wishes, I'mma let you have the West. But the *first* time ya ass fuck off, I'mma have to beg his forgiveness for what the fuck I do to ya ass," Trouble snapped, standing up and mugging Kong.

I stepped back, and Maine tightened his grip, trying to keep me from doing what he knew I was about to.

"Mia, let that man handle this shit. You pregnant," he whispered, but he knew damn better.

Stepping back again, he let out a heavy breath and released his grip on me at the same time. I took one more step back before turning around and walking to stand beside Trouble. That was my brother. Daddy wanted us to run this shit together, and we were about to start now.

"Settle down, guys... and Mia. There's no need for the hostility," Abraham said, trying to diffuse the situation. There was so much fear in his voice that it made me feel bad for him. But he knew what King did for a living, so he had to know that this shit could go left at any moment.

"This nigga been hostile since his flaw ass daddy shot his disloyal ass off in my mama's womb. He don't know no better," Trouble snapped, making me giggle. This nigga was shot the fuck out. I ain't know if Dallas was ready for the two of us together runnin' these streets.

"Mannnnn, fuck you!" Kong said, showing weakness and that Trouble had gotten under his skin.

"You hear that nigga? *Mannnn, fuck you!*" The nigga who came in with Trouble mimicked Kong. "Nigga, you sound like a whole bitch. T, this the nigga that thought he was gon' run some shit?" he asked Trouble, pointing to Kong. Trouble nodded his head yes, and it looked like he was trying not to laugh himself. "For real? My nigga, you a whole heaux. I bet you bleed once a month, too, huh?"

He was laughing so hard he had to wipe his eyes. I couldn't take him seriously right now. We were about to knuckle the fuck up with this nigga and his minion, or draw down on his ass, and he was over there laughing like a hyena and shit.

"Nigga, mind ya business," Kong's little sidekick said.

"See that nigga right there?" he said, standing up and pointing at Trouble. "That's my brother. Y'all don't know him or respect how real that nigga is, but I done been 'round him since he was a lil' sprout ass nigga. And if you knew the kinda havoc he could cause for real, you'd understand why King's decision was the wisest one. So if you a problem for him, you a problem for me." He walked to the other side of Trouble.

"So, this how it's 'bout to go down?" Kong asked, taking a step toward Trouble.

"You can't even respect King in his death, Kellen? Is that how you're built? And you wonder why shit just won't work out for you?" Nate asked, standing up and crossing his arms across his chest.

"Nigga, what you know about any fuckin' thing? You just patch up wounds and shit. You ain't got no parts in this, at all. As a matter of fact, I'on know why you and that bitch Marissa even in here. Maine, I get. Mia and this fuck nigga here," he said, eyeing Trouble up and down. "I guess DNA states he has a right to be here, but you—"

Nate stood there laughing at Kong. I thought he'd lost his mind, because there was nothing funny being said. When he cleared the distance between him and Kong and snatched him up by his collar, head-butting him, the sound of the impact made us all step back and flinch. Kong's mouth started to swell up immediately, and his nose was gushing. I was sure that shit was broken.

"That's one way to shut that nigga up," Trouble said with a shrug. "I was just gon' shoot his punk ass."

"There will be no gunplay in this damn office, y'all hear me?" Nate said, turning to look at us, throwing Kong back onto the couch where he had been sitting. "Y'all gon' respect King and his last fuckin' wishes. And as far as why I'm here… I was there when ya daddy met ya damn mama. When she damn near destroyed everything that nigga worked for," Nate said, pointing to the still image of Daddy on the screen. "You got so much of that bitch in you that I hate he ever laid eyes on her ass. I was here. Before you. I was here when he tried to raise ya simple ass right. And I'm here now. So you gon' show me some muthafuckin' respect. You don't know the whole story, so stay in a child's place. A lil' hair on ya fuckin' chest and ya nuts droppin' don't make you a man. Manhood is all in how you carry your fuckin' self. You don't deserve the right to be called a fuckin' King. Last name or not."

We all stood there in awe. He'd told us all some shit that we knew nothing about. I wanted to know more, but I could feel the tension heighten in the room and knew Kong well enough to know that he was about to do some dumb shit.

"Now, I'm pretty sure I broke ya fuckin' nose. But since all I do is patch up wounds and shit, I'mma let you handle that shit on ya own. 'Cause, in case you hard of hearing, I don't work for you no more. I'm on Trouble and Sa'Mia's payroll. Unless they give me the go-ahead, you ain't gettin' shit from me. You couldn't afford it anyway, wit' ya one territory on probation runnin' ass." Nate played the hell outta Kong, and this time, I laughed. I don't care what nobody said, that shit was funny.

"Naw, I ain't payin' for the nigga to get his shit fixed. He lucky you just busted his face up, 'cause I was gon' Swiss cheese his ass," Trouble said.

"Yeah, I'm with Trouble. That nigga can bleed to death for all I care. Daddy would still be here if it wasn't for his wannabe kingpin ass."

His sidekick reached for his waist, and Maine stepped forward and in front of me, almost nose-to-nose wit' the nigga.

"You hard of hearin', too, mane?" He gritted, his big body blocking me protectively. "There ain't gon' be no fuckin' gunplay up in here. So, let's take this nigga to get the medical attention he so desperately needs, before y'all both be bodied up in this muhfucka."

"Let's? What the hell you mean let's? Where the hell you think you goin', Maine? Wit' dis nigga?" I asked, my hands on my hips, because I knew I better be tripping.

"Mind ya place, Sa'Mia. I know what I said," Maine snapped, not even turning around to look at me.

I went to hit his monstrous ass in the back of the head, but Trouble grabbed my arm and shook his head. I wanted to pop him, too. They were both on my fuckin' nerves and made me wanna just leave Dallas and take my baby somewhere safe. This nigga leavin' with the man who caused my daddy to die like shit was sweet. Then tellin' me to mind my place. I'm the new HBIC, so he was the one who needed to mind his shit before he ended up un-em-fuckin-ployed. As a matter of fact, that was gon' be my first order of business.

Maine and the minion nigga helped Kong up and threw an arm across each of their shoulders. I watched Maine's back as he walked out the door with Kong leaking all over this white man's nice carpet. I bit my bottom lip that was quivering and tried not to cry, but I couldn't hold that shit in.

"Wh-wh-whyyyyy would he leave with hi-hi-himmmmmm?" I asked, falling back into my chair, holding myself.

"He knows what he's doin', Mia. Just let him—"

"Fuck youuuuuuuuu!" I whined, tears racing down my cheeks like they were on a motor speedway. I could barely see Trouble through them, so I planned to cuss his voice the hell out.

"Man, don't start that spoiled shit again. If you want me to be honest, you ain't ready to run this empire, in my opinion. You spoiled, short-sighted, and selfish. That's the kinda shit that'll get you killed or caught. Watchin' you and that nigga make me happy that I wasn't raised wit' y'all asses. I know the value of family and self-respect. Naw, I ain't know King as long as y'all did. But the nigga was my daddy, too. I lost my pops right when I found him, and y'all had him all y'all lives and still don't know how to respect the nigga. He *died* protecting you. He *died* at the hands of that nigga that just limped his injured ass outta here. And y'all ain't learn shit."

"You don't know me. You think you do. We shared a womb and share DNA, but you just came around a couple months ago. How I know *you* ain't behind his death. All this shit started happening when you came along."

"Is she for real?" the nigga that stood on the other side of him asked. I was just about over his ass and was starting to feel like Kong. Like, why the fuck was this nigga here?

"Yeah, I'm for real. You 'bout only here for a come-up. The fuck is you? Talkin' about he yo' brother and chimin' in where ain't nobody invite you to be. Don't do me, bruh. That's the quickest way to get done in," I popped, done crying now.

"Sa'Mia, that's *enough*!" Marissa yelled. I'd almost forgotten that she was in the room. "You have been a pain in your dad's ass for as long as I've known him. And you keep pointing out everybody else's flaws but refuse to face your own. Your brother is right and gave an accurate read of you with only knowing you for a short time. You're about to be some-body's mama. You got a man who just left with your brother to protect your ass, and all you can see is what *you* want. And I'm speaking from the place of a woman who *knows* what it's like to be you. But my daddy wasn't *half* the man Alonzo was. So if you couldn't grow up for him, then grow the hell up now, before it's too late and you lose everything." She tried to school me, but this bitch was just arrested for fuckin' her student and was part of the overthrow plot at first before she switched damn sides, so she could kiss my ass.

"You know what? Fuck all y'all. How about that? Y'all acting like I don't have the right to be hurt. Let a bitch act out because she pregnant and hormonal, in her feelings because her nigga just left with the enemy *once again*. I was just given an empire I don't fuckin' want. And... *and* I just lost my fuckin' daddy. Y'all gon' let me make it." I checked her irrelevant ass before jumping up and heading for the door. I didn't need this kinda negativity in my life while I was mourning the hardest loss of my life. They really were being disrespectful as hell.

"Well, she's quite the feisty one, isn't she?" the Tatiana bitch said when I stormed out of the room.

"That bitch better shut her vanilla ass up before I put some spice in her life." I went off to myself, stomping toward the elevator.

"Mia! Sa'Mia!" I heard my name, making me press the button fast and hard over and over again.

The door finally opened, and I pressed the button for the lobby before pushing the button to close the door just as Marissa rounded the corner. She could catch the next one, and by then, my ass would be gone.

Chances were slim as hell that Marissa was gonna beat me to the lobby. When the door opened, I continued my tantrum out the door and shook my head when reality hit me.

Wait... me and Maine rode together.

MAINE

What the fuck am I thinking? I asked myself, helping Kong inside his car. I'd just left Mia up there when she needed me most, but I had to. This nigga was on some fuck shit, I could feel it. I couldn't look Mia in the face, because her pain would've broken me. I was doing this for her. For us. I thought she would've known that by now.

"You loyal as fuck, bruh," Kong said, and he was right. I had betrayed the ones who were here for a nigga more times than I liked to admit and let his punk ass bleed all over my damn clothes. His mouth was his problem, but he could barely use that muhfucka right now. Doc Smith had fucked him all the way up. I ain't know the old head had it in him, but with the company he kept, I shouldn't have been too surprised.

"Yeah," was all I could get out dryly, and the Nick nigga shot me the side eye. "You gotta fuckin' eye problem?" I barked at him.

"Nah, my eyes work just fine, and I can see through that snake shit niggas be tryna pull. Like, you was just hugged up with Sa'Mia, and now you on Kong's side? You been playin' both sides, nigga, but I know who you loyal to. Niggas don't walk out on pussy, especially pussy that's carryin' they seed, for nobody. So, you stupid loyal, or you tryna keep an eye on my nigga, and pillow talkin' about that shit when you go to bed to sleep with the enemy?"

"Nigga, you talk a whole lotta shit about shit you don't know, mane. I was here before you was here, and I'mma be here when ya ass be six-feet in a hole, and I'm throwin' dirt on top of ya ass."

"Is that a threat, my nigga?" he asked, walking up on me.

"You playin' witcho life right now, mane."

I squared up and was done talking. If he was gon' move some shit, he needed to start moving before I rearranged his face and have his ass swole up like Kong was right now.

"Nigga, yeen 'bout to move shit. I see how ya bitch handle ya weak ass—"

Whap! Whap! I two-pieced his ass and picked him up, slamming him into the open door of Kong's car.

"Aye, watch my shit, nigga!" Kong barked, sitting up from where he had his head leaned back on the headrest of the car.

He laid back and watched the show as I whacked that nigga a couple more times in that big ass mouth of his. I grabbed him around the throat and started squeezing. I was choking that nigga for King, for Mia, because I had to fuck with Neisha's bitch ass as long as I did. For every lie I had to tell, every shady-looking ass move I had to make. He was scratching at my hands like the bitch nigga he was, but his movements were getting weak.

"Arkino! That's enough!" I heard the last voice I expected to hear behind me and turned around, meeting eyes with Sa'Mia. "Put that nigga down. He ain't worth no ghatdamned jail time. Dafuq wrong with you?"

She had her face balled up and her left hand resting on her stomach. Even though she wasn't showing, knowing that my baby was in there was enough to calm the beast in me. I dropped Nick's ass on the ground, looking back and forth between him, Kong, and Sa'Mia. There was so much I wanted to say to her. I wanted to explain it all, but then I realized that if she didn't trust me by now, she wasn't worth my breath, and I couldn't spend the rest of my life tryna prove my loyalty to her. Yeah, I made some dumb ass moves, and I wasn't tryna excuse them shits. But I'd been about Sa'Mia before Sa'Mia knew I was about Sa'Mia. I was 'bout to be over the whole King clan and take my damn losses. Marissa could get them to mail me my diploma. I just wanted to get the fuck away from this fucked up ass family.

"See—*couuuuuuggh*—that bitch got his ass on a leash," Nick's dumb ass said from the ground. This nigga ain't know when to quit.

Stomp! Stomp!

"Arkino!" I heard Mia say again, and I ignored her little annoying ass. "Maine!" Mia called my name again, and I turned to look at her in a way that told her if she ain't gone somewhere, she was gon' be my next victim. I was fed up, and she was getting in the way of my stress release.

"Dafuq you want, Sa'Mia?" *Stomp!*

"I need the car keys so I can go get my shit from yo' house. You can ride witcho new crew and shit," she hollered, pissing me off.

"Mia! I'm busy, and I ain't givin' you the keys to my shit. Catch a fuckin' Uber, and make sure all your shit gone before I get there. I'm good on you." *Stomp! Stomp!*

I stomped that fuck nigga to sleep, letting my feet do the talking. When he stopped talking and his head hit the concrete that one last time, I stopped. Looking over my shoulder, Sa'Mia was gone. I bit my bottom lip and held back the frustration that was beating in my chest. I had to let Mia go. I was tired of chasing her ass, and all I could think about was what King said in the video. He lost everything loving a woman, then lost it again trying to do right by her by raising Kong's ass. We could co-parent or what the fuck ever, but I wasn't about to spend the rest of my life on this kinda bullshit.

Walking off, I went to my car, looking at Mia sitting outside the Starbucks on her phone. I saw the envelopes on the table, but I didn't care about that shit no more. I'd learned a lot from King and had invested wisely. I was rich at a young age and had enough blood on my hands and bullshit coursing through my veins to last me a lifetime. I wasn't beat for the money, so I would be straight. Shaking my head, I popped the locks on the truck and hopped in. I had two months before I graduated and hit the road. Where to, I had no idea. Maybe I'd head to Alabama and test the waters where Trouble grew up. At least that nigga seemed like he had a lick of sense, enough to balance out his fucked-up genes. Somewhat. 'Cause his ass still wasn't wrapped too tight.

Damn, my baby got half that King DNA. Hopefully my shit will cancel the dumb shit out, I thought.

I sped out of the parking deck, getting caught by the light right outside of Victory Plaza. I was hurting and wanted to look at Sa'Mia one last time, but I had to fight that urge. I was *not* looking back.

Skkkkrrrrttttttttt!

MARISSA

"*I* swear, that little girl is allergic to reason," I fussed, watching her throw a fit like she was a child, not almost an adult and about to be someone's mama.

"Let her go, man. She gon' have to figure that shit out on her own. I don't fuck with Maine's ass, but even I could see that he was trying to protect her ass. It's time that we stopped protecting her ass and let her fall on her face. Mia needs some humbling, and I'm tired of talkin' to her ass. I don't know how King did that shit for as long as he did."

I heard him and had no response. Everybody babied Sa'Mia. You'd think that she would've learned something with all the shit she'd been through recently. But you can't teach some people nothing. Only life could. And sometimes, they still didn't learn. Sitting back in my seat, I put my face in my hands, trying not to cry. I hadn't mourned King and felt like I was failing him. I wanted to be a role model for Mia, but I couldn't blame her for not trusting me. Nate stood over me, rubbing my back, tryna soothe me, but it wasn't working.

"They left their envelopes," Abraham said, rubbing his hand over his balding head.

"She's mean as a snake, huh?" Tatiana asked, her mousy voice making it sound almost humorous. But this was no laughing matter.

Jumping up, I saw the opportunity to try and talk to Mia again. I picked up the envelopes and made a mad dash for the elevators, because I knew Mia wasn't gonna take the stairs.

"Mia! Sa'Mia!" I yelled behind her.

She was pushing the button so hard on the elevator that I was sure that she was gonna end up stuck in the damn thing. The door closed on me, and I ran to the stairs. Mia may have been above taking the stairs, but I wasn't. Nineteen fuckin' flights of them.

"I can't believe I'm doin' this shit. I shoulda just listened to Trouble and let her go." I fussed to myself on my way down the stairs. But something was urging me to try and reason with her one more time.

I saw her crossing the street and didn't know where she was going. I knew she came with Maine, but the way she was wiping her eyes, she didn't seem to be trying to leave with him. I couldn't leave her out here alone. She was a bitch and a pain in the ass, but nobody deserved to have to deal with what she was alone.

"Mia! Sa'Mia!" I yelled, running across the street behind her. I was waving my arms in the air with the envelopes in it, like she didn't have her back to me.

She stopped at the coffee shop across the street, sitting at the table on the outside. I jogged to her, but her face was in her phone, so she didn't see me at first. I sat down at the table with her and she finally looked up from her phone. Sitting it down on the wrought iron table, I saw that she had her Uber app open.

"You need a ride? You can ride wi—"

"I don't want shit to do with none of y'all. I just wanna be alone. Me and my baby. We don't need y'all."

"Well, ya kinda do. I was reinstated with apologies from the Board of Education, so you gon' have to deal with me until I sign your diploma, or you gon' be flippin' burgers tryna pay for daycare."

"Fuck you, Marissa. Yeen no better than me. You worse, as a matter of fact. Yeen love my daddy. You was with him because of his money. Bitch, you had Neisha's triflin' ass with my damn uncle. But now, 'cause you done found the Lordt, you over here judging me. Yeen gotta play mama to get the funds Daddy left for you, boo. That shit's money in the bank."

"See, that shows what the hell you know. You don't know about love.

You don't know about loyalty. All you know about is that half-cocked shit you let out ya mouth from the moment you open your eyes. You stupid as fuck, Sa'Mia. You don't see what the hell is right in front of you, and even if you do, you so petty, you'll cut off your nose to spite your damn face." I looked at her like the small ass wannabe woman she was. "And you're right. I was fucked up, and that made me fuck up with the one man that truly gave a damn about me, you, your brothers, and even Maine. You talkin' about me judging you, when you're the one spoutin' all that judgmental shit. You think you better than all of us, huh? Why? 'Cause King treated ya ass like a princess? You ain't have to work for shit ya whole damn life. Still don't. So, you'll never know my struggle. Ya know what?" I said, sliding the envelopes over to her side of the table. "Gone and leave so you don't get what King worked his whole life for. You need to be taking orders at somebody's damn drive-thru window. Get some struggle in ya life, then maybe you'll deserve to be somebody's mama and wife."

I stood up, turning my back to her and headed back across the street. I was about to slap the shit outta her ass if I didn't walk away. Her and Kong were more alike than they realized, and I meant what I said. They never had to struggle, so they didn't respect or understand what it meant to have to work for shit. That's where I felt that King and I both went wrong. I didn't give Neisha all that King gave his kids. I didn't have the means to. But she still didn't appreciate what I did do for her. It was the same with Kong and Mia. Maine and Trouble were the balance to their bullshit, but there was only so much balance that could be given, and Kong and Sa'Mia's big ass heads tipped the scales every time.

"Marissa! Marissa!" I heard from behind me, but I was over her ass.

She was right. I was gonna take that money King had left me and say fuck it. When their caps got tossed in the air and they moved toward their futures, it was gonna be bye-bye Rissa and bye-bye Dallas.

"Marissaaaaaa!"

"*What*, Sa'Mia? You don't give a shit about what I have to say, and I wasn't shit but a gold-diggin' bitch tryna leech off ya daddy, right? Gone on somewhere," I said, stopping in the middle of the street, grateful for the red light. I'm sure the cars that would be oncoming soon were looking at me like the idiot I was, standing there bickering with a child looking like an idiot.

"Listen, I'm sorry. You're right about e-e-everything!" she said with a frown. Tears started running down her cheeks. "Can I—we get that ride? I need to get my shit from Maine's house, and this little gremlin got me hungry." She tried to make a joke, but I still wasn't moved. I rolled my eyes to let her know I wasn't swayed. Hell, my daughter was Ray'Neisha Brown, and I had seen every manipulation method known to man. She'd created some new ones. So Mia was gon' have to come better than that.

"Cut the shit, Mia." I seethed, mad that she was tryna play on my emotions.

Vroooommmm!

I saw Maine in his truck, speeding out of the parking deck. His eyes were facing forward. He would've been gone if he hadn't been caught by the light. Looking at Sa'Mia's face, I knew she was hurt. I knew she regretted whatever she'd said or done, but she might've just lost him for good this time. When a man was fed up, he was fed up, and there was nothing that would change that.

I turned back around and looked at the back of the truck, hoping that he would get out, bust a U-turn, something. For Sa'Mia's sake. When it didn't happen, I reached out and wrapped my arm around her shoulders, leading her out of the street before the traffic light changed and we had bigger problems on our hands than a breakup. Dallas drivers showed no mercy.

Skkkkkkrrrrttttt!

The sound of burning rubber made my eyes dart to the parking deck, and I saw a car skid out, flying in our direction.

"Sa'Miaaaaaa! Watch out!" I got out before pushing her back toward the sidewalk we'd left from just in time. She hit the ground hard and rolled, but she was safe. "Ugh! Ugh!"

I was clipped by the car, rolling onto the hood, hitting the windshield, over the top, and down the back of the car onto the ground.

"Oh my God! Marissa! Marissa! Helllllllppppppp!" Mia shrieked as my head fell to the side and my eyes rolled back into my head. "Marissa! Please stay with meeeee. Don't leave me, tooooooo!" she cried.

I knew that shit was too good to be true. A good man wasn't meant for a bitch like me. King dying proved that. A better life sure as hell wasn't. Karma is a bitch, I thought, knowing that this time, it was the end for me.

TROUBLE

"*T*hank you so much for everything, Mr. Abraham," I said, reaching out to shake his hand. "I apologize that things got a bit out of control. And I'll pay for your carpet to be cleaned."

"You're definitely Alonzo King's son. Always the peacekeeper, huh?" he said, shaking my hand firmly and laughing lightly. "And don't worry about the carpet. I'd rather it be from a nosebleed than from real bloodshed."

I had to say I was shocked that he didn't seem to be as upset as I expected with all that went on. Maybe he'd seen worse dealing with Pops. Or maybe his other clients had been worse to deal with. I could imagine handling legal matters for people involved in illegal activities could be stressful.

"I'll call the cleaners," Tatiana said, and I couldn't help but to look at her and smirk. She was somebody I could take down through there, and I wanted to see what it was goin' for, for sure. I needed to get some stress off my chest, so I planned to have the attorney's assistant assist me with that.

"I'll see you guys out," Tatiana said, and I smiled at the invitation, but held up my finger asking her to give us a minute. She nodded obediently and left the room. I had to say that was refreshing after being around these bitches who were always with the bullshit.

"Nate, I wanna hear more about the history of all this shit. I'm still new to all this—" I paused, realizing that I was actually an OG in this street shit, even at this young age.

"I gotchu. I just sent a text to tell all the old heads to meet us at the spot. We all came up wit' ya pops. We can school you on that shit, no doubt. But you know Kong is gon' be a problem, right? I get you wanting to respect Zo's wishes and all, but you really trust that nigga with one of your territories with all the shit he's caused?" Nate spoke, and I could honestly say that I wasn't sure.

"OMG! Y'all come on! Marissa! She's been—somebody—Sa'Mia—" Tatiana burst back into the room screaming. Well, I think that was screaming. She didn't seem to be able to get much louder than her normal tone. That was cute, but the shit would probably get tiring after a while.

"Slow down. What's going on?" I asked, trying to get her to make sense.

Bzzzzzzzzz

Bzzzzzzzz

Bzzzzzzz

Mine, Nate's, and Tatiana's phones all started vibrating at the same time. I looked around, and an eerie feeling came over me. I looked down and saw that it was Mia calling. I let out a deep breath, happy that she was calling, and whatever Tatiana had been rambling about wasn't her being hurt.

"Mia? Mia, calm down, what's wrong?" I asked her. She was so hysterical that I couldn't make out what she was saying.

"What, Maine? Yeah, I saw it from the window. We—we'll be there in a jiffy," I heard Tatiana saying into her phone.

The look on Nate's face was a grim one. One that made my heart break. I ain't know his history, but I recognized a man who had lost more than he could bear, and this was his breaking point.

"I'll be right there," I said to Mia. "Don't move! And you know not to tell the cops *shit*," I reminded her. We didn't get the cops involved in our shit. Especially after dealing with Officer Purty's ass. "Come on, E. Somethin' happened with Mia and Marissa downstairs," I turned and said to my brother.

"I'll call the cleaners and come down to meet y'all shortly. I have a feeling you'll be needing my services," Abraham said, and I looked at him gratefully.

"'Preciate you, man. You've more than earned everything my pops left you, and then some!" I yelled over my shoulder on my way out the door. If he wasn't trying to retire, I was definitely gonna keep Abraham on deck. Pops had a solid team. I hate that I didn't get to learn more from him. He was about keeping shit in order, and that's something you need in the world we operated in.

Tatiana went for the elevator when we all made it out of the office. Me, E, and Nate all headed straight for the stairs. We ain't have time to waste, and I took the stairs two at a time, with them right on my ass. When we got to the lobby, we rushed through toward the door, pushing our way through the crowd that had formed, blocking the exit.

"Move! Damn! Get out the way! Bet not na'an one off y'all peepin' asses done called the cops or the ambulance. Is that bitch recording? Nigga, get her phone. The fuck she think this is?" I snapped off, telling Eli to confiscate the bitch's phone that had probably caught the whole thing. I would get Abraham to pay off security to get the surveillance tapes, too. Because we ain't need the cops getting a lead before we handled the cowardly muhfucka who thought it was ok to pull this shit.

"Mia! Sa'Mia! Where are you?" I yelled, pushing my way through another crowd and the cops and Medics that were blocking my path and my view.

"Over here, Trouble!" I heard a crying Mia yell.

I made my way to her, but a cop put his hand in my chest to stop me. "This is a crime scene, son. Can't let you through," he said, his hand still in my chest.

"Nigga, I ain't yo' damn son. But I *am* Alonzo King's son, and if you don't move I'mma show you just what the fuck that means, if you don't know already!" I barked, looking him in the eye. When I mentioned my pops' name, his stiffened arm relaxed, and his expression softened. He moved to the side, letting me through, but tried to stop Eli and Nate. "Nah, they with me."

The cop let them through but grabbed my arm, making me stop and turn around. I was half a second from popping his ass in his shit.

"Your old man was a good man. My condolences for your loss. You gotta lotta us in your corner, son. We *know* who you and Sa'Mia are. That's why I was so cautious," he advised me, his tone low enough for only me to hear him.

"Thank you, Officer Monroe," I acknowledged and appreciated genuinely. He pulled a card from his front pocket and slid it to me discreetly. I took it and put it in my pocket before moving along to get to my sister.

"Mia! What the fuck happened?" I asked her, as she sat on the back of an ambulance being checked out for injuries.

"He—they—Marissa is deeeaaddddd," she cried, and I saw Nate's eyes roll back into his head as if to say, 'this shit can't be happening'.

"Dead? Who did—ya know what? Ma'am…" I turned to the EMT that was checking Mia. "Can she come home?"

"No, she needs to come with us so that we can check her out and make sure that the baby is okay."

"I'm her doctor. I'll take her into my care, and we'll make sure that she's fine." Nate spoke up, but there was something in his voice that let me know I should be concerned about him.

"Are you suuuuure?" the EMT asked him, and he nodded, showing her something. I guess it was his credentials, and she looked at them before agreeing.

"I'll sign the papers showing that she was released into my care. What's the status of the o—*ahem*—other party of the accident?" he asked, his voice getting weaker by the second.

"Marissa Hervey? She's been transported to St. Vincent's. But we expect that she'll be DOA. She was hit head-on and run over by the vehicle in the hit and run. Speaking of—" the EMT said, suddenly realizing something. "The police might have some questions for you, Ms. King," she said, looking at Sa'Mia.

"I ain't see shit," Mia snapped, and I stepped in.

"I'll handle the police," I said, walking back to Officer Monroe to request a favor.

"Yes, sir, Mr. King?" he asked eagerly. I liked his devotion.

"It's Mr. Nobles. I kept my mama's last name. But I appreciate the respect. I need a favor, and I know we just met, so—"

"No, sir. What you need?"

"Mia didn't see anything, and we need to get her home to make sure that the baby is okay. Her doctor is here and ready to take her, but we don't have time to *talk to the cops*, ya know, because the baby may be at risk and all. If you can get us out of that, I'll make it worth your while."

"Gotcha," he said and looked at me with a smile. "I'll come by later to complete my report. I was the first officer on the scene, so I can postpone the report until then."

"Thank you, man. I appreciate that," I said before turning around. I stopped and looked back at him. "I'll send you the address that we'll be at. I'll make sure you get her *full* cooperation." I spoke in code, but he understood. He was fast on his feet. I liked that.

"I got it handled," I told them when I came back. Nate was just coming back from the front of the ambulance signing the necessary papers.

"Where's Maine?" Mia asked, and that made my jaw tighten. *Where is he, for real? If he's involved in this shit, I'mma shoot his ass again. And this time, I won't miss my kill shot.*

"Oh me! Oh my! Oh Mia! Are you okay?" Tatiana finally made it through the crowd with Maine right behind her. That nigga ain't realize he'd just saved his own life.

"If y'all don't get this Petticoat Junction Rated G speaking bitch the hell away from me, *she's* gonna need the ambulance!" Mia was on one, as usual. Tatiana hadn't done shit to her ass, but she had to make somebody the victim of her anger. My question was, why not her nigga, and where the fuck was he when she almost got hit by a damn car.

"Yo! Chill with all that. You trippin'. She ain't did shit to you. You mad at the wrong muhfucka. Where was ya nigga when you was almost roadkill?" I checked her ass.

"Nigga, you for real swelling up on me behind this vanilla wafer ass bitch you wanna fuck? Ya dick makin' decisions for you now?" She turned her attack on me. *Big* mistake.

"If I was, how would that make me any different from ya nigga?" I shot straight. Yeah, I knew what Maine's assignment was, but Mia needed some straightening, and I was tired of handling her reckless ass with kid gloves when grown-up shit was always happening around us. "And how would I be any different from *you*? You in bed with the nigga who shot me!" I gritted, putting her ass on mute. Again, I knew what the circumstances were in all of that, but what if that wasn't the case and Maine was really on some fuck shit? She needed to sit her judgmental ass down somewhere.

Mia jumped up from the spot she was sitting in and rushed me. I sidestepped her ass and kagged her with my cane. Maine caught her and saved her from a face dive to the concrete. Yeah, I knew she was pregnant. But hell, so did she, and she came at me. But that was my mistake, because without my cane holding me up, especially after that sprint down the stairs to get to her ungrateful ass, my legs gave in. Falling forward in slow motion, I felt arms catch me. They were feminine but strong as hell.

"Oh, wow. You're rock solid, aren't you?" Tatiana said into my ear, and it made me blush. Nah, I wasn't blushing. Niggas don't blush.

"Nigga, get that goofy ass grin off your face, and let's get outta here before y'all give these folks more to see with the Frick and Frack Fraternal Twins Show." Eli laughed, helping me to my feet.

Maine had Mia in his arms bridal-style, and all of us moved through the crowd toward the parking deck.

"What happened?" Nate asked when it was just us in the deck.

"Kong hit Marissa with his car. He was aiming for Sa'Mia, but Rissa pushed her out the way," Tatiana said, pressing play on her phone and turning it so that we could see the footage. *This bitch can get access to anything*, I thought, watching the video.

Seeing Marissa save Mia's life and get hit, rolling over the top of the car and hitting the ground behind it, I couldn't believe it. It was like some shit from TV. It was almost unreal, but I knew it was very real. Nate walked away and punched the concrete wall. He worked with his hands, so that was all anger right there. I had to take the initiative.

"Maine, take Mia to the hideout, then meet me at the spot. E, go find the bitch you took the phone from, and, you remember what we used to do for our CI's back home?" I asked, and he nodded his understanding. "Get two. Gotta take care of that cop, too. Tatiana, delete all the footage of this shit, and then meet us at the warehouse. I know you don't like people and shit with you on yo' computer hacker moves, but I need you close and don't wanna handle that shit over the phone. Bring my brother witchu. Nate—" I looked at him, and he was pacing and talking to himself. "Nate! *Nate!*" He finally paused and looked at me. "You come with me. Mia's fine. Her mouth proved that shit."

"Fuck you, Trou—"

"Shut... theeeee... hell... up, Sa'Mia, before I drop ya on ya ass. Since ya talkin' out that bitch, it should cut that hot shit you been spittin' short." Maine spoke with authority, and Mia shut up.

I chuckled under my breath, shaking my head because he'd really checked her ass, and that shit worked. *That nigga got that Magic Stick*, I thought, walking to the driver's side of the car. Nate and I had much to discuss. We were gonna take the long route to the warehouse.

"Well, let's fuckin' get to it!" I snapped, realizing no one had moved. They all scurried in their respective directions like I'd just lit their asses on fire. All but Nate, who was moving like he had the world on his shoulders.

"So, tell me what's good, man?" I asked Nate once we were in the car and on our way to the warehouse.

The man looked like he'd lost everything that mattered to him in the world. That was something that I could relate to. I had lost both parents in a year. One that I just met and the other that was in my city but so strung out that she abandoned me with her mama.

He was staring back and forth between his bloody hand and out the passenger side window. I didn't want to push him, because he seemed to be most like me. He didn't speak on his feelings and shit until he was ready to, and I could tell that he may not be ready to.

"Sa'Mia is ya mama's child, and Kong definitely belongs to Kellz," he said, through gritted teeth, catching me off-guard.

"What makes you say that?"

"Your mama and Kellz were behind the death of my college girlfriend. And, just like you, your daddy was still tryna make peace with muhfuckas who had shown themselves to be trifling. He ain't stop 'til they killed his ass, too, now," he ranted, not making much sense.

"I ain't following, man," I told him honestly.

"Listen, the past is the past for a reason, and Zo meant well. He just had hope for niggas and bitches that ain't have hope for themselves. Don't be like that. He kept you a secret from the world for a reason. He gave you the empire for a reason. Mia don't want it, and Kong don't need no parts of the shit. But I'll handle his ass."

His phone vibrated in his good hand, and he unlocked it and looked at what I guess was a message. I kept my eyes on the road and my mind on my own business, so I wasn't tryna read his shit on the slick. I felt like that was some bitch shit to do anyway. His whole demeanor changed. I think I even saw him smile.

"Aye, make this right," he said abruptly, making me take the turn on two wheels.

"Where we goin'?" I asked, the change in direction taking priority over the schooling he was giving me. But I heard him, loud and clear. Believe that.

"Take me to the house. I need to patch this hand up. Then I'mma go to the hideout to check on Mia. I know she seems alright, but I gotta make sure she good. That's just—"

"The kinda man you are," I finished for him. "Aye, you sure you ain't my pops or uncle or some shit?" I cracked, but I had seriously considered it.

"Nah, I brought you and Mia into this world, but Zo is definitely your old man. You're so much more like him than you are me. You just don't see the resemblance because he was on his 'can't we all just get along' moves lately. But once you get to the warehouse, you'll get it, trust me. Get off on this exit."

I drove in silence, taking the directions he gave me to his house. Other than 'turn here' or 'get in this or that lane' nothing more was really said between us. I was in my thoughts and he was in his, too. That's why it would always be bros before heauxs with me. If I was in the car with a bitch, she would've been all "whatcha thinkin'?" and "what's wrong?" but with the niggas, silence was valued, appreciated, and understood.

"This is me," he said, pointing to the house on the corner. The old heads are waiting for you at the warehouse. I don't want no parts of this drug shit. And I really wanna make sure Mia's okay."

"Even after everything, you still lookin' after our asses," I pointed out with a chuckle.

"Yep. Zo was more than a friend to me. He's the reason I am who I am and where I am. It's only right," he said, getting out and closing the door. Once I made sure he was in the house, I headed to my original destination.

KONG

They had me fucked up. Yeah, I brought a lot of this shit to fruition, but Pops handled the hell outta me. Through a damn pre-recorded video. And in front of everybody. I know I should be grateful to have walked away with my life after all the shit I did. But the nigga even said he understood. So why would he hand that shit over to a nigga that he ain't even raise? I had something for all their asses, though. Then Nate's bitch ass gon' lay hands—well his damn head—on me, and now these niggas out here fighting like that shit is gravy.

Nick still hadn't woken up, and I debated picking his ass up and putting him in the car and leaving him on the ground. Easing out of the car, I walked over to him, picking him up under his arms, and moved him. I sat his body up against the concrete of the parking deck. Somebody would find him and call 911 for him, or he'd wake up himself. Either way, I ain't need that kinda dead weight with me. He'd get over it, or not. I ain't care. His mouth, and his ass being weak and getting beat the fuck up, was the reason he was in the predicament he was in.

Limping back to the car, I slammed the door shut and cranked it up. I had to figure some shit out. Trouble and Mia had to go, and I had to make it happen ASAP. Paying the fee and leaving the parking deck, I felt like something or somebody was on my side, because Mia's ass was in the middle of the street, arguing with Marissa. I figured I would kill two birds with one stone, or two bitches with one hit. Revving the engine, I knew I had to make my move before oncoming traffic started moving again. I knew Maine was nowhere in sight because of the way he'd reacted to Mia's ass when she stuck her nose in when he was beating Nick's ass.

I sat there watching them for a few seconds, making sure that they didn't see me. They were so caught up in their little argument that they didn't know who or what was coming for them. All the better for me, because the shit would happen so fast, they wouldn't know how to react.

I pressed the gas pedal to the floorboard of the car, and it skidded and fishtailed, almost making me lose control and hit the wall. I caught it, though, and just in time. I'd aimed for Mia, but Marissa pushed her out of the way, making me hit her ass head-on. Cracked my windshield and shit, and I'm sure that big ol' ass of hers left some dents, too. I grinned because, even though she wasn't my first target, thinking about what Pops had said in the video when he gave her and Nate the green light to be together, this was my revenge on that nigga for putting his hands on me. And for her ass turning on me and running back to Pops after she had started all that shit with Kellz in the first place. You don't get away with that kinda shit and get to skip off into the sunset with a nigga and my pops' money after all she did. Nope. First name, Dat Nigga Karma. Last name, Ghost, because a nigga was outta there before Marissa's ass hit the ground. If I'd had more time, I would've jumped the curb and turned Mia's ass into a speed bump, but in due time.

I thought I was in the clear, until I got to the light and looked over to see Maine's ass look from the rearview mirror right in my face. Busting a quick right, I headed to the house that had once been my pops', but now belonged to me. But not before seeing Maine bust a U-turn in that big ass SUV of his, heading back to the scene. I had to wonder if he was gon' tell her it was me, because this was a burner car and I would get that handled as soon as I got settled in at the house.

I knew I should've probably gone into hiding. But when Maine 'nem were buying multiple spots, I was biding my time for this big ass mansion to be mine, and look how that worked out for a nigga, so I really ain't have no place to go. I mean, I could call and see if Chica would finally answer the phone for me. She'd been hot with a nigga since I killed DeRico. I was tryna let her calm down, but I'd given her long enough. She was about to make me pop up on her ass.

Me: *Chica, cme on girl. You can't still b mad w a nigga. I need ur tenda luvn care rhet nih. HMU*

I shot my shot. Wasn't gon' sit around like a bitch and wait for her to respond. Right now, I was gon' lay down and deal with this damn headache Nate's ass gave me. It was worth it after the heartache I'd just caused him.

I sent a text to the cleanup crew, too, telling them to come get the car and laid my head back on the couch with my feet up on the arm like King hated. You know why? Because this was my shit now. Letting my eyes slide closed, I went to sleep, hoping that a nigga didn't have a concussion and would be able to reopen these bitches in a couple hours.

"Nigga, you don't value yo' fuckin' life!" I heard, making me jump outta the sleep I didn't even get into good.

Looking around, Nick was standing behind the couch, looking like he'd just got his ass whooped in real life. It took everything in me not to laugh at his appearance. Waving him off, I checked my phone and saw that the car had been picked up and replaced, but nothing from Chica. *I see this bitch wanna play. I just gotta remind her who that nigga is wit' a hit of this double D... Daddy Dick.*

"You gotta be the stupidest muhfucka in existence. You don't think they know you tried to kill Mia and hit Marissa instead? You don't think they gon' creep up in here like I just did on ya ass. And yo' pussy ass in here takin' a fuckin' cat nap!"

"Pussy? I'll show you a pussy!" I hollered, jumping up, ready to finish what Maine had started. But I got lightheaded and was seeing two of the nigga. That's aight. I had two in the chamber and would shoot the shit outta both of their asses.

"Yeah, pussy. And I bet you *can* show me one. Word on the streets is that shit you walkin' around with, always tryna fuck a bitch, ain't much bigger than a clit. Word is, that's why you always in the middle of shit and tryna prove your manhood. 'Cause you know ya manhood don't measure up!" he said, busting into laughter that ended with violent coughs and blood that his disrespectful ass spit on my damn floor.

"You over here talkin' about a nigga dick like a bitch! You must wanna see for yaself," I offered, grabbing my dick and blinking, trying to focus and merge the two of him into one.

"You mad, so that shit must be true." He grunted, leaning onto the couch's back for support. Maine mollywhopped that nigga's ass, for real. "And *you the bitch!* You left me for dead at the ghatdamned parking deck like I ain't come there in the first place to protect yo' ass. You foul as fuck, my nigga. And I got half a mind to turn ya ass in for that bounty they got on ya damn head."

"But you ain't, 'cause yeen no snitchin' ass nigga," I reminded him, tryna feel him out.

"I'on know. A quarter mill is a lotta money for a nigga. I could do a lot with that lil' piece of change." He stood up and challenged me, seeing if I would flinch.

"Well, make that call, then. But know this, you won't get to spend that shit, 'cause ya ass gon' die today if you do."

"So are you if ya dumb ass stay in this fuckin' house like this ain't the first place they gon' look. You either stupid as fuck or the most arrogant nigga on the planet. Both meaning you stupid as fuck in my book. Dafuq yo' head at? Yeen think past hittin' Marissa's ass wit' that car, huh?"

I already knew that he was spouting real shit, because I'd had the thoughts myself. But to hear it from him drove it all home. I had to get outta here. Heading toward the door, Nick followed. We were both moving slow as hell. *Might as well do a pop-up on Chica and get my dick wet before I have to hide out and figure some shit out.*

"Naw, I'm driving." Nick snatched the keys from me. "Act like I ain't see you tryna focus. How many of a nigga you see? Two or three?"

"You ain't in much better shape than I am, hell. Maine whooped dat ass." I deflected.

"But I got here and in yo' shit without makin' a corner boy move like you did with that hit and run shit. Glad you at least changed cars and shit. I can't believe you let Maine see yo' ass."

"Man, Maine ain't gon' tell'em shit."

"That nigga suckin' yo' dick or som'n? He's... fuckin'... Miiiiii-iaaaaaa... sheeeee... gottttttt... hiiiiisssss... seeeeeeed..." he said slow as hell with stupid ass hand motions like he had to use sign language for me to understand what the hell he was saying.

"Nigga, I know. But I'm tellin' you what it is. And naw, that nigga ain't suckin' my dick. Gone wit' that gay shit."

Nick looked offended by what I'd just said, but he ain't speak on it. *Was he mad because I vouched for Maine or because I said, 'gay shit'? Had to be the Maine shit, 'cause that nigga ain't gay. Not the way him and that soft-speakin' ass bitch was lookin' at each other,* I thought. He was gon' see that when it came down to it, Mia had a pussy, but Maine was my nigga, and it was always MOB. Even if the B was my big sister, and she had my niece or nephew in her belly.

"I'mma say this shit, but you ain't gon' hear it, though. Maine gon' be the death of you."

I didn't respond, just got in the car and went along for the ride. I thought I'd told him I wanted to roll up on Chica, but I guess I just thought it in my head. We pulled up to a house that had a wall as tall as it was. There was a gate, but he didn't pull up to it. Instead, he drove past, looked onto the property, and then rolled on down about a block, turning the car around to face the house that was at the end of a cul-de-sac. I looked at him, and he was so intent on studying the house that I decided not to say anything. Instead, I turned the radio up just a little so I could hear what was playing, but he reached over and turned that shit right back down. Like he needed full concentration to stare at somebody's house. Instead of saying anything, I pulled out my phone and saw that Chica still hadn't responded.

Me: *U gotta nigga lookin like a simp hittin u up b2b. U aight?*

I put my phone down and stared down the street, trying to see what the hell Nick was looking at so intently. I was really trying to take my mind off of Chica and how she was handling a nigga, but I wasn't gonna let myself admit that. I was soft for her, and then she just left me hanging like this. Made me think that she was fuckin' wit' more than just me and DeRico.

"Got that bitch!" Nick hollered, making me realize that I'd zoned out. "Ahhh shit!"

The car that came from the house we were watching came straight for us. Nick ducked over into the passenger seat, his head landing in my lap. I alternated between looking at the car that was making its way toward us and this nigga's face in my dick. I wanted to punch him in the back of the

121

head, but my curiosity distracted me, because I wanted to know who we were stalking. When the car passed us, it was the cute lil' receptionist from the lawyer's office earlier today. I knew something was up between them and intended to ask him about the shit. But him getting his ass stomped out by Maine kinda postponed that. *My nigga mud dragged my nigga. Damn.* I laughed a little in my head thinking back on the shit. Luckily for us, she was on the phone, so she didn't even take notice of our car. I saw a nigga in the car with her, but I couldn't make out who it was. Hell, I was barely able to see her through the tint. The streetlights were the only thing that let me get a glimpse into her shit.

I only knew it was a nigga because of his silhouette. Even with that knowledge, though, I wasn't about to tell Nick's stalker ass that shit until I knew what the hell was going on. I didn't want to be in the middle of no dumb shit popping off without all the details. I felt like I was at the level where I ain't have to ride for and with a nigga. Hell, niggas risked their lives and freedom to be down with me. That's what comes with being a King. When she was gone, I popped that nigga in the back of the head.

"Get the fuck up, man. What we stalkin' that bitch for?" I asked and took notice that he took his time getting up out my lap.

"She fucked me over, bruh," he said, but for some reason, I knew there was more to the story.

Before I could say anything else, though, he had the car cranked and was following her. I was gon' watch this shit play out, because I had a feeling it would be entertaining, if nothing else. A few turns and I regretted my decision. This dumb ass nigga followed the bitch—or the bait —right into the lion's den.

MIA

This coward ass nigga really just tried to run me over. After all that shit Daddy said, he was still—mannnn, I was over this shit. Then Maine talking to me like that and Trouble kagging me, I'd never felt so alone in my life. Especially now that Marissa was gone. I didn't care for the bitch, but she was the closest thing to an understanding that I had. Nobody else got me. They ain't get that I was always on the defensive because, as Alonzo King's Little Princess, I was always seen as weak. I had to fight my way outta so much shit all my life that the need to fight became an instinct. I decided to get the niggas and bitches that tried me before they got me. Nobody knew my struggle, though. And not because I didn't want to talk about it, but because nobody ever asked.

"Mia, you almost got hit by a car. Is that enough to get ya ass to calm the fuck down?" Maine asked, more like fussed.

I looked upside his head like he was stupid. Was this nigga blaming me for somebody tryna kill me? He couldn't be. But he ain't say shit about Trouble tryna make me face dive and shit. Our baby could've been hurt if I'd hit the ground—again.

"Yeen got no response? How the hell am I supposed to look out for you when you stay puttin' yaself in dumb ass situations? I swear, you was gon' kill ya pops if Kong hadn't."

Now, he'd hit a nerve. I get that he'd been around forever. I get that he looked at Daddy like he was his father, too. But the reality was that he *wasn't*. He was *mine*. I had just got my memory back after the bitch *he* was fuckin' tried to kill me on multiple occasions, fucked up my reputation, and, again, was fuckin' my man. This nigga was about to get his mind right, or he could kiss my ass. He pulled up to a house, threw the car in park, and turned his body to look at me.

"Before you pop the fuck off—" he started, but I held up my hand to silence him.

All the shit I had in my mind to say, all the cussing out, all the name calling, all the pointing out all the fuck shit that he'd done, swole up in my throat and choked me. The tears ran down my face, and he reached over to touch me and try to wipe them away, but I leaned back, pressing my back up against the door. I didn't get it. If I was such a burden, then why was everybody always in my shit? Did any of them really know me? Or did they have their ideal of me and had attached their expectations of me onto my back like a 'kick me' sign, without asking me what I might have wanted or needed for myself?

Like, don't act like a baby, Sa'Mia, but they stayed babying me. Don't act spoiled, Sa'Mia, but they spoiled me and didn't let me do shit for myself. Grow up, Sa'Mia, then they stunt my growth. Now, I'm pregnant and about to be somebody's mama, and didn't even know who I was. I never knew my mama, never had a female role model, but I'm supposed to be good at being somebody's mama? I just lost my daddy, and the brother I was raised with had been the reason he was dead. Then, I was damn near grown and found out I not only had another brother, but he was my twin. The one man I ever wanted got more miles on his dick than I got on my pussy, and we lost our virginity *together*. And he was fucking the bitch who was trying to kill my whole family, keeping secrets from me, shot my twin while riding with and for the brother that betrayed us all.

But people wondered why I was halfway out my mind my whole life. Niggas stayed talking about how women be on some bullshit and driving them crazy, but these niggas, all the muhfuckas around me had driven me over the edge.

"Listen, Arkino, I need a break. This has been a lot. I just need to process it all," I told him honestly, and he looked at me like I'd just called his mama a bitch. I'm not sure if he expected me to go off on him and me not doing it was what had him shook, or me asking for a break.

"Ain't no breaks, mane," he said through gritted teeth.

"See, that's the issue right there. First it was Daddy, then you, then Trouble, then Daddy and you and Trouble. I have a mind. A strong one, Kino. I'm graduating top of our damn class. But y'all treat me like I need a helmet and a drool cup or some shit."

"Mane—" he started, but I held my hand up again. I wasn't yelling, and he was gonna hear what the fuck I had to say.

"When have I been able to make my own decision? When have I been able to move without one or more of y'all breathing over my shoulder? If life was a test, I would fail that shit. As a matter of fact, I feel like I am! Do you really know me? Like what I want for myself? Or are you tryna pick up where Daddy left off? Like, he gave me an empire I don't even want for real. Trouble out here acting like he done known me my whole life, and I ain't seent that nigga since we shared a fuckin' womb. And you bouncing back and forth, Mr. Friendly Dick..." I paused, looking him straight in the eyes so that he felt what his actions did to me. "Even if Daddy *did* tell you to keep an eye on Neisha and Kong, yeen have to fuck her, but you did. She made sure I knew about it."

"Damn," he said under his breath, letting what I had to say sink in. But I was far from through. Everything that had been simmering was spilling over like a volcano.

"In the last couple of months, I have been embarrassed. My *first* time was aired for the world to see. My man went to prom with the bitch who posted the shit, and I went with my *brother*, Maine. I lost my memory. *Twice.* And honestly, I regret getting it back. I don't feel like I know myself anymore with all these memories than I did without them. Do you know how that feels? Everybody I've known my whole life has left or betrayed me in some way. Back to back to back to back to back! So, yes, I need a break. Some space. To breathe. To be Sa'Mia De'Shay King. Not Alonzo King's daughter. Not Kellen King's sister. Not Tywan Nobles' twin. And not your main, or woman, or bitch, or baby mama. I need to figure out who the fuck *I am*. And I can't do that right now."

I blew out a heavy breath, feeling like a weight had been lifted. I didn't wanna go anywhere or be in the middle of no shit. I wanted to really sit alone and think about some shit. And if he thought I couldn't take care of myself, then he really ain't know how I was raised. Or know me at all. His head was hung, and his shoulders were slouched. That hurt, because it was true that he didn't know me. The sad thing was that he *just now* realized that shit. How the hell you claim to know somebody, to be in love with somebody, to want to build with somebody, and you don't know or allow them to be an individual? That's some nigga shit for you, I swear. Women stay losing their identities to their fathers, men, and children. Well, before I transitioned from being my daddy's daughter to being Maine's woman, wife, or whatever, and this little bitty person's mama, I was gon' get to know myself.

And fuck anybody who ain't like it.

Getting out the car, I walked up to the hideout. The house that my father was kidnapped from. The house where he took his last breaths. I had a bit of a limp because of how I landed when Marissa pushed me out of the way of Kong trying to kill my ass. But it could've been worse. He could've killed my ass. I looked over my shoulder and could see that Maine was struggling with whether or not he should get out the truck. I waited until he looked up at me and shook my head no before waving 'goodbye'.

"Hey, Mia. I thought I heard the truck out there," Nate said, his eyes swollen and puffy. I was surprised to see him because he'd left with Trouble, and I thought they were handling business, but I ain't question it. "Where's Maine?"

"He's not coming in. I need some time to myself right now. How's your hand?" I asked, looking at his bandaged-up hand and changing the subject from something I didn't really want to discuss.

"It's fine," he said, looking at it, and I could tell he was lying. I had seen blood through the bandage when he helped me into the house. "Let me check you out, and I'll go handle business with Trouble and let you have the time alone."

"Nate—"

"Yeah?" he asked while he helped me into the bed and opened his black doctor bag.

"I don't know much about you and Daddy's relationship, or about my mama. I mean, I thought I did, but apparently, I don't. Can you tell me about all that?"

"You sure you wanna hear that shit right now, Mia? Maybe we can wait until things have calmed down—"

"No. No more waiting. No more protecting poor little Sa'Mia. How the hell am I supposed to know about myself and my legacy when y'all— well, they—been spoon-feeding me lies or only bits and pieces of what they thought I could handle. Don't be like them. Please. I need to know. I don't wanna make the same mistakes my mama did. Hell, the same mistakes my daddy did," I begged while he checked my blood pressure, pressed on my stomach, and put his stethoscope on my chest. I stopped talking so he could hear my heart, but our eyes were locked, and I could tell he was battling with something.

"I wasn't a fan of Danielle, so I might not be the best person—"

"You're the *perfect* person to ask, then. She came to me when I'd lost my memory the first time. Something about her ain't sit right with me. I *need* to know the real."

"Okay, so your vitals are great," he said, checking the bandage the EMT had put on my knee. "I'm gonna head to the house, and I'll be back with some takeout for you and the little one. And we can talk about it then. If you're sure," he said, like he was giving me one last chance. That made me curious. *Am I right about my mom not being the person Daddy tried to paint her as?*

"I'm sure. But I have one more request," I said hesitantly, hoping that he'd give in one more time.

"What's that?" he eyed me skeptically.

"Can I come to your house? I mean, I never been there, and I promise I ain't on no bullshit. I just wanna be somewhere that Maine and Trouble and Kong don't have immediate access to me. I know they'd never look for me there."

"I don't think that's a good ide—"

"Pleeeeeease," I asked, giving him the puppy dog face. I was playing the innocent role to death, but I really, really needed him to say yes.

"Aight, Sa'Mia. Come on," he said, closing his bag, and he helped me off the bed. He blew out a breath, but I was so happy that I had gotten him to agree that I didn't say anything about it. I didn't need him changing his mind on me.

We got in the car and rode the twenty-minute drive to his house in silence. He lived modestly for someone who made as much money as I knew he made. He had a single-story house with a garden and bird bath in the center of his small yard in one of those communities where all the houses looked almost identical. There were little things that helped you tell one from the other, the owners putting a splash of themselves on their houses, but nothing major. Maybe a painted mailbox or different shrubbery, or a team flag hanging on the flag post by the door.

I liked it. He wasn't flashy, was quiet and to himself. He minded his business and stayed under the radar. I could see why Daddy fucked with him like he did.

Walking inside, the house was decorated beautifully. It was more extravagant than the outside by far, but you wouldn't know that unless you were invited in. His décor was black and blue. From sofas to vases to the rugs that covered the hardwood floors. He didn't have the usual "nigga with money" shit, like a huge ass TV like his ass was blind.

He had maybe a fifty-inch on an oak entertainment center that was carved with African relics and hieroglyphs. There were African and African American pieces of artwork everywhere. I was loving the whole space. But what caught my attention was the record player and a shelf of vinyl on one side of the entertainment center and the shelf that rose to the ceiling and was stuffed with books. I mean, everything from urban fiction to medical books to poetry to history. I definitely looked at Nate as more than a doctor in the short time that I was in his space.

"Welcome to my humble abode," he said, motioning with his hands around the foyer and living room that had me on stuck. "Let me show you to where you can chill. There's plenty of food and leftovers in the fridge. You can have anything you want, except my liquor, 'til I come back."

"Thank you for letting me come here." I thanked him genuinely, following him to the room at the end of the hall. "I swear if I could finish this last couple of months without having to set foot in Lincoln, I would."

"You can take online classes," I heard from behind me and turned to look at one of the rooms that had the door closed when we walked past.

"What the fuck—" I snapped, mad as hell. *What the hell is she doing here?*

TROUBLE

*W*hen I walked into the spot, I went straight to the conference room. Like Nate said, the old heads were there, ready to school a nigga on some real shit. I had to pause because something felt off, but not in a bad way at all. I looked at everybody in the room, and they all looked like somebody I knew from back home. It was weird, and my brain thought my eyes were playing tricks on it.

"Listen, Lil' Zo, we been watching you for a minute," one of them said, his voice starting the wheels to turning. I studied his face, and he let me. A smile crept across his face when he saw the light come on.

"Mr. Nixon?" I asked, getting up and hugging the owner of the corner store back home that I used to go to all the time.

"Yep. It takes a village," he said, moving his hands around the table in an all-inclusive gesture.

Mr. Nixon's corner store was where I stole my first Grapico when I was eight, because Mama Pearlie wouldn't buy me one. Of course I got caught. Instead of calling the cops, he made me work that shit off. I worked there every weekend for three months, stocking shit in the back and helping him do counts. He'd sit with me and talk while I worked. Nah, he ain't work, he just talked and watched me work. I'd learned that he was my pops' cousin, and when I'd paid off my debt, he let me work there after school and on the weekends. It was good money, and I used it to invest in my dope when I got older and as my legit move, so that it looked like that's where the money came from for me to get the shit that I stayed fresh in.

I was starting to see that everything my pops did was intentional. He had his niggas around me all my life. The same niggas who schooled me on life in one way or another were here.

"Don't look so surprised, knucklehead," Mr. Hill, my Middle School Principal said, standing from his seat. I always thought he had more hood than book in him, and he'd shown that shit a couple times when I was smelling myself, and he checked me. He was tall and muscular. Looked like he played football in college, so it didn't take much to make me bow down. Well, that's a lie. It took him body slamming me in his office when I was in the seventh grade and then calling Mama Pearlie to finish that ass whoopin' to drive that shit home. But, after that, he took a special interest in me, and now I knew why.

"Juke?" I asked, shocked. "You clean up nice than a muhfuckas, man!" I said, making my way over to Juke, the nigga that was *always* on the corner up the street from Mama Pearlie's house.

He did his jig when I made it around the conference table to him. It was like a shoulder lean mixed with the Bankhead Bounce and the Harlem Shake. He bounced, threw it up in the air and I caught it, imitating his moves, before he wrapped me all the way up in a hug. He was the one that taught me the side of the game E and Doe didn't want to give me. He taught me how to cook that shit up, bag it up, flip it, and even how to take my cut before re-ing up. *"Always pay yaself first, then you invest in ya business, youngblood,"* was his motto, and it was what I lived by, even to this day.

With Juke in my corner, I had lil' niggas on my squad, and we were all paid, and fly as hell, but never too flashy. Him being in the streets like he was, he knew when there was some beef brewing and when one of mine was about to betray me. He'd saved my ass more times than I could count. And now, the question about why, if he knew what he knew, he was on the streets was answered. He wasn't. But he had a role to play, and he played the fuck outta that shit, too.

That made me think about Maine, and I had to say that he was just as devoted as Juke to Pops and played his role. I gained a new respect for him in that moment.

"Every kingpin in the making needs a prayer warrior," Luther, the usher at Church of the Highlands, which we were dragged to every Sunday and Wednesday said. "Especially a loud-mouthed, hotheaded one like you."

Everybody laughed and nodded in agreement with his statement. I had to agree, too, because I was a muhfucka when I wanted to be, which was most of the time. Luther gave me a pat on the back and dapped me up, but I pulled him to me, making him give me a brotherly hug. He wasn't big on being touched. I remember him shaking one of the little girls off his leg like a dog when she wrapped around it one Sunday. Funniest shit ever.

The smile on my face was so broad, my full grill flashing in the room's overhead lighting. It was like a damn family reunion in here. So many memories and so many lessons were in this room. *Thank you, Pops,* I said a silent prayer to him for being the angel on my shoulder before he was the angel on my shoulder. After I'd walked around giving hugs and dap, I sat in the seat that was left empty at the head of the table.

"Trouble, ummm, we have a problemo," Tatiana came running in saying frantically, squeaking like a mouse. My ass hadn't even settled in the seat, and I was back up on my feet, ready to react.

All eyes fell on her and Eli, who was looking around the room the same way I had. "That nigga King," he said, with a chuckle.

"Right!" I co-signed before looking back at Tatiana who was in an obvious panic. "What's goin' on, N0B0DY?" I asked, and she hit a button on her phone that made the wall open and the security footage come up.

I watched Kong and Nick get out of the car. They had no business being here, especially after the shit Kong's ass had just pulled. Before I could react or give any instructions on what to do, I watched Maine creep up on them and punch Nick in the back of the head, planking his ass on the ground and then wrap Kong up in a bear hug until he put his ass to sleep.

"So, that must be Maine," Juke asked, and I nodded, never taking my eyes off the screen.

Maine walked them both to the car they'd come in and searched both their bodies. He found the keys in Nick's pocket and used the key fob to pop the trunk. He tossed Nick in first and pushed him back, struggling to get Kong up and into the trunk with him.

"I'mma go help hi—"

"Naw." I cut Eli off. I needed to see what he was up to. "Let him handle that shit. This the job Pops gave him. Let the nigga earn his keep."

Shrugging, Eli leaned up against the wall and watched Maine with the rest of us. He got Kong in the trunk and closed it before walking around to the driver's side of the car. He looked up at the camera in the garage and gave a head nod, letting me know that he had the shit handled, before getting in. He adjusted the seat, cranked that shit up, and left out.

"Can you track him and tap into what they sayin'?" I asked Tatiana, and she nodded, sitting down in the chair in the corner, pulling a MacBook from her bag. She went to work, and for a minute, the room was filled with the sound of key clicks.

"Aight, while she's handling that, let's get down to business. E, you handle that?"

"Yep. Grabbed the prepaid cards and put the ten thou max amount on both. Met up with the cop. NOBODY can find any damn body and any damn thing, I swear, nigga. I'm just glad she on our side, for real." He sang her praises, confirming that she really was as good as I'd heard she was. "And we handled the phone issue. She might even be givin' a young, fine nigga a call later on, on her shit," he said with a laugh and a pop of his collar, making me ball my face up.

"You know we don't shit where we eat, bruh," I fussed. He was about to let his dick cause a potential problem for us. All he had to do was stop calling the bitch after knockin' her down, and she'd be at the precinct tryna snitch on some get back shit.

"Nigga, gone wit' that shit. Can't even take a joke and ummm," he said, his eyes drifting to Tatiana, as if to say, 'you can't talk nigga,' letting me know he'd read my mind and knew I had every intention on getting familiar with her insides.

"Anyway." I dismissed the assumption, and he laughed 'cause he knew he'd called the shit. "I wanna say I 'preciate all y'all's parts in raising me up in Pops' absence. It feels good to know that he always had a nigga's back, front, and both sides," I said, getting emotional. Eli started playing an air violin, and I was about ready to cuss his ass out. He was gon' let me be grateful, ol' hatin' goofball ass nigga. Before I could say another word, Tatiana clapped her hands together loudly and started laughing hysterically, letting me know that she might just be crazy as hell.

"Got 'em! It looks like they're goin' to King's house. I have devices all over, so we'll be able hear everything," Tatiana said in her tiny voice, blowing her fingers proudly.

I shot her a smile and nodded my head approvingly. I tried to take my eyes off of her, but something about the way she was looking at me, more like looking *through* me, made it hard. I heard Eli chuckle and already knew what he was thinking. I swear I hated that nigga sometimes. But even that didn't make me turn away from her. The shit was obvious, so I knew that E wasn't the only one who'd peeped what was happening between the two of us.

"Alright, CK2s! We got two months to whip this little knucklehead into shape!" Mr. Nixon announced, bringing my attention back to the issue at hand. I snapped back to reality, but I was shook, to say the least. *I need to stay away from her ass. She just feel like she'd have a nigga's head fucked up*, I told myself, but knew that was gonna be easier said than done. She'd piqued my interest now. You know what they say… Curiosity killed the cat. Call me curiosity, 'cause a nigga had been known to kill a cat or two, and now her kitty was on my hit-list.

"I'on know if he's ready." Mr. Hill eyed me skeptically, making me sit up in my seat and match his glare.

"I ain't that young nigga you DDT'ed back in the day, Mr. Hill." I growled. I was ready to fight for this shit, even his old ass if I had to.

He just laughed like something I said was funny before softening his stare. "Yeah, and I don't beat up on the handicapped. But feel free to holla at me when them knees stop bucklin' every time you take a step," he jabbed, because I was back to using my cane.

"Fuck all that, it ain't shit but a lil' wobble baby, wobble baby, wobble baby, wobble. I'm rockin' witcha, youngblood," Juke said, doing The Wobble in his seat. I swear I used to think this nigga stayed high on something. But on the real, it turned out he was just high on life.

"'Preciate that, Juke. You always been *that nigga*!" I said honestly. I used to think he was cool as fuck for just being himself, regardless of what anybody else thought.

"Mannnnnn, if he anything like Zo, and that gal there anything like Danielle... Lettuce pray," Luther said, pressing his hands together and bowing his head. "Lawd, and Zo, 'cause we know you up there by now, please guide this man's moves with his mind and not his heart or his dick. We know where that can get us all. And if he doth fall victim to the power of the P, as we all have at one time or another, please let this young lady be as humble as her voice implies and not send him down the road of death and destruction that his lineage has laid for him. Create for him—for them —a new path, oh Lawd. In your humble, son's name I pray. Amen. Amen. And Ashé!"

"Amen," everyone said collectively. Everyone but me. When Luther opened his eyes, he was met with me mean mugging his whole life. All he did was burst into laughter.

"Oh well, we lost, y'all. He wasn't even praying for his own soul. This gon' take Pearlie, some oil and holy water," he continued to joke. They all thought that was the funniest shit.

I expected Eli's goofy ass to join in, but when Tatiana started laughing, I gave up. I was outnumbered, so I just leaned back in the seat and let them get a good laugh at my expense. Once the laughter died down, I looked around the room and smirked, not even mad for real, because pussy had got *me* in enough trouble, just being here in Dallas, for me to understand what they meant. And then, even with Nate not going into detail, I could tell that Mama was a problem for Pops wayyyyy before she was one for me.

"Y'all gon' school a young nigga or what?" I asked as humbly as I knew how, which wasn't humbly at all.

"Sounds like he ready. Let's give him what he askin' for," Mr. Hill spoke up and said, making the butterflies flutter in my stomach. It was a nervous feeling, but it was more excitement than anything else.

The opportunity that I'd come to Dallas for was coming to fruition in more ways than I could've imagined. Just hated that Pops couldn't see me take his shit to the next level. But I knew that he was watchin' from up above, and I was gon' make sure not to let him down.

MAINE

I pulled up to the warehouse just in time to see some fuck shit about to pop off. Nick had followed N0B0DY to the warehouse with Kong's ass riding shotgun, and I knew they were about to get themselves killed. My loyalty was to the King Empire, but I had been given a job and was gon' make sure that I handled that shit. I parked on the side of the building and made my way to the garage door right before it closed. I slid in and waited for them to get out of the car and walk around.

"Nigga, you realize where we are, and we ain't armed?" Kong snapped at Nick. He sounded scared as hell, and he should've been. He'd been given redemption by King and still violated, trying to kill Mia and killing Marissa instead. I knew that he couldn't come back from that shit and had a feeling that if I ain't move quick, they were gon' be murked. Not that I was against that shit, because I was sure Trouble would just hand me the West, but I was worried about what might happen if they asses got lucky and got a shot in. Couldn't risk it.

"I stay ready," Nick said, raising his shirt and showing a gun on either side of his waist. "Here," he said, pulling a Glock out and handing it to Kong, who reluctantly took it.

Creeping up, I didn't make a sound. I punched Nick in the back of the head, making his ass fall forward and hit his head on the concrete of the ground. Before Kong could turn around and see who was workin' on their asses, I grabbed him in a bear hug and applied pressure until he stopped fighting. I tossed their asses in the trunk after patting them down to find the key fob I needed. I got in the car, but not before looking at the camera to let that nigga Trouble know I had this shit handled. I knew he was watching, and that's what had me at a loss. I had to wonder if Kong was just arrogant as fuck or that damn stupid that he didn't think about the cameras that were in every corner of the damn warehouse, and every location that King used. N0B0DY had made sure that there were up-to-date cameras and wire feeds everywhere. It was a precaution that King took a little while ago, and I thought he was paranoid. That nigga was a chess player in this game of life. I had to give him that. I was honored to have been brought up by him and to have learned from him. The only thing I hated was that he left me to babysit this nigga that was in the trunk of this damn car.

I drove carefully, making sure not to get pulled over. King had DPD pretty much on lock, but with this transition and his death, there was bound to be some tension and some niggas who might just jump ship. Trouble was a new face. And nobody liked new faces, no matter what their bloodline was. I was 'bout to have to play diplomat 'round here. I already knew it.

Pulling up to King's mansion, I knew that even in leaving the crib to Kong, there was a method to his madness. N0B0DY had cameras and wiretaps in every part of the house, so we could track and trace his every move. That was one of the reasons I'd just gone on and brought their asses back here instead of killing 'em and disposing of the bodies. That was my first thought. Hell, it was my first, second, third, and fourth thought. That would save me a lotta headache and get me back to Sa'Mia. I knew she said she wanted space from me, but there ain't no space 'round this bitch, mane. It was me and Sa'Mia 'til death, and her ass was gon' accept that shit or else. I was tired of playing with her.

Pulling into the garage, I closed the door behind me. Not that anybody could see what I was about to do, but better safe than sorry was my motto nowadays. I unlocked the house and walked in, turning on all the lights to make sure that they got good video. I went to the fridge and grabbed an apple juice, popping the top and drinking it. Sitting at the kitchen table, all the memories of dinners and holidays and great times with King and the family flooded my memory. All the laughter, all the fights, all the knowledge King dropped on us all. The first time I saw Sa'Mia, the moment I knew I was in love with her. So much was here in this house. Even all the dumb, disrespectful shit that Kong would do when King was on business trips or he thought no one was watching. All the shit I got his stupid ass out of. And that tradition was continuing.

I knew *why* King chose me, but I ain't wanna be tied to this dumb ass nigga no more. The more I sipped my apple juice, I contemplated taking the nigga out. But that wasn't my place or my call. It was Trouble's now. That nigga had his work cut out for him. This shit wasn't for the faint of heart. There were many nights when me and King were the only ones awake, and he was stressing about some shit that was popping off. He had to think for everybody and stay two steps ahead of what they might think, plan, and how they might move. That was some *Black Mirror: Bandersnatch* shit. It would drive even the strongest mind over the brink of insanity.

I finished the apple juice and decided I'd go get dumb and dumber out of the trunk of the car. One or both of them should be up by now. I threw the bottle in the glass recycling receptacle and laughed because that was a habit that King drove into us. He used to say, "We can't keep the niggas who buy the shit from us from buying it, all we can do is not add no shit that'll kill 'em tryna stretch the shit. But just because they choosing to put poison in their bodies don't give us the right to poison the planet."

He was all about trying to do one right for every single wrong that he did. It was an honorable way to live, for real, and the shit had rubbed off. I'd learned so much from the old man. My eyes got wet, and I used the collar of my shirt to wipe my face. I hadn't cried about his death for real, and this time, I was shedding tears over what his death would mean—for all of us. *Damn, we lost a real one*, I thought, walking back into the garage.

Boomp! Boomp-buh-boomp-boomp-boomp!

I heard muffled yelling and what sounded like kicks in the trunk. I stood outside and listened, thinking of what my lie was gonna be. I didn't want to open the trunk, but I knew I had no choice. I reached into my pocket and hit the button on the key fob. The trunk unlatched at the same time that a foot flew upward trying to kick it open. The shit was hilarious. I leaned back against the wall and watched Kong climb out of the trunk—ass first. He fell backward and landed on the ground, making me shake my head. Nick came out after him and damn near stepped on Kong on his way out. The shit could be a TV show. I'd watch it. They looked like the clowns that they were.

"Nigga, you just gon' stand there hee-hawin' and shit, and not help a nigga out?" Kong asked, mad as hell.

"Not my circus, shole the hell ain't my monkeys," I told him, still not moving.

"What the fuck happened?" Kong asked, struggling to catch his breath. This nigga was in bad fuckin' shape.

"I'on know, mane. I came in and ya car was in the garage, but you wasn't in it. I went up to the lil' meeting Trouble was havin', and you wasn't there, either. I ain't know what the fuck was goin' on 'til I heard y'all kickin' at the trunk," I explained to him, and he looked at Nick, shaking his head.

"Nigga, you 'bout got us killed witcho stupid ass!" he hollered, foaming at the mouth. "Following a bitch on some fuck shit."

Kong stomped off in the house like a spoiled kid throwing a tantrum. I shook my head and watched while Nick followed like a lap dog. I walked over and slammed the trunk shut before going into the door that they'd left wide open with their disrespectful asses. I followed the sounds of Kong cussing Nick out toward the living room but fell back a little to see what I could hear that they might not want me to hear when I was in the room. I knew that I could listen to the recording later, but this might be something that I could use in the moment.

"Man, I can't tell you," Nick argued.

"You gon' tell me somethin', my nigga. It almost got me fuckin' killed. What the hell were you chasin' that bitch for?"

"Man, I can't—come on, Kong. Put that shit away." Nick's tone changed, and it was time for me to intervene.

"Yo, mane, what you doin'?" I asked, walking into the room with my hands in the air. "I ain't against you shootin' this nigga, but you gotta be smart about this shit."

"Nah, he need to tell me what the fuck is goin' on."

"I'm wit' it. Nick, nigga, you better start talkin' befo' I start walkin' and let this nigga do what he gon' do." I tried to reason with him, and the way that he hesitated let me know it was something this nigga was willing to die to protect. I tried another angle. "Listen, mane... if you was knockin' Tati down, don't nobody give a fuck about that shit. Whatever it is, it ain't worth dyin' for."

"You don't know, man, so shut the fuck up! I ain't fuck that bitch. She ain't my type. Stay in yo' lane, bruh. This ain't ya business."

"But it's mine! So start fuckin' talkin'!" *Pow!*

"Ahhhhh!" Nick hollered. Hell, even I flinched, and my eyes squeezed shut. "Are you fuckin' crazy, nigga? You coulda hit me! The fuck wrong witchu?"

Hearing Nick's voice, I knew Kong hadn't shot his ass. When I looked down, I saw that he'd shot a hole in the wall behind Nick. I knew that King's house wasn't gon' make it long with this nigga living in it.

"That was a warning shot and a fuckin' courtesy, my nigga. Just know that next time won't be a warning, and I won't miss ya ass."

"Kong, chill out, mane. You don't need nobody on you right now. You already got enough heat on ya ass. You don't know who mighta saw you hit Marissa, or if they had traffic cams on ya shit or what. And you gon' make sure they take ya ass down for shootin' this fuck nigga?" I asked, making it known that I still ain't like or trust Nick's ass.

"I gotcho fuck nigga." He tried to swell up, and I laughed.

"You might wanna mind ya mouth and start tellin' this nigga what he wanna know before I stop talkin' and let him bang on ya ass 'til ya body look like Swiss cheese 'round this muhfucka. Ain't neva met a nigga let his ego have him comin' for the nigga that's tryna save his fuckin' life," I said, but my words trailed off after that, because Kong's ass did the same thing. I guess birds of a feather. But I had to admit I wanted to know why this nigga had such a hard-on for NOBODY. I knew she'd crossed a lotta niggas and had dirt on every fuckin' body. But I couldn't understand what the issue coulda been with her and Nick. I was gon' ask her, too, but this nigga was 'bout to have to tell Kong somethin' before his body wound up floatin' somewhere.

"You heard anything from Chica, Maine?" Kong asked me, catching me off guard. I didn't think this nigga would even miss her after finding out that she'd been fuckin' DeRico. Guess I was wrong.

"Nah, man, what's up?"

"She ain't responding to a nigga texts and shit, and I was about to pull up on her when this nigga wanted to play Stalk-A-Hoe and followed the bitch to the warehouse. We gon' go pull up on her when we done with this nigga, aight?" he asked, looking back at me to make sure I was down, and I nodded my head. I would deal with that shit when we got to it. "Nih, tell a nigga what's good, Nick. You lookin' more and more suspect by the minute."

"Man, aight. But you gotta put the damn gun down," he bargained. The arrogance of this nigga to think he was in any position to bargain.

"I ain't puttin' shit down, nigga. Talk!"

"So, there's something about me y'all don't know. Somethin' that I'd rather keep on the low and shit, and that bitch knows about it."

I walked back into the room and sat down while Nick's ass weaved the tale of his encounter with N0B0DY. I'd heard more than a few, and she was a *beast* with them keys. I was ready to hear what she had on his ass. Kong followed my lead and sat down on the couch while Nick stood in front of us, wringing his hands like he was nervous or some shit. I mean, if being held at gunpoint had him all scared like this, then his ass may wanna reconsider the line of business he'd decided to get into. Especially when dealing with Kong's ass.

"Continue," Kong urged, and I kicked up my feet.

"There was this nigga I worked with before you put me on that I used to hit licks for named Joose. Nigga got an organization that spans the south, for real. Big time shit. Anyway, he had me and this nigga Logan workin' for him and runnin' the Dallas Division. But Logan got greedy. I found out about it and was about to put Joose up on game, but he was already hipped and had that bitch Tatiana on it. She had us under surveillance from her crib, my nigga. Like, tapped into our Smart TVs and phones recording video spy movie kinda shit."

"Well, if you knew the nigga was on some bullshit and you wasn't involved in it, what kept you from tellin' the Joose nigga what the business was?"

"I was getting to that," Nick said, blowing out a long, heavy breath. "It was more than business with me and Logan. It was..." He hesitated and looked at us like he knew the next thing he said was gon' be the nail in his coffin. "Complicated."

"Complicated?" Kong and I said at the same time.

"Yeah."

"Complicated?" we asked in unison again, this time the pitch of both of our voices getting higher.

Nick just nodded, waiting for what was gonna come next. Kong bust out laughing, and both me and Nick looked at his ass like he'd lost his entire mind. I sat there silently, and Nick kept looking back and forth from Kong to me, confused as hell.

"So what, you was fuckin' his sister or some shit?" Kong asked.

Nick shook his head no.

"Cousin?"

Another head shake.

"Mama?" Kong asked.

It was my turn to laugh. I knew his ass wasn't that stupid, and he was just grasping at straws because he didn't wanna state the obvious. I laughed 'til tears leaked from my eyes, and Kong leaned back into the couch like he was hoping it would swallow him whole. He started scratching his head with the muzzle of his gun, and I watched him, in case that shit went off by accident so I could try to get as little of his blood and brains and shit on my clothes as possible.

He kept scratching his head, though, and my concern for him making a fatal mistake shifted. I hoped that he wasn't about to shoot his damn self behind the next nigga's secret. Then again, that wouldn't be such a bad look if he did.

"So, you gay?" Kong asked, finally resting the gun in his lap and staring at Nick intensely.

"Yeah..."

"Nigga, you was about to get me killed behind a bitch having evidence that you like dick? For real?"

I had to say, even I was shocked at how well Kong was handling the news. He'd never acted like he had an issue with anybody being gay, but in our work, we weren't around too many of them—well, at least I didn't think we were. I knew Nick was a fuck nigga, but I wouldn't have given him gay. Not that it mattered, like Kong said.

"As long as you don't let that shit fuck wit' our money, I don't give a fuck who and what the fuck you do in your own time."

Nick blew out another breath at Kong's statement, and I couldn't agree with him more. We all had made some stupid ass decisions behind pussy and love, so as real niggas, we understood.

"But..." Kong picked his gun up again and pointed it at Nick. "What happened to the nigga you was caught fuckin'? Logan, right?" he asked, showing me that he still had his head on at least some of the time.

"I had to take the nigga out. He fucked up a good thing by fuckin' up our business *and* by putting me in the position to have to make the choice between his life and mine behind a dollar," Nick said honestly, and I could tell that shit was still eating at him. I could understand because I was in the same position with Sa'Mia. I couldn't imagine having to make that choice, or if I would make the same one that he did if it came down to it. I still ain't like his ass and still felt like there was something he was hiding. But, just like this, it'd all come out in the wash. Or I'd just hit up NOBODY to see what else there may be that he didn't want us to know.

We both waited for Kong to speak, but when he did, the nigga reminded me why he was, by far, the most ignant muhfucka in the whole city of Dallas.

"Well then, I ain't gotta kill ya fairy ass. You just as dumb as the next nigga behind matters of the heart and ass. You just like giving and takin' it in the ass." Kong laughed at his own insensitive ass joke, and I knew that was his discomfort coming through. "Hell, Maine torn between fuckin' with my ass after I kidnapped and got my pops killed, and almost hit his pregnant girl, my sister, with my car. And I'm runnin' up behind Chica's ass, and she was fuckin' the nigga who was in your position before you right under my nose the whole time."

I knew what Kong was doing, because we all had secrets and demons and shit. There was so much bad blood in this empire that we could drown in it. But there was a time for business and a time for pleasure. I just hoped that he was as understanding as I was being about him tryna kill Sa'Mia when I told him about Chica's ass. I wasn't gon' do it in front of Nick, 'cause some shit just wasn't his business.

"Say, mane..." I spoke up, noticing that Kong was grimacing and remembering Nate handling his ass earlier. "Maybe you should lay down. Chica's ass gon' be wherever she at. You might need to go get checked out. You, and ya lil' side bitch here." I pointed at Nick with a chuckle. "Y'all might wanna get checked out. Y'all done been victim to a couple ass whoopins today. But I wouldn't go to Doc Smith. He might just finish the job."

"Nah, I'm good," he said, trying to stand up and falling backward.

"You ain't good, my nigga. Now, you can either sleep that shit off and hope yeen got a concussion and don't wake the fuck up in the morning, or you can get checked the fuck out and live to be a dumb ass another day," I scolded. He looked like he was listening, so I kept going. "You got the chance to do better. Yeah, you fucked up tryna run Mia down, and I can't save you from what's gon' happen to you behind that shit. Not that I would even want to, 'cause on some real shit, my respect for and loyalty to ya pops is the only thang keepin' you alive and the only reason I'm even talkin' to ya dumb ass after you tryna take out my nigga and my seed. But *because* of my loyalty to King, you still breathin'. Know that."

I had to get my mind right. I was letting my emotions show, and it would impact his trust in me. I'd come too far for that shit to go down. Rubbing my hand over my face, I blew out a breath and pulled out my phone.

N0B0DY: *Trouble needs you ASAP*

"Listen," I said, trying to recover from my tangent, feeling both their eyes on me. "Lemme call a nurse to come through and check y'all out. If she say y'all good, then y'all good. But I can't let y'all go to sleep with the possibility that them hands that was laid on y'all caused more damage than y'all think." I met eyes with Kong, so he saw that I was concerned for his ass and not just spoutin' no bullshit. One thing King had taught me was that you could make a man believe a lie if you looked him in the eyes when you told it. "And what's the worst that could happen if I'm wrong? You get a lil' TLC from a sexy RN and we find out that the only thing that y'all got was some sense knocked into ya asses," I said, finally looking at Nick, happy they both found that shit funny.

"Aight, nigga, whatever. A nigga in need of a lil' TLC, especially with Chica on the shit she on," Kong agreed, bringing her up for the second time. I felt my jaw tighten. Shooting a look at Nick, he smirked, letting me know he saw the shit. I was gon' have to watch his ass harder than I thought.

"What about some TLC for me?" he asked, taunting me.

"That's what Grindr is for. Figure that shit out. Dafuq I'm supposed to ask? Aye, when y'all send some nurses over, make sure the nigga nurse is gay. You a special kinda stupid, mane," I said, shaking my head at his dumb ass.

Getting up, I headed for the door.

"Yeen stayin' for the party?" Nick asked.

"Nah. I gotta wife to go check on." I gritted, keeping the rest of my thoughts to myself.

"Aye, Kong, I'll hit you and let you know when the nurse is headed your way."

Without another word, I walked out of the house and off the property. Hopping in the car that was waiting for me, I had no words. I rode in silence. I had a million questions, but that would have to wait. How Mia was doing, why I hadn't heard from her, and what Tatiana really had on Nick were in the back of my mind. But what Trouble was cookin' up, and I knew he had some shit brewing because he was Alonzo King's son, was gonna make or break what I could do about any of that other shit. *"Business before pleasure, at all times."* I heard King's voice repeating in my head as I laid it back on the headrest and tried to sort through my thoughts before we made it to the warehouse.

KONG

"*N*igga, where you think you goin'?" Nick asked, looking at me like I was crazy as hell when I stumbled toward the garage.

"To mind my fuckin' business. You should try that shit," I snapped. I couldn't get Chica off my mind, and I wanted to see if she was alright.

"Aight. You get pulled the fuck over, you gon' be fucked. Yo' ass know you hot as fuck right now, so it ain't gon' take nothin' but one swerve for ya ass to end up in them cages," he said, annoying the hell outta me. He was right, but I ain't wanna hear none of that shit right now.

"Man, I know how *not* to get pulled over. I just wanna check on Chica," I admitted.

"That bitch must got heroin in her pussy or some shit, bruh," he said, getting up and grimacing. The pain was settling in from the whoopings he took today. "Gimme the fuckin' keys."

He snatched the keys from me, and I looked at him like he was dumb as fuck.

"Last time I let you drive, I ended up in the trunk of my own damn car. I got a better chance seeing four lanes on the road than trusting yo' ass behind the wheel. Gimme them shits," I snapped, grabbing for the keys.

"You tried it," he said, stepping out of my way. I wanted to swing, but I ain't have time to be wrestling with his ass. I was losing time.

"Aight, my nigga," I said, stomping off toward the door. I stumbled down the stairs, catching myself, but not before Nick saw me and chuckled. But he knew better than to say shit.

I opened the door and got in, waiting for him to do the same. I sat there watching him in his phone, wondering who he was texting that he *had* to text right now. I just shrugged it off, because he got his ass in the car. I plugged Chica's address in the GPS and laid back and let him follow the directions to her house. I needed to make my head stop hurting so that I could face her and only see one of her. I knew I looked pretty fucked up, but I ain't care. I needed to know that she was good, even though something was telling me that she wasn't. I felt the car slow down and knew that we were close. I could feel the turns that were being made.

It was weird that Nick hadn't said much the whole drive. Most of the time, I couldn't shut his ass up. I figured he was still waiting for me to say something about him being gay, but that shit really ain't bother me. I mean, his head in my lap when he ducked so that Tatiana bitch couldn't see him when he was stalking her was suspect as hell, but I wasn't about to open that door. The nigga had never tried me, so we were good. Seeing that we were close to Chica's house, I shot her another text.

Me: *I hope u aight. A nigga need u, man. Wya?*

Still nothing. I checked and rebooted my phone, hoping that I'd lost signal and I'd just missed her message. But when the phone finished rebooting, the only message that came through was from Maine.

Maine: *Ya nurse gone b there in a half 2 a hour. Enjoy. Lol*

I shook my head, because I wasn't on that shit. If I could have Chica, I wouldn't need nobody else. Especially now. I needed a real bitch like her to help me come out on top of this fucked up situation. Yeah, she'd fucked around on a nigga, but niggas cheated on their bitches all the time. We just needed to get an understanding. On some T-Pain type shit. I could do me, she could do her, and we could do us together. As long as we were loyal to each other, we'd be good. That shit would be heavenly for any nigga with some sense, for real. As long as she ain't fuck my squad. Which would be easy to make happen with Nick chasing dick and Maine with his head up Sa'Mia's ass like he was.

Nick pulled into the parking lot of her apartments, and I hopped out before the car was even stopped all the way. Running up the stairs, I started beating on the door!

"Chica!" *Boomp! Boomp! Boomp!* "Bae!" *Boomp! Boomp!* "You in there?"

"Nigga! The fuck wrong witchu? She ain't there, ain't been there for a hot lil' minute," Moni, her nosey ass neighbor hollered, sticking her bonnet-covered head out her cracked door from across the street.

"Where she at, then?" I asked, looking her in the face. She licked her lips, and it pissed me off. In the past, I would've been tryna ease up in her house and knockin' her down. But the sight of her ain't do shit for me. Not because she was unattractive. Hell, she was badder than Chica. But she wasn't Chica. And that's all that mattered to me.

"You hear me, King?" she asked, her door all the way open now.

She was standing in her doorway with nothing but a t-shirt on and some dingy ass house shoes that you could tell she wore as regular damn shoes all the time. Her hands were on her hips, raising her shirt up a little bit, showing her thick ass thighs.

"Nah, what you say?" I blinked, realizing that I had been staring at Chica's door like I was waiting for her to open it and prove Moni to be a lie. That didn't happen. Turning to face Moni, I noticed her smile get bigger. I guess she thought she had my attention, but she ain't know how far from that shit she was.

"I said…" She paused dramatically, popping her lips. "I'on know why you runnin' up behind her skank ass no way. She have niggas in and out that bitch before and after you would come through. You need you a real down ass bitch like me on ya team. Jus' sayin'."

"See, I wouuullllddddd," I responded, giving her the attention she was begging for. I walked up on her, taking her fat ass in my hands and squeezing it. "But I don't do bitches with loose ass lips," I whispered, smacking her ass and pulling back.

I'd just had a handful of ass, and my dick wasn't even hard. It was official. I was in love. Turning to walk away, Moni couldn't leave well enough alone.

"Fuck you, Kong. I hope that nasty pussy havin' bitch give you somethin' that take both y'all asses out. Lame ass nig—"

Before she could finish talking shit, I had my hand around her throat.

It hurt like fuck to move that fast, but I ain't take kindly to threats, and she was playing with fire. Pushing her back in her house, I slammed the door and turned her around, pressing her back up against it.

"Now, what was you sayin'?" I asked her, my face so close to hers that our noses were touching. I could feel her breath, and the trifling ass bitch pushed her chest out so that her body was pressed up against mine.

Even with me choking the hell outta her, she was still tryna get chose. I couldn't deal with this kinda shit right now. My head started to spin, and I was seeing two of her. The only reason I knew which one was the real one was because I had my hand around her throat. I could feel my grip loosening, though, and she took full advantage, kneeing me in my dick. This was the first time I was grateful for Sa'Mia's ass and her abuse. That shit ain't hurt half as bad as it used to. I guess my shit was numb to it at this point.

"Stupid biiiiiitchhhhh!" I used the rest of my strength to reach back and slap the shit outta her, making her fall to the ground. I was able to pull the door open before I fell forward on my face, hitting the concrete *hard.*

"Kong! Kong!" I heard Nick holler before I blacked out.

"You brought him with you?" I heard a woman ask, alarm in her voice.

"The nigga unconscious. Just tell me what you need so I can get this shit over with," Nick snapped, trying to whisper.

"Whatever, Nick. What the hell you got me out here this time of night for?" she asked, and I could hear her attitude shift.

"Come on, baby. You know what we tryna do. I need help, and you was the only one I knew could gimme what I need." I heard him begging the bitch. Him calling her baby had me lost as hell, 'cause I thought the nigga said he was gay. *Maybe he's playin' the bitch,* I thought, waiting to hear the rest of the conversation.

"How's that?" the woman asked. I opened my eyes, trying to get a clear view, but was blinded by the headlights of the car that was in front of us.

"He crazy about that bitch Chica. Obsessed for real for real. His head ain't in the game. I need you to help me find her."

"Oh, I know where she is," she informed him with confidence.

"Oh yeah? Where?"

"Dead."

"Dead?" Nick asked, his voice raising a little. "How the hell I'mma tell that nigga that shit?"

"Easy, tell him that Mia killed her ass, and Maine helped cover it up by throwing her body in the Trinity River," she informed him, matter-of-factly. Hearing that made me try to sit up, but I was hurting too bad to move.

"That's just what I need to show him that nigga Maine flaw as fuck. 'Preciate ya."

Pissed was an understatement, but I had to say I was grateful that my nigga Nick was tryna help me find my bitch. That made him aight with me. At least I had *one* real nigga on my team, 'cause Maine's ass was number one on my hit list after what I'd just heard.

Damn, that nigga sat right next to me and pretended he ain't know shit about my bitch goin' missing. Even tried to check me about what he wanted to do to me for tryna kill Mia's ass, when he'd already bodied my woman, I thought, closing my eyes and pretending to still be out when he got back in the car. *This nigga on some bullshit. But I know this... Maine gon' have to fess up about Chica. And pay for his disloyalty with his life, Mia's, or both. And their seed's. Fuck all of 'em. And if that nigga Trouble stick his nose where it don't belong, his ass can catch it, too.*

EPILOGUE

GRADUATION DAY

Two Months Later

NOT ON MY WATCH

TROUBLE

"Come on, Tywan, just one more picture. How many times does your favorite grandson graduate from high school." Mama Pearlie fussed over me, straightening my tie and holding that old ass Polaroid camera up to take another picture.

"Favorite?" Eli snapped like he was hurt by what she'd said.

"Three better be the damn—I mean dang-on answer," Doe whined, and she shot him a death glare behind that slip-up.

"Y'all asses got through high school. *Barely*," she said, eyeing both of them sideways, making me snicker. "This one is my baby and the last of the NegroTeers." She reminded us of what she used to call us, a spin on the Three Musketeers. She choked up and wiped her eyes, making me shake my head. She was about to drive me with all this crying and shit. A nigga was graduating high school. Not dying.

"Mama, go catch them tears before you mess up that beautifully made-up face that I paid all that money for," I teased, and she play hit me on the shoulder before going to do just that.

Knock! Knock! Knock!

"You expecting somebody?" Doe asked me, and I shook my head no.

I wasn't strapped, but him and E stayed ready and pulled theirs before

152

walking to the door. Doe stood to the left of the door while E stood to the right, and I walked to answer it.

"Who is it?" I yelled, standing a bit to the side, in case somebody wanted to fire off into the door tryna shoot me.

"Luther!" he hollered from the other side of the door, and I looked at Doe and E who both shrugged.

"Luther who?" I asked.

"Boy, move out the way," Mama Pearlie fussed, pushing me to the side and rushing to open the door. "Hey Bab—I mean, Lu. Awwww, are those for me?"

Seeing him grin from ear to ear and hand Mama Pearlie a dozen tulips and a box from Tiffany Inc., I saw red.

"Yo, what the hell is goin' on here?" I yelled, my voice cracking. Yeah, Mama Pearlie was grown, but that ain't mean she could date. She needed to be gardening or going to play Bingo or some shit.

"Boy, watch yo' mouth," Mama Pearlie snapped, turning around and staring at me like she was about to lay me across her knee.

"Nah, Mama, Trouble ain't wrong with this one," Doe said, him and Eli stepping into view and standing on either side of us with their guns pointed at Luther.

"Put them things away, youngbloods. Ain't no callin' for all that," Luther said, his hands raised in the air.

"Geez Louise, did I just walk into the OK Corral?" I heard a soft voice say from behind Luther. "Don't shoot," Tatiana said, giggling with her hands in the air like Luther's were, a gift bag in one of them.

"I'm not gon' say this but once. Put... them... guns... away..." Mama Pearlie threatened in a voice that made a chill run up my spine.

"Man, fuck all this. I'm out!" I snapped, walking past her and pushing past Luther with Tatiana hot on my heels.

"Tywan! Come back here! Tywan!" I heard Mama Pearlie yelling at my back, but I stood on the passenger side of Tatiana's Prius because it was the last car in my driveway. This was *my* day, and she had a nigga poppin' up with flowers and expensive gifts and shit. A nigga who was in the same drug game she tried to keep us from all our lives. That nigga was 'bout as Godly as Lucifer, and that shit had me pissed the hell off.

"Sooooo, you wanna tell me what all that's about?" Tatiana asked, pointing to the house.

I pulled on my seatbelt, not wanting to talk. But the fact that she wasn't putting hers on and hadn't cranked up the car let me know that she wasn't budging until I did. In the last two months, Tatiana and I had gotten close. As badly as I wanted to knock her down, she was more like a sister to me. She was the closest thing to a friend that a nigga like me had ever had, outside of E and Doe, but they were family.

She was there when I didn't think I could take any more training with Mr. Hill, who seemed to wanna beat my ass for everything I'd done as a kid. When I was sore, she'd give me massages, ice packs, and even go to the gym with me so that I could be better conditioned for the physical training. Or when I didn't see the point in taking dance classes with Juke, but she showed me that it reminded me to have fun, but also that it taught me that every step is important in the process. She was even my practice partner. She helped me with the math that Mr. Nixon taught me and made sure that I knew the ins and outs of the business the way Pops had been running it, while helping me flush out what could and couldn't work with the improvements that I had in mind.

And the most important thing was that she prayed with me, even though she was Agnostic, and made sure that I studied the scriptures that Luther would give me, telling me that I would need a strong foundation in faith to make it in these streets.

Tatiana was there with and for me and would be wife material. But a nigga wasn't lookin' for a wife, so she was just my bestie. We'd pinky swore on the shit, with her lame ass. She was my voice of reason, but even she couldn't talk me off this ledge.

"All that prayin' and scripture, and this nigga ain't say shit about him bustin' my mama open," I said under my breath. It was eating me alive.

"First of all, ewwwww," Tatiana said, balling her cute little face up. "Second of all, she got all y'all grown. Like officially today. So what she does while y'all out livin' y'all's lives isn't your business Troubie." She called me the goofy ass pet name she'd given me. "And this is a man who has been around you your whole life. Your dad trusted him. *You* trust him."

"But not with my mama. Ain't nobody good enough for my mama!" I pouted, folding my arms across my chest. There were two things I ain't play about, my family and my money. This nigga was fuckin' with Unfuckable Item Number One, and the punishment was death, by gun squad. Me, E, and Doe would light that nigga up, no questions asked.

"You look like a whole child right now, Tywan." She said my name, letting me know that she wasn't about to pull punches with me.

See, Tati was underestimated. People thought that because she "hid" behind the computer and had that soft voice and demeanor, she was weak or a pushover. She was actually one of the strongest women I'd met. And she was a beast with anything she put her hands on, not just electronics. That's why I ain't fuck her, as bad as I wanted to some days. I *needed* her on my team.

"Man, shut up," was all I came up with. I was mad that she was face checking me, and even madder that she hadn't cranked her lil' ass car up.

I looked at the doorway, and everybody was staring at us like we were as crazy as I felt like we looked.

"Man, shut up." She mocked me, putting the gift bag in my lap. "You sound juvenile as hell right now. But I'm gonna let you be great. I mean, I get it. Nobody wants to think about their parental units gettin' busy, or bustin' it open, as you so eloquently put it. And again, ewwwwww. But what she does isn't your business. That's the long and the short of it. Just be happy that you know she's doin'… whatever it is that she's doin'… with somebody you know. 'Cause if it was somebody else, and they mistreated her, I'd be hunting down that nigga's whole family and wiping their entire footprint off the record so y'all could handle they asses," she told me matter-of-factly.

I smiled at her because I knew she wasn't lying. She'd made sure that we kept up with Kong's ass, and the only reason he was still alive was because he seemed to have come to his senses. Maybe it was the Nurse that Maine had sent him. That bitch's pussy must've been lined with platinum, and her tongue must've had a battery in it, 'cause she'd changed that nigga's whole tune. And, even though Maine didn't know, she'd helped me find Mia so that I could keep tabs on her. I'd talked to her and Nate and knew that she just needed time to clear her head. But I couldn't deny that I felt like they were keeping something from me. But as long as she was safe and he made sure her and my niece or nephew were good, I ain't care. I'd learned that some secrets needed to be kept secrets. And if they needed to come out, they would.

"Man, why they still standing there starin' at us all stupid?" I asked, deflecting.

"Because they're waiting for you to finish throwing your tantrum," Tati said, holding her phone up and showing me a message conversation between her and Eli that I didn't even know she was having. *Yeahhhh, I gotta watch her,* I thought.

Elijah: *Y'all coming back inside?*

Her: *Yeah, as soon as he's done with his tantrum*

Elijah: *Well tell dat nigga 2 hurr the hell up b4 he miss his own graduation*

Her: *Okie doke Lol*

I shot her a side eye and then looked at E, who was laughing his ass off. I flipped him off, and the stance that Mama Pearlie took made me drop my hand, hitting it on the bag.

"Fuck all y'all."

"When and where?" Tati asked, leaning over to whisper that shit in my ear. My dick jumped. *Down, boy,* I thought, trying to keep my head in the right place, which was outside of Tatiana's walls. "That's what I thought. Now open your presents. I know *children* love presents."

Reaching in the bag without a response, I pulled out a fresh ass diamond-encrusted Rolex with the matching bracelet. I know that shit set her back, and I couldn't take it from her.

"I can't take—"

"You can. And you will. I just wanna Rolly Rolly Rolly with a dab of ranch. I already got some designer to hold up my pants. I just want some ice on my wrist so I look better when I dance. Have you lookin' at it, put you in a trance." She started singing Ayo and Teo's song "Rolex" while dancing in her seat. "Aye. Aye. Aye. Ayyyyeeee!" She laughed before looking at me and switching up on me. "Aye, Tywan? You ugly. You yo' daddy's son, ayeeeee!"

Dabbing, she hopped out of the car and ran toward the house. I put the gifts back in the bag and shook my head. She was too damn silly, man. But I needed that light in my life. Getting out the car, I walked up to the house slowly, giving Luther the up-down.

"Now, can we talk about this like adults so I can see my baby walk 'cross these folks' stage?" Mama Pearlie asked, her arms crossed under her chest.

"Nah, ain't nothin' to discuss. Luther know if he mess this up, he gon' have some hittas on his ass," I said, mugging the hell outta him. He matched my mug, and that's when I saw the gangsta come out of him.

"As good a woman as Pearlie Jean is, I'd beat my own ass if I messed this up, youngin," he informed me, and I nodded. *As long as his old ass knew. 'Cause fuckin' wit' mine, his ass would be on borrowed time, and I was the one who would come to collect. Personally.*

LET THE PAST STAY IN THE PAST

MAINE

 I stood in the mirror, taking in my reflection. A nigga was dapper as hell. I hadn't heard from Mia or Kong since the night after the hit and run and the will reading. I figured Kong's ass was layin' low, and we had a trace on his ass, so I knew he wasn't making no moves we ain't know nothing about. The nigga was definitely enjoying the care of the nurse I sent to take care of his ass, though. And she was helping us keep an eye on him, too.

We were watching Nick, too. And he kept having meetings with this woman. We ain't know who she was, because all we could get was audio. They went through a lot of extra measures to make sure that we couldn't tell who she was. But today, I wasn't worried about all the drama. Today wasn't about business. I'd made it, and I was proud of myself and sick to my stomach at the same time.

I missed Mia. I'd spent the last couple of months waiting to hear from her. Searching for her. I knew Trouble knew where she was, but he wasn't giving her up. And I wasn't about to ask him. To say that shit between us was tense would be an understatement. There was a mutual respect there, but it was no secret we ain't fuck with one another. As long as no lines were crossed, that shit was fine with me. As long as Kong stayed in order, and our money was straight, all he had to do was supply. That was fine with me. All I wanted that was attached to him was Sa'Mia. But I could find her ass on my own. As a matter of fact, she wouldn't be able to dodge me today. And I had a surprise that would hopefully change her life, and the state of our relationship, forever.

Walking out of the house, I popped the locks on my car and turned to lock my door. Hearing footsteps, I reached into my waistband and pulled my gun, ready to handle whoever was stupid enough to walk up on me. Yeah, I was paranoid, but who wouldn't be with everything that had been going on? Taking it off safety, I took a breath, hoping I ain't have to shoot nobody on my graduation day. When I turned around, I got the shock of my life. *What the hell?* Was all I could think, looking at the woman standing before me.

"Hey there, Arkino. How've you been?" she asked, and I blank stared her like she was crazy.

"What you doin' here, man?" I asked her, waiting for her to say something that made sense.

"You look just like your daddy, you know that?"

"What do you want?" I asked again.

"You graduating today. I had to say I never expected you to make it this far, but when I got the word, I wasn't about to miss it."

"You could've. Like you missed the rest of my life. What do you want, Mama? You ain't never just showed up because you proud of a nigga, or wanted to see a nigga, or hell, to make sure I was still breathing. So, what's your motive today? 'Cause you ain't never gave a damn about my learnin'."

"I know, Arkino. I know, and I'm sorry. You look... so nice," she said, sniffling and wiping her eyes. I wasn't buying that shit, though. There was always something behind her pop-ups. She ain't give a fuck about me as long as her bills were paid and she ain't have to be a parent.

"Mama, I got shit to do. So I'mma ask you one more time. What... do... you... want?"

"I told you I wanna come see you on graduation day. Here, I got you somethin'," she tried to hand me a card that I looked at like it was made of snakes.

"I'm good. Thank you, though. I gotta go, aight."

"How long you gon' be mad at me, Arkino?" she yelled at my back while I moved past her.

"Gimme about eighteen years, when my seed is getting ready to graduate, and I'll see if I can understand how being a parent is so hard that a nigga could be abandoned."

"Oh my goodness, Arkino! I'm about to be a granny?"

"No." I turned and looked in her face to make sure she felt my meaning. "I'm about to be a daddy. But you ain't nobody's grandma. Not no child of mine, no way."

The look on her face was filled with pain, but I wasn't about to deal with her shit. Not on my day. Not when the only parent I ever had wasn't on this earth no more, but her greedy, absentee ass was still breathing. Not when I hadn't seen my woman or my child in months and felt like the worst parent in the world, because I knew I was missing appointments and shit. But this woman was standing in front of me like her missing out on my whole fuckin' childhood was something that could be forgiven with a smile, some fake ass tears, and a greeting card. These bitches blew me. Sa'Mia, too. If she ain't talk to me today, I was gon' have to take other measures to make sure I was allowed around my child. Wasn't nobody gonna make me like the woman who was watching me drive away.

"Aye," I said, rolling the window down and hollering to get her attention. I watched her perk up and wipe the sad look off her face, but that shit was about to be short-lived. "Make sure you get outta my neighborhood the same way you came in this bitch."

Rolling my window back up, I pulled off, not even looking back. Artina Shane was the last woman that I needed in my life, even if I didn't have these problems with Sa'Mia. She wasn't to be trusted, she just ain' know I knew that. NOBODY had spent a year fixing my credit after all of the credit cards and loans and utilities that she took out in my name. I wasn't going to have her around my child so that she could get his name and do the same to him. Not on my watch and over my dead damn body.

"Man, you need to check that bleeding heart of yours, and stop letting folks in my shit," I snapped at the security guard when I was leaving out. I planned to report his ass before I killed him or somebody he let through that damn gate with a sob story. I gave him a look to make sure that he felt me and planned to report his ass when I got back. But right now, I had somewhere important to be. *Damn, I wish King was here,* I thought. Shit just didn't feel right without him in the stands cheering us on. This was gonna be a great day, though. I was claiming the shit. For me, but especially for Sa'Mia. She deserved everything that she had coming. Everything.

Sitting in traffic, I looked over and saw a Maserati. It caught my eye because it was like the one that Mia had a million pictures of between her phone and plastered all around her room. King and I had even gone and looked at one for her before all this shit hit the fan. I wanted to get it for her, but I didn't want to overstep my boundaries. I would wait until we were in a better place and see if she still wanted it. Buying it may remind her of her dad, and I didn't want anything to upset her. *Damn, I missed Sa'Mia,* I thought, still staring at the car. I couldn't see inside because of the tinted windows but thought it even stranger that they were headed the same way that I was. I mean, turned into the parking lot of the school and everything. But while they went to the back, I headed to the front. Something told me to check the shit out, but when I checked the time, I saw that I was running late. *Thanks, Ma.*

Getting out the car, I pulled on my cap and gown, checking myself out in the window of my truck. I looked damn good as a high school graduate. I took a moment and thanked the Most High for making it to see this day, and to be able to close out this chapter in my life before starting a new one as a dad. *Damn, mane, I'm 'bout to be somebody's pops,* I shook my head in disbelief. Not that I wanted to change the shit, but if there was a way that I could, I wouldn't. I was having a child with the woman I'd loved since the first time I'd seen her. I had more money than I could spend in a lifetime. And between the two of us and what King left our child, that lil' nigga's kids would be good.

I smiled proudly at that thought and the fact that I'd broken a curse of poverty and parental abandonment, even if it was through the drug game. But I was gonna follow King's example and raise my seed to be better than me. That's all we could want for our children, that they were better than us. Whether Mia and I were together or not, that was gonna be our mutual goal. If I wasn't sure of anything else, I would bet my life on that shit.

I ran into the school's auditorium, just as everyone was getting ready to line up. I looked around but didn't see Sa'Mia. I didn't see Kong or Trouble, either. I was starting to get disappointed and felt like maybe there was something that had happened that I was out of the loop of. Checking my phone, I saw nothing. Blowing out a breath, I realized that it was possible to feel alone, even when you're surrounded by people. Especially if the people who were there weren't the ones that mattered. The only family I had, the only family I'd known, were the Kings, and not one of them were here, even though they were supposed to be.

We walked into the auditorium to the sound of "Pomp and Circumstance" and took our seat. Waiting for the teachers to come in, I looked around and saw Trouble walk in and take his seat in front of me, but still no Mia and no Kong. When the administration came in, there was a collective gasp from all of us when Sa'Mia and Marissa walked up on the stage hand in hand. *What the hell has been goin' on?* I asked the question in my head that everyone else was asking themselves as we all looked around at each other. When Marissa walked up to the podium, we all quieted down, waiting for our questions to be answered.

KARMA REALLY IS A BITCH

KONG

"Nigga, we 'bout to be paid!" Nick shouted, rubbing his hands together. "You gon' let that nigga have Dallas for real, and take ya money and build ya own team?"

He looked at me like he was uncertain. I had been on the fence about the shit, but I knew that I wasn't strong enough to take Trouble on by myself. Not right now, anyway. I gave Maine the West 'til I came back. Tellin' him I just needed a lil' vacation. He ain't need to know all my moves. Nobody did. Not even Nick. He was rocking with a nigga, but if it was one thing that I learned through all this shit, it was that anybody could be bought or sold, and egos caused more issues than cash flow ever could.

"Yeah, I gotta get my own shit. Prove myself to myself, ya know," I answered him, and he nodded his understanding.

"Where's ya bitch?" he asked, referring to Kymbrea, the nurse who had been taking such good care of me I'd made her mine.

"She gon' meet us at the school," I informed him. She'd said she had a surprise for me, and I ain't gonna lie, I wanted to know what it was.

I checked myself out one last time and got ready to head to this bull-shit ass graduation. That piece of paper was the last thing I needed before my come-up hit. Yeah, it was inheritance, so a nigga wasn't gon' have to get it on the streets like the rest of 'em, but that ain't mean that I wouldn't have to do my due diligence to come back and get what's mine. I wasn't against the running the shit with Trouble, but that nigga had a hard ass heart, and I didn't think he would let that shit happen, even after what King said. He was like King, but not at the same time. So if he wasn't gon' give me what was mine when I came back, I would just take that shit.

Boomp! Boomp! Boomp!

"Who the fuck beatin' on my shit like the cops?" I asked. I wasn't expecting anybody, so I grabbed my piece and nodded toward the door. "Go see who there," I ordered Nick.

"Aight," he said, pulling his gun from his back, heading up the hallway. We looked like some Original Gangstas in our expensive ass suits, guns drawn and shit.

"Kong!" Nick shouted.

"Yeah!" I responded, walking toward the front of my house, once King's house. He'd left it to me in that manila envelope, with a couple of properties in the Hamptons, Las Vegas, and Paris, France. I ain't even know the nigga had it like that.

"It's a graduation gift for you, my nigga!"

That made me put my gun away and walk up to the front fast as hell. As soon as I rounded that corner, though, I regretted it. Turning to try to run, I heard the word every black man feared hearing.

"Freeze!"

Obediently, I stopped moving, mid-stride, with my hands in the air.

"Don't shoot," I stated, and they frisked me and found the gun. The cop snatched my arms down and slapped the cuffs on me.

"Kellen King, you're under arrest for the attempted murder of Marissa Hervey. You have the right to remain silent—" He started reading me my rights, but I zoned out when I turned around, and Nick's ass was standing there with a smirk on his face. When Kymbrea walked up beside him in a police uniform, a nigga was confused and even more pissed than before.

So they was in this shit together? I wonder if Maine knew about this shit. He had to, because he was the one who sent the bitch to me. All they asses gon' have to pay. Wait... did he say, 'attempted murder'? Did she survive? Damn, I'm fucked.

On the way to the police station, I exercised my right to remain silent. If they had something against me, they weren't about to get shit else from me to use against me on the way to that cage. I watched the city of Dallas pass me by, knowing that this was probably the last time I would see it as a free man. In that moment, the graduation that I was saying wasn't a big deal was huge to me. It would've been a milestone in my life. I didn't have nearly enough of those. I wasted my time on the shit that didn't matter. Funny how it took a nigga being about to lose his freedom to think about all the stupid shit that I'd done.

They escorted me into the precinct, and this was the first time in a while that I missed my pops. I never saw that shit coming, but Nick disappearing all hours of the night that I didn't know where he was going should've told me he was up to some foul shit. I thought he was on some Tindr hookup, late night creep shit. That's what the hell I got for assuming. I had to say, though, of all people, I would expect Nick to fuck me over. But Kymbrea's ass was the one that really threw me. I really liked her and thought she liked me. See, this was why I was on my fuck these bitches shit. They wasn't loyal to shit but a big dick and a dollar.

Sitting me in an interrogation room, I wanted to get this over with, but knew that wasn't how these cops worked. So I sat there, looking at my own reflection in what I knew was a two-way mirror. A nigga looked good in a suit with my dreads braided up in a man bun. Kymbrea had just twisted my shit last night. I hoped she was the one that was gon' bring her ass in here. I couldn't put my hands on her, but I was gon' let my mouth loose on her trifling ass. After sitting there for what I knew had to be a couple of hours, I finally laid my head down on the table. Of course, that's when the door opened, and I heard someone come in. I didn't raise my head up immediately, because I wasn't ready to face my fate... or the person who was coming in to let me know what that fate was.

"Kellen," I heard the familiar voice say, and my head popped up from the table. If looks could kill, her ass would be on the floor shaking right now.

"Bitch, you dead. You know that? You're dead!" I hollered at her, spit foaming at the corners of my mouth.

"Threatening an officer of the law is a felony, Kellen. I would advise you to be mindful of your words."

"Bitch, now you a cop. Last night you was a nurse. All I see is a heaux that likes to play dress-up. So fuck you and that shit you talkin'! Get a real cop in here."

"You're a hardheaded one, I see. I thought he was kidding when he told me that, but he had that shit right on the nose."

"He? He who? Not Nick's gay, snitchin' ass. I knew I shouldn't have trusted a nigga who liked dick. It was the equivalent of trustin' a bitch. And obviously, I can't pick bitches, either. Or was it Maine's two-faced ass?" I was so mad that I felt the veins bulging out of my neck.

Kymbrea didn't seem to be bothered. She stood there, a smug look on her face that I wanted to slap off her ass. She was really getting under my skin, and I wasn't with that shit. I had to get a grip. Switch up on her. She pretended to like me, but she pretended too well. I knew that she couldn't have been faking the whole thing.

"Listen, Kellen, I really like you. I just want what's best for you," she offered, finally sitting down, the smile being replaced with a serious look. It was like she was reading my mind, and that shit was creepy. "I had faith in you, but listening to you talk, I knew that you were about to get in over your head. I had to intervene. Trust me, it's for your own good."

She sounded genuine, but she was talking to me like I was her child and not her man. I wanted to speak, but I'd said too much. I wanted to know what she was talking about, who'd sent her to me, and what was for my own good.

"Listen, man, gone and lock me up. I hit the bitch with my car. Aight. I thought she was dead, though. It's whatever. All the shit I done did in my life, I knew I would have to pay sometime. Karma is a bitch with good pussy. 'Cause yo' shit A-1, baby girl."

"Nick is Chica and Tank's cousin. That nigga wanted your head on a platter, and you were about to give it to him. He thinks he's a CI, and that's how we got him to cooperate with me, and how we gon' keep you from doin' football numbers behind these bars," she advised me, and I leaned back and let her talk.

"You still ain't told me who the *we* is. So all this talkin' in circles ain't gettin' us nowhere," I said, sitting up and looking her in the eyes.

"I think it's better for him to tell you," she responded, getting up and walking toward the door.

"You have *got* to be fuckin' wit' me right now. There's no way in the hell, man… No fuckin' way," I spoke in disbelief, just above a whisper.

"I really like you, Kellen. I hope you take this chance to get your shit together, and we can give this a real, honest chance. Everything we been doin' has been to protect you from yourself."

Kymbrea left out of the room, and I watched the man she'd left there walk to the table and take the seat she had been in.

"You need to sit here for a little while, son," Pops said, looking at me like he was disappointed. Like his ass hadn't lied to all of us. Like this shit was ok by any means. "Of all my children, you always were the hardest one to learn your lesson. Maybe seeing what can happen to you if you keep up the shit you been up to will simmer you down a lil' bit."

He got up and walked out, his back turned to me. "Don't turn your back on me! You played me! You played all of us! You—"

"I what? Survived dying at the hands of the nigga you sided with to take over an empire that you didn't earn or deserve. An empire that you would've ran in the ground. That I shed more blood and tears than you will *ever* know about for. All you saw was what you wanted. *All* you saw was power, Kellen."

"You *lied to me! You* ain't even my daddy. My whole life was a lie and you act *surprised* that I acted like I did. Nigga, *you* set all this in motion. You pretend that you're this upstanding nigga, but you lie and shit like the rest of us. Yeen no better than any of us!"

"And that was punishable by death, but you ain't willing to do a lil' time behind bars? Miss me with that shit," King went off, getting on his soapbox. This nigga couldn't be serious. "Everything I did, I did because I loved you. I *raised you* instead of my own son. The child made from the betrayal of my wife and brother. I gave Kellz the same chances that I gave you, and look what that shit got me. From *both of y'all niggas. Ungrateful asses.* Where did I go wrong?"

"Where did you go wrong? Look at me. Look at Mia. Hell, look at Trouble. We're all fucked up because of choices you made. *You!* You know math, right? The common denominator here, my nigga, is you. This is the life you chose, the life you put all of us into, and then you're *surprised* by the way we turned out. Fuck you, man. Fuck… you…"

"I hope that this time to think about your actions will help you take some responsibility. I beat myself up about y'all and all the bad that happened to y'all. I beat myself up about every moment I wasn't there. About what I might have done to push Kellz and Dani together. My guilt started before you were even made, Kong. But your selfish ass don't see that. You don't see the sacrifices that I made in *my life* to make this life for y'all. And you never will. You never will."

Grabbing the door, he snatched it open and walked out, leaving me in there alone. I looked at the door that Alonzo King had just stormed out of and felt more betrayed than I ever had in my life. He looked at me like I had let him down, when he was the one who let me down. He took care of me to prove that he was a bigger man than the ones that had done him wrong. But I never felt like I was his. Even now. He hadn't made Sa'Mia's ass sit in jail. Or Trouble. No. He sent that white ass lawyer of his to get them out of there.

I heard what he was saying, but he had just been on some kumbaya shit, and now I needed to be caged? Just me? These niggas were about to fuck around and bring out the *beast* in me. A beast that they hadn't seen. One that I didn't know was lurking but could feel awakening. And he was thirsty for revenge.

"You really should think about what he said, Kellen," Kymbrea said, coming back into the room. I hadn't heard the door open the anger was ringing in my ears so loud. I didn't respond to her ass, either. In my eyes, she was the enemy. All of them were.

I would do my time. Ain't shit else to do when you locked up but think. But I wasn't about to think on the shit they wanted me to. I planned to plot on some shit, and I had plenty niggas to plot on. Alonzo King would be the first on my fuckin' list.

LET'S FUCK SOME SHIT UP!

MIA

"You ready to do this, Mia?" Marissa asked me, holding my hand.

She'd been there for me this entire time. She never missed a check-up or appointment with the baby, and we'd had what felt like a million of them because I was high risk. I wished that Maine could've been there, but I wasn't ready to see him yet. I needed to make sure what I wanted to do. I couldn't let seeing him and my love for him, or us having a child together, cloud my judgment.

"I don't think I'll ever be ready, but I don't have much of a choice, huh?" I asked honestly.

"Nope. Not at all. And before you ask, yes Maine is out there."

"I expected him to be," I said, getting nervous all over again. Trouble had done the best that he could to protect me, but I knew I would have to talk to Maine eventually. I'd had two months to get my head together, but now, I wasn't sure what I was gonna say to him when he approached me. And he was gonna approach me, I knew that much for sure. I think what worried me more than anything else, was whether or not he was gonna be on his angry black nigga shit, or his begging for forgiveness moves. And I didn't know how I would respond to either one.

"It's time to go," Marissa told me when the rest of the administration stood by the doors of the room we were sitting in. I was Valedictorian, so I was with them and would be sitting on the stage instead of with my classmates.

Grabbing her hand, she squeezed it to give me the reassurance that I needed, and we went to the end of the line, ready for our processional. Walking out, I saw Trouble first, and he winked at me, settling some of the nervousness that was dancing around in my stomach. I would've loved to be able to blame that on the baby, but it was too soon for that. Too soon to find out what the gender was, too. Even though that was one thing that I wouldn't have done without Maine, whether I loved his ass to death or hated his ass to death. That just wouldn't have felt right to me. I kinda hoped we could get it sorted out before that time came.

All eyes were on the stage, but they weren't on me. The loud sounds of surprise were definitely for the woman walking beside me. The woman who had been taken out of our prom in handcuffs. The prom that was held in this same auditorium. She had been reinstated but had foregone the position. All she asked was that she be allowed to say her goodbyes to our graduating class. We were her "babies," and she wouldn't have felt right just leaving.

"Welcome, graduating class of 2018. I can tell by the looks on your faces that I'm the last person y'all expected to step onto this stage. I have to say that I didn't expect to be here, either. But, I didn't think some of y'all would make it to graduation. So the day is just full of surprises, huh?" she joked, and everyone laughed. Hell, there were some people that I ain't expect to graduate that were sitting there, so she was right. "Today marks a day of new beginnings for all of us. Parents, you've done your due diligence, and now it's time to send the children that you cried over, went broke for, and prayed over more times than they will ever know out into the world. Honestly, I'm both excited and fearful for the world and don't think it's ready."

The auditorium erupted in laughter again, and hearing Marissa speak and face down all the faces, judgmental eyes, and thoughts with no fear helped me to calm down. She was so strong, and I would never understand how she'd birthed and raised a daughter like Ray'Neisha. But then, she was half Kellz's, so I could understand partially. But, if I'd had a mom like her, I had to think that I would've turned out differently. Not that I was complaining about the way I turned out or no shit. Just thinking back over my life. Graduation tended to do that to you. I felt eyes on me and saw Maine staring at me. I tried to look away, but I couldn't. Our eyes held a whole conversation that neither of us was prepared to have with each other just yet. Feeling my eyes fill with tears, I blinked them away, using that as an excuse to break eye contact with Maine. Coming out of my own thoughts, I tuned back into Marissa's speech.

"We all have our whole futures ahead of us. Some of us will stay here, while others will embark on their own journeys. I have so much faith in all of y'all and can't wait to read about you in journals, the news, and Alumni mailers. One person that I am especially proud of, whom I have watched grow into her own woman will give you all words of encouragement before we give you your walking papers and send you out into the world to cause all kind of problems." She paused, allowing everyone else to laugh at her very real joke. "Please help me to welcome the 2018 Lincoln High School & Humanities/Communications Magnet Valedictorian Sa'Mia De'Shay King."

Everyone cheered as I stood up. That was a warmer reception than I expected. Maybe everybody was excited. My speech got us that much closer to getting out of this damn ceremony and to the parties, dinners, and other celebrations that were going on tonight. Making my way to the podium, Marissa wrapped me up in a hug.

"You got this," she whispered in my ear before letting me go and taking her seat. Taking a deep breath, I cleared my throat.

"You can't keep a good bitch down. That's word," I started my graduation speech. I knew that this wasn't what they expected when they asked me to speak, but hell, this was graduation, so who was gon' check me.

"Whoooooooo!"

"Yeahhhhhhhh!"

"That's right, girl!"

My classmates cheered, making me smile. I knew they would feel me, even though I knew the teachers behind me were cringing. I rested my hand on my swelling belly and took a deep breath. It was time to speak my truth.

"Most of y'all know me because of who my daddy is… was. Alonzo King was a lot of things, but more than anything, he was a great role model. Now, those of y'all who *knoooow*, know that calling him a role model is kinda strange. But while he did what he do, he was showing me that there was more to life than what was right in front of us. See, our generation wants everything fast. And why shouldn't we? Everything is at our fingertips with little to no effort, right?" I looked around at the head nods before continuing. "But my daddy was old school. He made me work for everything. I mean, I'm Valedictorian right now because I had to make all A's in order to get this Maserati I wanted. I know that seems like first world problems to you, but it's no different from you wanting your parents to give you something that you really want, and they make you work to earn it. It sucks, but they know what they're doin'. At least, I hope they do. We'll see at the ten-year reunion," I said, laughing at my own joke and them joining in. "I won't let my daddy down, and I hope that y'all will join me in my promise to show them that their hard work wasn't for nothing. So, Class of 2018, let's step out into this world and fuck some shit up!"

Everyone stood to their feet, cheering loudly. I hoped that my speech motivated them to be as different as writing it had made me. I rested my hand on my stomach and did the Beyoncé belly bump reveal, making them cheer louder. I smiled, looking at Maine and felt so much love for him. I hoped that we could work this shit out. We'd been through so much in such a short time. I knew he loved me, but I also knew he was still in the game. I didn't know if I could deal with sitting up with a baby every night, hoping he would make it home to us alive. I didn't want any parts of the dope game. I just wanted to have my family and the life Daddy was never able to have. I wanted to go to college and get a degree in English. Mama was a writer, and she'd passed that down to me. Daddy had left me his Marketing Firm, and I planned to take that shit to the next level, like Trouble planned to take the drug empire. That was #Goals for me. And if Maine wasn't onboard, we'd be some co-parenting asses.

When Marissa got up and started to call names to hand out diplomas, I got a text. *Noooooo, this shit ain't happening!* I thought, hoping that this wasn't some kinda joke, or a setup. I wasn't in the mood to be kidnapped today.

SURPRIIIIIIISE!

KING

*M*e: *Miss King, this is Martin from Park Place Maserati. I have a gift that was delivered here for you for graduation.*

Mia: *A gift?*

Me: **MMS Message* Yes ma'am. It's in the parking lot. Section G. Space 36. The code is 0415*

Mia: *Ummm ok.*

I sat back and thought about how close I came to missing this big day. I never wanted to come that close to death again. The way that shit played out was insane, though. And I was glad I was still alive to tell my story and survive to attend my daughter's graduation. In the flesh.

Her speech had made me so proud, and I snuck out when they were close to the last of the names on the list. I had to say seeing Marissa was a surprise, but I meant it when I said I wanted her and Nate to be together. I wasn't tryna be tied down to anyone or anything. I'd got my kids grown, it was time for me to do a little travelling.

I smiled and waited for Mia to come out. I figured she was gonna be upset with me for faking my death but seeing the look on her face would make it all worth it. I knew she would be skeptical, so I made sure to send her a pic of the car that she'd sent me a million pictures of in the last six months, including the spot that I had just texted her about in the picture.

When she rounded the corner to the more isolated portion of the parking lot, she had her 9mm drawn with her finger on the trigger. *That's my girl. Protecting herself by any means.* The shock that registered on her face was all I needed to let me know that coming out of hiding wasn't a mistake. Her not lowering her gun or taking her finger off the trigger made me laugh, though, because she stayed ready.

"Daddy?" Mia asked in disbelief as I leaned up against the Maserati I had promised her if she kept her grades up. It was her graduation gift now.

"In the flesh," I said with a smile, my arms outstretched for a long-overdue hug.

"Wait. But… it can't be. You can't—you're dead. Maine said so," she cried, running into my arms and burying her face in my chest. Her warm tears were ruining my silk shirt, but it was worth it.

I pulled her away and looked her over. She was glowing, and there was no way she could hide that baby bump if she wanted to.

"Look at youuuuu. Soon you're gonna be trading this Maserati in for a minivan," I teased, and she sucked her teeth.

"Nah hell. This baby gon' be in the garage for when mommy needs to get away and let her hair down."

I laughed. That was my Mia. I missed her so much. But I knew that time was winding down, so I had to get to the point and get gone. At least for now.

"Listen, baby girl, I need a favor. Can you get Trouble and Maine in the same place for the graduation dinner?"

"Mannnn, that's a lot to ask, but I can try. What's up?"

"You'll see. That number I texted you from is my new number. Let me know where y'all are gonna be."

"I'll see what I can do, but them niggas hate each other. I wish you coulda seen how they were lookin' at each other at the reading of the will. Speaking of, that was real fucked up, Daddy. Had us all thinking you were dead and shit. I mean, I get it. But still." She pouted. I felt bad. Even though I felt like that was the best course of action, it didn't take away from the fact that it had caused my children more pain.

This life, the life I'd gotten into to make things easier for them, had caused so much chaos. And it was time for me to fix that. All of it.

"Just get them there, Mia," I said, hugging her again. "Please?"

"I'll try my best. What if they give me pushback?" she asked, pulling back and looking in my face like she was searching for the answer.

"Use your—*mmm mmmmmmmm*—special charm." I laughed. "I got you some backup on the inside. Mama Pearlie. She can handle Trouble if need be. You, you focus on Maine."

She nodded with tears in her eyes, and I leaned down to kiss her on the cheek. "Were you inside? Did you hear my speech?" she asked.

"You know I wouldn't miss any of that for the world, baby girl!" I told her, and she looked surprised. "Yeah, I know about all that. Your old man still plugged in," I said with a laugh. "I'm so proud of the woman you're becoming, Sa'Mia."

The tears streamed down her face and she gave me another tight hug. I wasn't ready to let her go, but I had a big dinner planned for her that Pearlie had helped me plan. Yeah, she knew that I was still alive. I'd been hiding out at her house. Smiling, I got in the car that I'd called to pick me up. This was the day I'd been waiting for since Danielle had told me she was pregnant. I had to make sure that the ties between my kids were tight. The most important one being between Trouble and Maine. Once that rift was repaired, I could leave the rest to them and officially retire. And then I would take a much-needed, much deserved vacation.

DINNER & A SHOW

KING

Two hours later, I was sitting in the private section I'd paid for at P.F. Chang's, waiting for everyone to arrive. It was decorated beautifully with balloons and streamers, and I'd ordered everything on the menu to be set out on the table buffet-style when we were ready.

I was nervous, and that was so unlike me. But I didn't know how everyone was going to react to my being alive. I was sure that after the shock wore off, things would be cool. But before that, though, they were gon' be mad, and I was sure they were going to let me know just how they felt about it.

"Mr. King... Mr. King," the hostess said, laying her hand on my shoulder gently to get my attention.

"I'm sorry. What's up?"

"Your party is here. They're in the lobby waiting to be seated like you requested," she said with a smile, loving being a part of this "secret plan".

"All of them?" I asked, making sure everyone was there.

"Yes sir. Party of fourteen. Thirteen plus you," she confirmed.

"Thank you, Monica," I said with a smile, rising from my seat and pulling five hundred-dollar bills from the money in my pocket. I knew she didn't need as much, but I was feeling generous today. *It's a celebration, bitches!* Taking the money, she scurried off toward the front of the restaurant to execute the next part of the "plan".

Getting up and heading to the kitchen, where I'd paid the manager to let me hide out, I watched my family be seated. There were so many stares and glares between everyone at the table that it broke my heart. I was glad that I had survived long enough to fix this shit, once and for all.

I watched the servers go around and take their drink orders, and there was very little conversation going on. I could feel the tension from where I was, so I knew they felt it. Mia kept looking at the empty seat at the head of the table, and I saw Trouble point to it and ask the server a question. I figured he was asking who they were waiting for. The look of frustration on his face made it evident that she didn't tell him what he wanted to know. Maine was staring across the table at Mia, and she was dodging eye contact. And Trouble alternated between talking to his brothers and my homies, but he was ignoring Pearlie, and there was something going on between him and Luther.

"We're ready to take the cake out," the server Olivia walked up and informed me. That was my signal to get ready to walk out.

They wheeled out the three-tier cake that I'd had made for them. One tier was New York Cheesecake, Sa'Mia's favorite, one was marble cake, Tywan's favorite, and one was peanut butter chocolate swirl, Maine's favorite. Each had their names and a special message written for them on it. They took turns reading the message and all sat back down, deep in thought. That was my cue.

"What the hell is wrong with y'all's faces? I thought this was a party! Hell, I got a lot to celebrate! Life! Health! Y'all asses being grown witcha own money and 'bout to get the fuck up out my pockets!"

"Holy shit!" I heard Trouble say, looking like his eyes were playing tricks on him. He stood up and walked up to me, a mug on his face like he was about to hit me.

"Tywan," Tatiana called to him, standing from her seat and placing her hand on his shoulder. He let out a breath, and I had to say I was impressed. I'd never seen him let a woman close to him, and she was close enough to calm him. I hoped that whatever they had going on lasted, because he needed that kind of balance to make it out here. His expression softened, and a smile came across his lips, the shimmer from his top and bottom grills blinding me momentarily.

"Pops. Mannnnnn. A nigga is happy as *fuck* to see you!" He turned and looked around at everyone at the table. "Who knew?"

No one responded, and I knew no one would. My not being dead was a secret, and the ones I trusted to keep it would never tell that they knew. I walked to the head of the table with Maine eyeing me and Mia's smile broader than I'd seen it in a long time. She had her hand resting on her swelling belly, and I was filled with pride. Most dads would be mad as hell that they'd gotten their child all the way through high school and they came up pregnant. But in my eyes, this child was what Mia needed to get her head on straight. And I couldn't have chosen a better man for her to have a baby with. If nothing else, I knew that Mia and that baby were going to be loved and spoiled, and not just by me.

"I know this comes as a surprise. And if y'all are upset, I completely understand." I spoke honestly, looking at Trouble and Mia who were visibly happy to see me, then at Maine, who I couldn't read.

"Mane, I can't believe... I just... thank God!" Maine finally spoke and I saw tears in his eyes. I knew something was bothering him, but I couldn't tell if it was my coming back from the dead or something else.

"Arkino, I love you like a son. Always have. And I wanna let you know that I'm grateful for you and your loyalty. You never questioned anything and even respected my wishes regarding Sa'Mia. You're a good man, and I'm glad to have you as a part of this family," I told him sincerely. "I—"

"Before you say anything else. Thank you for raising me to be the man that I am and taking me under your wing. A nigga don't know where he'd be if it wasn't for you. And with the mention of family, there's something I need to say... and do."

Standing up, Maine walked around the table to Mia, who was looking at him like he was insane. She appeared nervous, uncertain of what he was about to say or do. I hadn't gotten all the details on what had been going on with the two of them. But with her being at Nate's, I had to leave there to keep my secret, so I knew things had taken a turn for the worst in their relationship.

"Sa'Mia De'Shay King, I've loved you since you threatened to bust me in the head with a bat. You're crazier than any bitc—woman that I've ever encountered in my life. But I wouldn't change a damn thing about you. Not a damn thing. Now, I wanna do this shit properly. But I ain't think I'd have the chance."

Looking at me, Maine stuck his chest out and all I could do was lean back in my seat and observe him. He had become a grown man right under my nose, and I had a feeling he was about to make a grown man move.

"King, Alonzo, I would be honored to have your daughter's hand in marriage. If she'll have me," he said, looking at Mia, and I caught her roll her eyes. Shaking his head, he turned his attention back to me. "I mean, I know a nigga did the shit backwards as hell, knockin' her up and all first, but I ain't never done shit the way they say it's supposed to be done."

Everyone at the table chuckled, and I stood up and walked over to him. Looking him in the eyes, he didn't flinch or break contact, just like he'd done when he came to me asking me to be put on. He was solid, and I was the one who would be honored to have him as a son-in-law. But I had to make him sweat a little.

"Mia, you interested in marrying this lil' nigga?" I asked teasingly, never breaking eye contact with Maine.

"I—"

"I object to this shit!" Trouble spoke up, jumping up from his seat.

Everyone at the table laughed, except for Pearlie and Luther. They looked at each other and at Trouble, reminding me that I had to find out what the hell was going on there.

"Nigga, sitcho dumb ass down. You object to the marriage at the wedding, not during the engagement. The hell wrong with you?" Eli asked, making everybody laugh even harder.

"Nah, they ain't gon' get that far. I ain't letting my sister marry this flaw ass nigga!" Trouble continued with his objection.

"It's not your decision to make." Luther spoke up, with more bass in his voice than I'd heard in a while.

"And this is *family business*. That means it ain't got shit to do wit' yo' ass. Just because you done took Mama out on a couple dates don't mean you got no stake here, patna. Know your role, play ya muhfuckin' part, and stay in ya lane."

"Lil' nigga, you 'bout to make me put my Bible down and show ya ass what a real OG capable of," Luther barked.

"Yeen said shit but a word, my—"

"Enough! Tywan, you're making a fool out of yourself. Just 'cause you wanna be lonely and bitter don't mean nobody deserves love. I hate the way ya mama hardened your heart, but that shows that you more like her than you know. Sit down. This ain't got shit to do with you, just like me and Luther ain't got shit to do with you. It's *you* who needs to play ya part and stay in ya lane." Pearlie checked him, mocking him with her last statement.

"Mannnnn, fuck this!" Trouble said, pushing his chair back so he had more space to walk away. It clattered to the floor and I blew out a breath. I knew shit was gonna get hectic, but I never knew that it would happen so fast. *Pearlie and Luther? Stella done got her groove back*, I thought with a laugh, even though this was no laughing matter.

"Sit! Down!"

A voice squeaked above all the chaos, and all eyes landed on Tatiana. Trouble froze and looked at her like she had lost her mind. I hadn't heard her speak in all the time that she'd been working for me.

"I have watched you go through hell. I have heard you crying in your sleep, calling for your mama, a woman who was never there for you. I have watched you push against everything and everyone that loved you. But today, you *will* respect all these people who put their lives on the line for you. Everything that's been done has been done for y'all. I wish I had someone who was willing to do that for me. Y'all are the most spoiled, ungrateful, entitled group of black men, and woman," she said, looking at Mia who met her look with one that said she'd smack the hell outta her. "That I have ever met in my life."

Tatiana didn't cower like most people would under Mia's threatening stare. Mia didn't put fear in her heart, at all. But I wasn't gonna let them get to the point where it escalated to them seeing who was badder, either. Maine was nodding his head in agreement, but I looked at him to let him know that he wasn't too far from spoiled his damn self.

"Geez. Y'all thought this man was dead. Show some respect for what he did for y'all before y'all were even born. What he's doing for y'all *right now*, and what he's gonna be doin' for y'all 'til the day he *really* takes his last breath."

She said nothing else, and the room fell silent. I was glad that we had a secluded space, because this was getting way out of hand. You could hear the thoughts and feel the aggression with each breath.

"Listen, I know that my actions caused some confusion, but NOBODY —I mean Tatiana is right. Y'all act out way too much. Y'all making me wanna leave y'all to fend for yourselves and see that the world don't give a fuck about none of y'all. Ya name don't mean shit without the work to go behind it. Tywan, of all of my children, you should know this the best. Still, you up in here making dumb ass moves based off emotions."

"You left me, man. You don't get to tell me how to act, what to feel, when you fuckin' left me... *twice!*" he yelled, and for the first time, I saw the pain that I'd caused him.

"He didn't leave you. Danielle left you. He did the best he could for you." Doe corrected him, his jaw getting rigid. "Get the fuck over yourself, nigga, and get your priorities straight. Ghatdamnit. What me and E worked for, all we ever wanted, you got that shit. A family. They ain't perfect, but they yours. Spoiled ass nigga, I ought to beat yo' simple ass up in these folk's fine establishment."

With every word, he walked up on Trouble, who squared up, ready to fight.

"Stand down, lil' nigga," Eli threatened from behind him. "We proud of you and shit, but this the real world now. Chillax before you get ya ass embarrassed."

"I ain't the same lil' nigga y'all used to have runnin' behind y'all like a fuckin' lap dog," Trouble threatened, stepping back so that both of them were in his view.

"Stand down, man," Hill and Juke said at the same time, getting up from their seats. Trouble wasn't moved. I knew and he knew that he couldn't take all of them—all of us. But his stubborn ass was willing to tear up this room trying to.

Nixon and Nate, who had been quiet this whole time, just shook their heads. They never really wanted any parts of the empire, but their loyalty to me had kept them in the middle of my shit for decades now. I knew that they could see me in my kids, but that they could also see Danielle, and that was the part that they hated the most. They'd never liked her, for me, or at all. But today was making them despise her even more.

Pearlie and Luther were holding hands, with their heads bowed, deep in prayer. I knew they were praying for all of our souls right now. And I had to say that we all needed it. At this point, I didn't know if any of us would make it out of this alive, and without being in handcuffs.

For the first time since I'd entered the space, Marissa and I met eyes. She looked to be in shock that I was still alive, and I could tell that she was torn between being happy that I was here and pissed that she had been left out of the loop. But this wasn't something that I wanted her involved in. I had to say she looked good as hell. I was glad that Kong didn't kill her, but I would admit that him hitting her was the main reason that I had to get his ass locked down. Even though I'd said that I was ok with her and Nate being together, looking at her now, I knew I couldn't let her go.

"Everything OK in here? Are you ready for your appetizers?" Olivia came in and asked nervously.

I wondered whether she'd lost a game of Rock, Paper, Scissors to be the one that was sent in here to check on us. *Poor girl,* I thought, sure we were putting on a hell of a show.

DAFUQ IS GOIN' ON?

MIA

"Yes, we're fine. Give us about twenty minutes, and we'll be ready for the appetizers," I spoke, rubbing my stomach, a habit that I had picked up to calm myself.

The waitress nodded and damn near ran out of the way. I couldn't blame her. My family was a bunch of trigger-happy, hotheaded asses, and I used to be one of them. Yep, used to be. I had to say that Maine shocked me with his marriage talk, and I was so stunned that I was speechless. Something that was new for me. But before I could respond, Trouble pulled a me and threw a whole bitch fit. Now, he was seconds from getting his ass beat, and I couldn't handle that. Worse, I couldn't let that happen. He was being a dumb ass, but that was still my twin brother, and he wasn't about to be in here fighting by himself.

"Listen, I was getting proposed to. Or auctioned off to the highest bidder." I cut my eyes at Daddy, letting him know that I didn't appreciate being put in the hot seat. "Trouble, you killin' my vibe and shit."

"Mia—"

"Naw, ain't no Mia nothin'! This is about me! Me! I get it. You wanna protect me. But you should take note from somebody else who tried to protect me." I looked from him to Daddy again. "This is *my dinner, too.* And as much as I don't know how I feel about it right now, marrying him... or *not marrying him*," I emphasized, looking at Maine so that he knew that I was undecided about it, "is my decision. Not yours. And regardless of what I decide, he's the father of my child."

There was a long silence, and I held my breath, hoping that I had managed to talk some sense into my brother. Trouble and I had grown close. Close enough that I would've laid down my life for him. Close enough that I had. But he was going to give me the same respect that I gave him, or he could get the hell on out my life, just like anyone else who wanted to be heavy-handed and in my damn business. Family or not.

"Well fuck you, Mia! Don't call a nigga the next time he fucks up," Trouble snapped, storming out of the private room and the restaurant. His words were like a slap in the face. They stung just that bad.

Daddy, Eli, and Doe exchanged frustrated and confused looks, then all started to follow him. I guess they were gonna try to talk—or beat—some sense into his stupid ass, but I was over him at this point. He wasn't about to ruin this day for me. Any other time, I may have tried to chase him and begged him to see reason. But not today. Or any other day after today, for that matter. Everybody wanting to run this whole grown ass nigga down pissed me off. He was really about to let his ego ruin shit for us. Even Mama Pearlie got up, but her man grabbed her hand and looked at her with an expression that made her sit back down.

"Nope. Nope-ty nope-nope-nope," Tatiana said to the men, grabbing her purse and rising to her feet. "Y'all enjoy your dinner. I got him."

Everyone looked at each other like they were deciding if that was a good idea. She didn't wait for them to make that decision, sprinting out of the restaurant behind Trouble's selfish ass.

I rolled my eyes and closed them for a few seconds, so that the tears wouldn't escape. I hated being pregnant and how emotional it made me. I felt a hand on my back and opened my eyes to Marissa rubbing up and down comfortingly. I plopped down into my seat, biting my bottom lip so hard it hurt.

"Hey, Zo! That boy that left up outta here... That's Danielle King's son, brutha," Nate said, and every one of the other men there laughed and nodded their heads.

"Mannnn, don't I know it," Daddy agreed, chuckling with a sadness in his face that made my heart ache. I never had the pleasure of meeting my mama in real life, but the more I heard about her, the less I liked her, and the happier I was that I was spared that trauma. Lord knows I had enough of my own between Daddy, Kong, Maine—and now Trouble.

"At least one of your kids got some sense," Nate added, nodding his head at me.

Now, that made me smile. In the two months that I'd been hiding out at his house, he'd told me about Mama and Daddy, about Kellz, and that had helped me learn so much about myself. He was smart, loyal, funny, and showed me that there was more to life than the streets. He and Marissa had even helped me come to terms with everything that I'd been through, and with their help, I'd been able to find *me*. Not Alonzo King's daughter. Not Tywan Nobles' or Kellen King's sister. Not Danielle King's daughter. Not even Arkino Shane's girlfriend or baby mama. But the real me. I would be eternally grateful to them.

"Now, before I was interrupted, I was tryna make this woman my wife," Maine spoke up. I had forgotten that he was standing there. When I shifted my body toward him, he got on his knee and pulled out a ring box that had Jared's on the outside in gold lettering. "If I have your blessing," he asked Daddy who nodded his head with a big smile on his face. "Sa'Mia De'Shay King, will you—"

"Listen, Arkino," I said, resting my hand on top of his, stopping him from opening the box. "I'm not saying no, but I'm not saying yes, either. I guess I'm saying not right now," I inflected because I wasn't sure if that was even what I meant. "I feel like we need some time, without all this bullshit going on, to get to know each other and see if this can really work. I love you, I do. But love ain't enough of a reason to spend the rest of your life with somebody. So, hold onto that. We got some time. Let's take a break from everything and date. Chill. Let me see the you that ain't under my daddy's watchful eye. The you that ain't fuckin' bitches to keep an eye on them. The you that I would be with for the rest of my life. Okay?"

Standing up, Maine looked hurt, but I could tell he understood where I was coming from. That was a relief. I wasn't trying to reject him, but I couldn't make a rash decision like this. Not because we were in a room full of people. Not because I loved him more than I loved my own breath. Not because I was carrying his child. I wanted to be sure. And I was gonna take as long as I needed to make that choice. He would either stick around until I made my decision, or he wouldn't. I had to worry about me and my child. I couldn't worry about him like that. Love or no love.

The fact that he was willing to take this step showed me that he was, at least, serious about us now. But I had a lot to forgive him for—a lot to forgive myself for—before we could make a move like this. Because when I said 'til death do us part, I meant that shit. And I would kill a nigga before I let him part from me.

So before I committed myself to him, I had to make sure he wasn't gon' make a bitch catch a charge. And with his track record, that shit ain't look too promising right now, just being honest.

The look of awe on everyone's faces let me know that either they were surprised that I said no to the one thing that most women want and wait for all their lives, or that they were proud of me. Daddy confirmed it, though, with a big 'that's my girl' smile on his handsome face. That was all the confirmation that I needed.

"Since we're all going balls to the wall, I have something that I wanna say," Daddy said, looking in Nate's direction. "Nate, I know that I said in my video that I wanted you and Rissa to give it a try. But in the time that I've been away, I've realized how much I love her," he said nervously, rubbing his hand over his bald head. Nate held his hand up and they shared a silent conversation that only their minds were privy to. I could tell they had been friends a long time, because they *just knew*. I longed for a friendship like that but feared that I would never have one with the way my "friends" had done me. "Thank you, brutha. Thank you so much."

Daddy got up and walked over to Marissa, taking her hand into his. He looked at her like Maine looked at me, and that made me reconsider my answer to his proposal. Then, I came to my senses.

"I bought this before I came back here. I didn't know what to expect, but I know that life's too short to be wasting time. Hell, we both done lived enough life, fucked up enough times, and lately almost lost our lives enough times, to know that we have to value what you got right in front of you." Daddy pulled out a box from Tiffany & Co. and sat it on the table.

"What... is... happening..." Marissa asked, tears streaming down her cheeks.

"You took care of my kids when I couldn't. You even seemed to be able to talk some sense into Sa'Mia," he said, giving me a wink. "I'm old, and my knees ain't like they used to be, so I hope you don't get too mad if I don't get my old ass down there on the floor."

"You better not, 'cause I ain't gonna pick ya ass up," Nate joked, and the other men at the table nodded, chuckled, and mumbled their agreement.

"Fuck y'all," Daddy barked, but all that did was make everybody laugh, even me and Maine. I looked at him and knew that we could have a forever kinda love. But I needed to be sure. And right now, I wasn't.

"Alonzo, gone and ask that girl to marry you so we can eat," Mama Pearlie fussed, speaking for all of us.

"Well, you heard the lady. Will you marry me, Marissa Hervey?"

Marissa stood there frozen, and all of us were confused as hell. We would've thought she would've jumped in his arms like the bitches on TV all excited and shit. But she wasn't moving or blinking. It didn't seem like she was breathing.

"Please?" Daddy added.

"Yes!" she yelled, jumping up and down while he put the ring on her finger. It was like somebody had hit the play button after pausing and muting her ass. We all clapped, and I had to say that I ain't like her ass to begin with, but she was definitely somebody I knew would take care of and do right by my daddy for the rest of his life. And if she didn't, I'd make sure her ass didn't get to enjoy the rest of hers.

Caught up in the romantic atmosphere, the man who was sitting beside the woman Trouble called Mama Pearlie stood up and started to get down on one knee.

"Pearlie Jean, I have loved you for longer than I think you knew. I wanna make an honest woman outta you in the eyes of our good Lord. Will you marry me?"

There was a pause, and she had a look on her face like she was trying to see if he was serious. When she saw that he was, she grunted, leaning forward and cupping his face into her right hand.

"Luther," she said, patting his hand that rested on her thigh with her left hand. "We been sinning a long time. And I'm 'bout sure that there are some other sins on our books that'll send us to hell long before what you talkin' about with this honest woman mess. You my husband in my heart, and I'm your wife in yours. But I'm old, and I ain't tryna do nothing but enjoy these last few good years I got on this earth."

Luther's face was unreadable. Everybody was looking from them to each other, and it was kinda sad but funny at the same time. I'm a bitch; I know. But it looked like that shit about women wanting to be wifed was being disproven, right here in this room. 'Cause for the one that said yes, the no's were at two. So much for that Disney bullshit. But ain't too many happily ever after's in our world anyway.

"We got a good thing goin'. Let's not ruin it with marriage, okay?" she asked, and he stood up. Everybody stared at him, waiting on his response. Surprisingly, he laughed, standing up. I was holding my breath, because I didn't know how he was gon' take her rejection, but their relationship was dope as hell in my book.

"Mama Pearlie shot the hell out, man," Trouble's brother Eli laughed, stuffing his face with bread, as ready to beast on the buffet as I was.

"Now, it's a celebration," Daddy said, clapping his hands and laughing so hard he had tears in his eyes before kissing Marissa. I couldn't agree more.

"So, Daddy, who are ya friends?" I asked him, motioning with my hands toward the men at the table that I didn't know, and even Mama Pearlie, wanting a formal introduction.

JUST CALL ME MOE

TROUBLE

"Tywan, are you serious right now?" Tatiana asked me. I was standing beside her Prius, waiting for her. I knew she would come out and try to talk some sense into me.

"As a fuckin' heart attack," I said, meaning every word. I kept looking over her shoulder, waiting for someone else to come out after me, but no one did.

"They're not coming. You shouldn't be acting like this. What's your dealie, yo?"

See the way she talked was cute sometimes, tolerable in others. But right now, the shit was lame and just damn annoying. And I wasn't about to stand out in the parking lot of this restaurant discussing the shit with her.

"You gon' take me home or not?"

"I should make you walk, but you need to tell me what's eating you." She huffed, popping the locks to her car with the key fob. "So because I like you, you're getting an escort home. But you better start chitty-chat-chatting before we get on the freeway, or you're getting out, and I'll make sure no Uber, Lyft, or none of that shit will be able to locate you."

I knew she was mad as hell, because she almost never cussed. I got in the car and reached for the knob of her radio. *Pop!* She hit the back of my hand like she was my damn mama or some shit, and I almost popped her ass back, but didn't.

"Tati, it's complicated. I don't even know where to start," I told her honestly because I couldn't tell her why I was as mad as I was. I just knew that I was pissed.

"Start at the beginning, Troubie. You almost started a war back there. You were acting just like Kong, and that's not you. You're not selfish and short-sighted. Hardheaded, stubborn, mean as a cobra, yes. But not selfish and short-sighted."

"All this shit started because my mama was an addict and my uncle was a fuck nigga. My whole life, everything was based on decisions that were made that I had no say so in. I ain't letting that shit happen no more. And I won't just sit there and watch some bullshit go down, neither. I thought my pops was dead for months, man. *Months*!" I punched the dashboard so hard, I felt my bone crack.

"So now we're about to be spending time in the ER, huh?" Tatiana asked, shaking her head and taking the exit toward the hospital. "I hope they sedate you, because you're being really animally right now."

"Animally?" I asked, laughing and holding my hand feeling like the dumb ass that she sounded like with that made-up ass word.

"Yes. Primal. Like you were raised in the wild. Like you don't have a loving family that you turned on because of a past that has nothing to do with the present. Your mother was a fuck-up. I get it. So was mine. Your father left you, mine, too. But at least yours left you in the care of a loving household."

"So were Kong and Mia, but they grew up with King. Kong's ass ain't even his seed, and he got an opportunity that I ain't get. I had to come *looking* for my pops. I had to find out that I had a twin. And then I had to watch a nigga do her dirty as fuck, fuckin' other bitches, then knock her up and propose? Kong wasn't no kinda brother to Mia, but I woulda been. That chance was stole from me. But fuck it if they thought I was gon' let the nigga she'd just been crying over for the million and first fuckin' time since I've known them ask her to marry him and sit there with my mouth shut like that that shit was okay."

"Regardless of how you feel, Tywan, it's not your choice to make. If your sister said yes and came back and cried on your shoulder about

Maine a million more times, all you can do as her brother is be there for her. You can't live her life for her. You think you had it bad? Imagine being Mia. Even *now*, somebody is trying to make decisions for her. Let her live. Just like you're trying to."

I knew she meant well, but I didn't wanna hear it right now. This was about me. She asked me about me, so I didn't need her tryna teach me some valuable life lesson. I'd had enough people in my damn life always talking over my head and treating me like they had to "teach me about life" and not let me live that shit. Regardless of what they said now, I was gon' do shit my way. I was far from a dumb nigga, and it was time that people saw and respected that.

"Fuck that shit you talkin', man!" *Sssssss*. The pain in my hand was kicking in, and it seemed like she was taking the scenic route to the damn hospital.

"See, God don't like ugly." Tatiana giggled. I rolled my eyes. "You know, you look like a bitch when you roll your eyes. That's not very masculine to do when you're so busy tryin' to convince the world that you're suuuuuch a manly man."

Tatiana was about to make me cuss her ass out. She had one slick ass remark, and I was gon' call her ass something that her mama ain't name her. When we got to the hospital, I ain't even want her to go in with me. She could kiss my ass like the rest of them.

"Fuck you, Tatiana! Yeen *NOBODY* to be giving advice." I used her hacker tag and the meaning that she'd shared with me against her. "What the fuck you know about shit in the real world? Your whole life is stalking people when they don't know you lookin' and bein' in other niggas' business."

"And you pay me handsomely to do just that, too, don't you?" She checked me, but I wasn't backing down.

"But without me, all you'd be doin' is runnin' up behind the last nigga that hit it and quit it and shutting his Facebook down when you see pics of him with the next bitch."

Whipping into the hospital's Emergency Room drop-off lane so hard it threw me into the car door, she slammed on the brakes. We sat there looking at each other angrily, but I could tell that I'd hurt her feelings. I meant to, but I didn't mean to. I wasn't apologizing, though. She coulda just left a nigga in his feelings until I got over them shits. But nah, she had to pry and wanna talk and shit. Now she was sitting there like she was about to cry.

"Listen, maybe you should just let me out here and I'll catch up with you later when things calm down," I offered, feeling bad.

"Wanna know what's funny?" she said, the tears finally breaking free. "You thought I was coming in. Goodbye, Trouble. You didn't lose your Tech Girl, but you just lost your friend."

"Tati—" I tried to apologize, realizing that I'd really fucked up and she wasn't gonna take my shit like everybody else had. She shook her head, making me stop talking.

"Don't worry about it. I'm a *NOBODY* anyway, right?"

Hanging my head, I got out of the car, feeling like shit. I realized what she meant by me acting like Kong. I was being reckless with my mouth and my actions. She didn't deserve that. None of them did. Regardless, though, I meant what I said about Maine and Mia. I couldn't fuck with her if she was with him because every tear she shed I wanted to put a hole in that nigga for it. This is why I didn't fuck with women. All this emotional shit. I knew I was wrong, and knew where I needed to improve, but there was still some shit that I wouldn't take.

I would talk to my family again at some point. But right now, I needed to focus on me. I knew I had fucked up the dinner and shit, but they had to see where a nigga was coming from. I couldn't talk to everybody at the same time, but I would clear that shit up. With everybody but Sa'Mia. I was dead assed serious. I would work with Maine, 'cause that nigga's 'bout his business. But if Mia married his ass, she was dead to me.

With Pops back, the empire was safe. So after getting my hand fixed up and shit, I was just gon' leave for a little while. I needed some time. As a matter of fact, I decided not to wait. Turning away from the ER entrance, I was sad because Tatiana had really left, and I knew I'd never get her back in my life like we had been before. Using my good hand, I called for an Uber to take me to the airport. I would get my hand fixed up when I got to where I was going. Wherever the fuck that was.

Sitting in the Uber, I had an epiphany. From now on, it was all business. Money over everything was my new motto. 'Cause Money was the only thing that never let me down.

THE END... UNTIL...

MIA

FIVE AND A HALF MONTHS LATER

"*M*ia! Did you hear me?" Marissa asked me, making me look up from my phone to see what she wanted.

We had been out for four hours and my big, pregnant ass was hot, annoyed, and this little monster in my belly was on one. I stayed hungry. Feeling around in my purse where I kept my snacks, I got even more upset when I realized I'd eaten the last bag of Lay's ten minutes ago. That took my frustration to a whole new level.

"You okay?" Marissa asked, walking over to me in the dress that she had to have taken out because her and Daddy's old asses didn't know what birth control was. How the hell was that shit gon' look? My child older than their Uncle.

"No. I'm hungry, I'm hot, and we been out here for fuckin' hours on what you called a 'last minute run'. I'm tired, Rissa." I pouted.

Laughing at me, she sat down beside me and rubbed my back.

"You gettin' yo' ass kicked, huh?" she rubbed my stomach. That was something I hated when people did. All but her. She was the only one who seemed to be able to calm this little monster down. This baby got crunk at the sound of Maine and Daddy's voices. We'd decided not to find out the gender until the baby got here, but had names picked out for both and a nursery at both of our houses.

"Yeah, man. This child needs to come on outta here," I fussed. "You hear me? Ya ass need to come the hell on. You're getting evicted. *E-victed*!" I said to my stomach. I was so big people were always asking me if I was carrying multiples. Not twins, though, more like triplets. My feet were swollen, when I could see them. My thighs chaffed. I felt like a whale. I could only imagine if both of them had made it.

"You still ain't heard from your twin? He hasn't RSVP'd yet," Marissa asked me when she noticed I was checking my phone again. I shook my head no. I hadn't talked to Trouble in months, and I still couldn't shake the hurt from his abandonment. I had spent so many sleepless nights thinking about it while I studied and did homework assignments for my online classes. "Damn, y'all some stubborn ass kids," she pointed out, and there was no lie there. All of us were stubborn and hardheaded as hell. That's the reason Kong's ass was still behind bars.

When Daddy first told me what he'd done, I ain't understand why he didn't just kill Kong's ass. It would've made more sense. But he wanted to give him a chance. He loved him just like he did the rest of us. And I believed that he felt like he owed it to our mother to try and turn Kong around. I knew better, though. That nigga wasn't gonna stop 'til he was dead or in jail doing some real time. But I had gotten tired of trying to get Daddy to see the flaws in his sons' ways. He could love them unconditionally if he wanted to, but my shit came with conditions. Fuck what they thought. I had a child of my own to raise. I ain't have time to be tryna raise their grown asses.

Finally looking at Marissa, I realized how beautiful she looked. Her dress had a toga top with crystal going over her left shoulder. The bottom was chiffon and flared right under her breasts, hiding her bump beautifully.

"You look soooooo prettyyyyyyyy," I told her honestly. I wasn't sure why I was crying, but lately, I didn't need a reason to cry. I would cry because the wind wasn't blowing.

Checking my phone again, Marissa took it out of my hand, and I went from tears to fuck her up in 0.5 seconds. I tried to jump up, but the way my belly was set up, I almost fell off the bench I was sitting on like Humpty Dumpty off that wall.

"What are you checking for, Sa'Mia? What's going on?"

"Nothing," I lied, crossing my arms over my belly, looking at the floor.

"Okay, I got time. You the one hot and hungry and shit," she threatened, walking back to the dressing room to put her regular clothes back on.

All this wedding shit had me in my feelings... more than usual. All it did was make me think about my wedding. Or the fact that I still wasn't sure that I was gonna have one. Or that I wanted to have one. Every day for almost six months, Maine had asked me to marry him. Every morning. Every night. He showered me with gifts constantly and had me spoiled rotten.

But today, he hadn't said or done anything. I had to say that I was starting to expect the gifts and the daily proposals, so him not doing that today definitely caught my attention. Then again, it could've just been the hormones and Daddy getting married tomorrow. Who knew? All I knew was that I felt like I was losing him. Maybe he'd given up and decided to just co-parent. I know I wouldn't spend damn near six months begging anybody for anything. That's what had me fucked up in the head.

Coming out of the dressing room, Marissa said something to the woman behind the counter of the boutique, handing her the dress that she'd just tried on. Then her ass had the nerve to walk past me like I wasn't there. I was tempted to trip her ass, but I knew I would have to kill my Daddy if I did. Grunting, I rocked back and forth until I got the momentum to get up out of my seat and followed her as fast as I could. It wasn't like she was walking much faster with her waddling ass.

"You gonna give me back my phone, Rissa?" I said, more as a demand than a question when I finally caught up with her at the car. I was out of breath and sweating, which made me madder than I already was.

"No. Not 'til you tell me what's wrong. Is it Trouble? He'll come around. I promise."

"That's not it," I said, getting in the car that she'd unlocked for me, happy as hell to be able to sit down. "Maine didn't ask me to marry him today. As a matter of fact, I ain't heard from him this whole time I've been gone."

"Ohhhhh, and you think that he's over tryna change your mind?" she asked to make sure that she was thinking what I was thinking. I just nodded. "Well Sa'Mia, I'm gonna be real with you. You done had this man beggin' and pleadin' for months. You had to know that he might get tired at some point, right? I ain't sayin' that he ain't deserve the shit with all you went through. But when are you gonna give him an answer? Y'all don't have to get married tomorrow." She paused. "As a matter of fact, y'all better not try to get fuckin' married tomorrow. That's *my damn day*!"

"I don't know if I wanna marry him, though."

That made her swerve the car a little bit because she cut her eyes at me so ugly it hurt my feelings. I didn't know why she was so surprised that I was unsure. Why the hell would I still have this nigga begging if I was sure? I mean, yeah, I'm petty as fuck on a good day, but that would've been petty on steroids.

"Mia, I can't tell you what to do, because it's your life, and I get it. You done had people tryin' to make decisions for you all your life. But I know this... you been lookin' like a sick ass puppy, checkin' your phone every five seconds waiting for something from that man. Stop playin', and when I take you to the house, talk to him. Be honest with him. Before you lose him," she schooled me, pulling up to the gate to Maine's neighborhood. He'd made me stay with him this last month, because he wanted to keep an eye on me and was worried about me going into labor. But I knew that he also wanted to be close to me. I had kept my word and wasn't rushing my decision to get married. Even though the closer I got to my due date, the more I wanted to say yes and run off to the courthouse. We'd been dating, and he'd managed to make me fall deeper in love with him than I was before.

Marissa punched in the code, and neither of us spoke the short distance from the gate to the driveway of his house. When I opened the door to get out, she tossed my phone into my lap and smiled when I looked up at her. "Go get yo' nigga, Sa'Mia."

I got out without a word. I planned to do just what she'd told me. But first, I needed to pee and take a damn shower, thanks to that involuntary ass workout she'd put me through.

MAINE

"*I*'m so ready for Mia to have this damn baby, mane," I said aloud to myself laying across the bed in my room alone.

A nigga had blue balls out this world, and the bigger and more uncomfortable she got, she made sure that I was just as uncomfortable. And to make shit worse, she still hadn't given me an answer on the proposal. I wasn't sure at this point if she was trying to torture me, or if she was really unsure about wanting to be my wife. Both of them were a bitch, and torture, on top of her being pregnant.

Sitting on the bed, I thought back on how far we'd come. I was grateful for King for making her and for giving a nigga a chance. He could've told me no when I told him how I felt about Mia, but he didn't. Even with all the shit that I handled, that he'd checked my ass on, he still let us handle us. I wish I could say the same shit about her brother. That nigga and I were barely cordial.

When Mia came into the house, she didn't say anything to me, just made a mad dash right for the bathroom. I didn't know if it was her bladder or her hygiene that had her wobbling her ass past me without a word, but I knew not to say shit. Lately, her mouth had been lethal.

It was then that I realized I hadn't said much to her today. A nigga had honestly been deep in his thoughts. Tomorrow King and Marissa were getting married. That had me thinking that if Mia hadn't said yes by now, maybe she wasn't able to forgive me and didn't wanna marry my ass. Something told me that she blamed me for her and Trouble falling out, and that me doing business with him, while he still wasn't talking to her had her feeling a way.

That nigga had got ghost for a couple of months and had just came back. King was mad as fuck, because he ain't wanna be in the game no more, but I refused to take over with Mia being in the condition she was in. Eli and Doe stepped in to help, and I learned a lot about Trouble's past through them. That still ain't excuse that nigga's behavior. He acted like he wanted my bitch or some shit, and if I ain't know they were blood, I would've had to handle his ass again. This time, though, there wouldn't have been no winning for his ass, 'cause I would've been talkin' in rounds of hot ass metal.

About a month and a half ago, Trouble came back, and I had to say the nigga had turned his pops' empire into some next generation shit. But he ain't have two words for my ass. We were cordial for the sake of business only. Whatever he did to NOBODY had her dealing with his ass at the bare minimum, and she ain't talk to him at all. Everything with his ass was in writing. I ain't know what happened between them two, but knowing Trouble's ass, I was about 100 percent certain it was all his fault. These King kids were a muhfucka. And my ass had just made another one.

Kong was still sitting his dumb ass behind bars, because he kept talkin' about how he was gon' kill all of us to his cellmate, not knowing that King had planted the nigga there for just this reason. That nigga King was always three steps ahead of every fuckin' move we thought we'd make. I ain't see how he did that shit, and watching him with his kids, and knowing how he was with me, too, I could only hope I was half the pops he was to his to mine. I'd take half the headache his kids gave his ass, too, though, 'cause I can't promise I wouldn't have killed one or all of us if I was King. Especially after this fuckin' year.

Sitting up in the bed, I decided to turn on a movie for a little Netflix and Chill with Sa'Mia. Even though she had a nigga ready to throw in the towel, I still treated her like she was the love of my life, because she was. She had never really seen how I would love on her and treat her if I wasn't caught up in this street bullshit, and she deserved that. Picking the movie

Nappily Ever After because I knew she wanted to see it, I hoped there wasn't shit in there that would set her off. Mia was a whole ball of feelings and shit, and it got worse the closer we got to her due date. One minute she'd be crying, because she's happy about something that happened or sad about it. The next minute, a nigga could get cussed the fuck out over some shit the nigga in the movie did wrong. And the next, she'd be ready to fuck the shit outta me.

And it didn't have to be just on TV. It could be a song on the radio, something in one of them damn books she's always reading, or a bitch that got her order wrong at the restaurant and she would swear it was because she liked me. Shit was hectic, mane. I hated to say the shit, but I was happy that she only had one baby in her right now. I couldn't imagine what shit would be like if there were still two.

Turning down the lights to set the mood, I ran downstairs and popped some popcorn, grabbed me a Pepsi and her a cold bottle of water. I mean almost frozen cold, 'cause I'd got tired of room temperature ones being thrown at my head. I was so stressed that a nigga wanted to try a beer or a shot of some shit, but we ain't have that kinda shit in any of our cribs. We were in grown folks' lifestyles and making big boy moves, but we were still under the legal age to drink, and Mia couldn't drink anyway. Yeah, we obeyed the law, sometimes.

When I came back in, I smiled. I was about ready to give up on us being together, but I was gonna enjoy tonight, and feel what it would be like if Mia and I were together. The only light in the room was from Netflix ads that were running of the shows that were trending. I put everything on the nightstand and pulled back the covers, putting four pillows on Mia's side like she liked it. I was fluffing them when I heard the door to the bathroom door open. But when she called my name... I knew some other shit was going on.

MIA

"Maaaaiiinnnnneee," I cooed, standing in the doorway to his bathroom. His mouth hit the ground at the same time that my towel did. That made me happy, because I didn't know if he still found me attractive being all swollen and shit. I was big as a house and tired of being pregnant, and sexy had been the last thing that I was worried about being. But thinking about the conversation with Marissa, I knew that I had to either shit or get off the pot.

Stepping out of the doorway and into the room, the light from the TV set the mood perfectly. It looked like he was tryna be on some Netflix and Chill type shit, but I was on my K. Michelle 'fuck you like I'm tryna pay bills' moves. I needed to show him tonight, that I'd made my decision—and that decision was him. I was still scared, but I honestly couldn't see my life without him, and definitely didn't want to have to swallow seeing him with another bitch. Or raising our child in two separate houses.

Maine wore a look of awe. I could tell he was expecting to see me in one of his big ass t-shirts and some jogging pants. My wardrobe was limited as hell, because I refused to buy maternity clothes. I felt like that would be me saying that I was willing to get pregnant again. Which I was *not*. So that would've just been a waste of money, because you only wore them bitches for a limited time. Yeah, I was stupid rich, but that didn't mean that I had to just throw money away. I was investing in the marketing firm, trying to expand it like I'd heard my brother was doing with the drug empire.

"Mia, whatchu doin'?" he asked with a pained look on his face.

"If you gotta ask me that, then it's been way too long since I did it," I tried to flirt, walking toward him as flirtatiously as I could with my big ass pregnant belly leading the way.

He stood there looking like he was constipated, and I knew it was because his dick was so hard, he'd probably lost all blood flow to his brain. When I reached him, I tried to get up on my tiptoes to kiss him, since he was still stuck standing there looking like a statue. My attempt was an epic fail, though for two reasons. One, my stomach was in between us and my midget ass arms only reached so far. Two, trying to lift all this extra weight hurt my ankles and I think I broke a pinky toe.

"Damn," I heard him say under his breath. I wanted to smile and be flattered because he was saying it as if to say I looked so beautiful, sexy, or I'd taken his breath away and that was all that he could get out. Instead, I stepped back, cocking my head to the side, before bursting into tears. "Awwww, come on, mane. Mia, what the fuck?"

"You think I'm faatttttt," I howled, waddling to my side of the bed and plopping down on my side. The baby wasn't here for that move because it started kicking the hell out of me, which only made me cry harder. I grabbed one of the pillows and wrapped my arms around it, letting the tears and the wails flow freely.

I knew Maine was probably still standing there on stuck, but every second that he didn't come tell me that he didn't think I was fat made me cry harder. I took this as a sign that we weren't supposed to be together, and that my failed attempt at trying to make us official was a mistake. He didn't even know how and when to comfort me, so I knew that we weren't gonna work.

"Mia," I heard his voice over me. I had been crying so hard that I hadn't heard him walk to my side of the bed over all the noise I was making. He placed his hand on my stomach, the baby had it jumping like it was twerking at the sound of its daddy's voice.

"No. Don't try to comfort me now. It's too late. Just leave me alone," I snapped, pushing his hand away, the tears stopping just like that.

"You need to gone have this damn baby. Yo' ass already bipolar as hell without being pregnant, but that lil' nigga in there gotchu tri-polar as a muhfucka. A nigga can't even admire the beautiful woman you are without you havin' a ghatdamned emotional meltdown. Dafuq wrong witchu!"

His frustration was evident, but that ain't move me, because he should've told me all that when I was trying to be affectionate with him and kiss his stupid ass. Now the only thing he could kiss was my ass.

"Kiss my tri-polar, emotional meltdown havin' ass, Arkino!"

"Okay," he said, walking away. *Wait, what? Did he say okay? It's that simple for him to be done. Well fuck him, then.*

"Ahhhh shit." I moaned when I felt his lips press up against my ass cheek. I arched my back more than it already was, thanks to this little monster living inside of me, and he took advantage. Spreading my cheeks, he stuck his tongue inside my pussy from behind. I gripped the pillow harder, burying my face into it and moving as much as I could with the in and out motion of his tongue. He took his time eating me, making sure to slurp up every drop that I released on the way to my nut. Reaching around, he massaged my breasts with his hands. They'd grown so big that he couldn't fit all of them in his hands. Pinching my nipples, he hummed against my pussy, sliding his tongue from my clit to my hole. He stuck his tongue all the way inside of me, so far, his face was pressed into the soft-ness of my ass. I came so hard I got lightheaded and had to close my eyes to regroup.

I felt Maine's body press against mine and he raised my leg up in the air. Placing the tip of his head at the opening of my leaking pussy, but he didn't put it inside. I was hurtin' to feel him and he was playing.

"Tell me I can have you, Mia."

"Fuck me, Maine. Quit playin'," I whined.

"Tell me I can have you," he commanded, still not pushing it in.

"Mainnnneeee."

"Say that shit, Sa'Mia De'Shay!" *Whack!* He slapped my ass so hard that it rippled through me, making me cum again.

"You... you can... ha-ha-havvveeee meeeee!" I moaned, another orgasm vibrating through me.

Easing into me, he gave me time to adjust to his size. He squeezed my thigh hard, and buried his face into my back, biting my shoulder. Then he kissed the spot he bit before biting it again when he got all the way inside.

"Damn baby, you feel so fuckin'—unhhhhhhh!"

Maine was moving in and out of me at a quick, gentle pace. He was being considerate, even though I knew he wanted to fuck me so hard he put the next baby in line to start growing after this one.

"Kino! I love you!" The words slipped free before I could stop them, and even though I might have regretted it after this was done, I wasn't gonna take that shit back now. And I *did* love him.

"I love you, too, Sa'Mia. Marry me!"

"Ask me again when you ain't knockin' ya baby in the forehead," I joked, right before I felt a pain that knocked the air outta me, and a gush of water.

"That's right. I know how to make that pussy squirt!" he said cockily, patting himself on the back.

"M-M-M-Maine," I uttered when I caught my breath.

"Miaaaaa!"

"Maine!"

"Yeah, say my name, Mia! Fuck, you wet!"

"Maine! Stop!"

"Come on, bae. I'm almost at my nut!" he pleaded, not wanting to quit. He started stroking me faster, trying to get his before I said anything else.

"Maine! Stop! Owwwwww!" I yelled, and he pulled out of me and hopped out of the bed, running around to my side.

"I'm sorry, baby! Did I hurt you? I'm so sorry!" He leaned over me apologizing, his dick right in my face.

"I'm in laborrrrr," I moaned, grabbing my stomach and balling up into a tight ball.

"Oh shit! Oh shit!"

Maine helped me out of the bed and ran over to the dresser, taking out a t-shirt and a pair of his sweats. Running back to me, his dick slapping his thigh, I was leaning on the bed trying to hold myself up. He helped me get dressed, before picking me up and running toward the door. I was in so much pain, I was grateful that I didn't have to walk. When he got to the door, he placed me on my feet, and I leaned up against the wall while he grabbed his keys and the delivery bag that we had packed and by the door of both of our houses.

"Maine!" I managed to scream when he threw the bag over his shoulder and went to pick me up again.

"What, Mia! What?"

"Nigga, you naked!"

Looking down, he looked back up at me, and I smiled as much as I could through the pain I was in. Him panicking was cute. And him making sure I had everything I needed, without thinking about himself was sweet. I watched him run back to his room and tried to breathe through the pain while he got dressed.

When he came back, he grabbed me and the bag and ran like hell out the door. Unlocking the truck, he threw the bag into the back seat and put me in the passenger seat as gently as he could. He was moving so fast that he almost hit his head when he leaned down to put me in. Slamming the door, he ran around the front of the truck to the driver's side before getting in, cranking it up, and peeling out of the driveway. We were on the freeway in no time. He was darting in and out of traffic, and I was breathing through these painful ass contractions. We were silent for a few minutes, and then he broke the silence with the dumbest shit he could've come up with at the time.

"Mia, I need an answer. I don't wanna bring our child into this world without knowing where we stand for real."

"Maine! You wanna talk about this shit *now? I'm in ghatdamned labor!*"

"Hell yeah I wanna talk about this shit now. I been tryna talk about it for months, and yeen gave a nigga a break. The time clock is winding down, bae. I need to know."

"And what if I say yeah? Then what? You gon' have a priest come marry us while I'm pushing your watermelon head ass baby out my pussy?"

"Yep, som'n like that," he said with a chuckle, and I looked at the side of his face so hard it should've hit his ass like a slap.

"Som'n like that! I wanna weddinnnnngggg. I want the flowers and shit, Maine. I want—"

"That's yo' bad for playin' wit' a nigga and having me wait half a fuckin' year for an answer. Now, you gon' be Mrs. Arkino Shane or not?"

Rolling my eyes as he pulled into the ER drop-off, I tried to get out of the truck, but he locked the doors.

"Nigga, I know you better unlock these damn doors!" I snapped, right as another contraction hit me.

"Not 'til you answer my question. Hell, I got time. You gon' be the one with a head hanging outcha shit in a minute. Your choice, delivery room, or front seat of my ride. I don't give a fuck. I'll just get the shit detailed or buy another car."

I wanted to hit his ass in the face, but it hurt to breathe, so I wasn't gonna take my chances with making any sudden movements. I bit my lip, massaging my stomach, trying to lessen the pain. Nothing was working.

"This is a hostage situation. You really want me to answer this shit under duress?" I asked, cutting my eyes at him and making a mental note to beat his ass once I got this child up outta me.

"Duress or no duress, I need a yes or a no. And your contractions are ten minutes apart, I was timing them with the clock on my radio, so we got time. But the longer you wait, the less the chance that you can take advantage of that wonderful modern medicine that they have to help you with that pain. You breakin' a sweat, so I'm sure them shits hittin' harder than you do when you mad right now."

This nigga was serious, and now wasn't the time to be stubborn. I gritted my teeth and popped my lips, trying the door handle again. Beating on the window, I tried to catch the attention of anyone outside the truck. But this was one of the few times that niggas in Dallas minded their damn business. *Just my luck. This some bullshit,* I thought. It wasn't that I didn't want to say yes. My issue was that I was being forced to make a decision that he didn't know I'd already made.

"Yes, Kino! Okay. Now open the damn door before we both be in beds next to each other in this fuckin' hospital."

"I ain't too worried about that." He chuckled, unlocking the door. "My baby boy lookin' out for his daddy. We just tag teamed dat ass."

I slung the door open and went to try to get out while he killed the ignition. I was in so much pain that my knees buckled when they hit the ground, and I almost fell on my face.

"Whooooaaaa," my daddy said, catching me just in time. *When the hell did Maine call him?* I wondered.

"She hardheaded as hell," Marissa fussed, walking back out of the hospital doors with Maine, who was pushing a wheelchair. "They're waiting for y'all. I already gave them all the information they needed. All you gotta worry about doin' now is have us a healthy baby, Mia," she said with a smile, but I wasn't smiling. I was hurting like hell, and the baby didn't like this shit any more than I did, because he was kicking me all in my ribs.

"Naw, we need a minister, too," Maine informed them, helping me into the chair and leading the way into the hospital.

"She finally made a decision, huh?" Daddy asked Maine.

"He ain't gimme no choice. He held me hostage in the truck and said he would make me have the baby in there if I didn't give him an answer," I pouted, snitching his ass out.

"Creative," was all Daddy said, and Marissa laughed. That pissed me off.

"Fuck all y'all! Ahhhhhhhh! Get this baby the fuck outta meeeeeeee!"

A contraction hit me so hard I passed out. When I came to, I was in a room, hooked up to machines. Daddy was sitting across the room with his head in his hands. Marissa was in the chair on the side of my bed, holding my hand. Maine was pacing and talking to himself. *See, this nigga crazy as hell. I'on know if I wanna spend the rest of my life with his ass or not. It's too late for the baby shit. But I ain't gotta marry him, though*, I thought. The thought of the baby made me lift my free hand to my stomach.

"She's up!" Marissa yelled, and everybody raced over to the side of me.

"Where's the baby?" I asked, my stomach feeling soft.

"Emergency C-Section. You passed out and the baby was under too much stress. They took him."

"Him? Is he okay?" I panicked.

"He's fine, Mia. I'll go tell the nurse you're awake and that you want your son," Marissa said, getting up from the chair.

"And I'll go get the minister," Kino said, leaving the room before I could object.

"He's for real…" I said, more to myself than to Daddy.

"Yeah, he is. Are you sure it's what you want?"

"Yeah, I'm sure. Like for real for real. I was gonna tell him that tonight, but then I went into labor."

"Yeah… you *went* into labor."

I didn't look at Daddy when he said that, because I knew then that Maine's big mouthed ass had told him how the whole thing went down. We had to talk about that shit. Daddy didn't need to know every damn thing about us. Especially not no shit like that.

"Man, that nigga."

"The nurse asked when you went into labor trying to get a timeline, and his nervous ass spilled the beans. It was way TMI, though. She only needed a time. Not a play by play." He laughed like he was remembering the whole thing. "Ya know, you're not gon' be able to make the wedding tomorrow."

"I know," I said sadly. "But it ain't like I'm missing the shit outta spite or nothing, like somebody else I know," I said, thinking about Trouble and rolling my eyes.

"One thing that I've learned is to let y'all do what y'all gon' do. Last time I didn't, I damn near got all of us killed."

"Hey there, Miss King. Let me check your vitals," the nurse said, coming into the room.

"Thank you," I said watching her check the machines, then taking my blood pressure, and pressing on my stomach. "When do I get to meet my son?"

"Look who it is, Arkino. There's your mommyyyyy," another nurse cooed, wheeling my son into the room. *Arkino?* I thought and smiled. *He gave him the name we'd picked out. Arkino Alonzo Shane. My son.* My eyes filled with happy tears at the thought.

"Good, he can be a witness to his parents making this shit official," Maine said, a few seconds later, walking in with a priest behind him.

"And his grandparents," Marissa said, looking at Daddy who looked just as confused as I was. "Baby, I don't care about the big wedding. All I wanna do is be your wife. I was willing to wait 'til tomorrow, but we got the minister already here, your—our—first grandson was just born. Let's get married today. And tomorrow will be for the niggas and bitches who were only coming for free food and liquor and to take pictures and video to be able to say they know us."

"Let's do it," Daddy said excitedly, rushing over to Marissa, kissing her on the forehead and resting his hand on her stomach.

Maine picked our son up gently and placed him in my arms. Feeling him lay up on my chest gave me a feeling I'd never felt before. I would do anything for this little boy. *Anything.*

"That's my cue," the minister spoke up, clearing his throat. The nurses looked on with googly eyes. "Your names?"

"Alonzo King and Marissa Hervey," Daddy said with so much excitement in his voice and his eyes that my heart melted.

"Arkino Shane and Sa'Mia King," Maine followed up with just as much excitement, looking at our son with pride. "And that's Arkino Alonzo Shane there," he said, pointing to our son who was in and out of sleep in my arms.

"Nice to meet you all, and I'm honored to be the one chosen to bind both of you beautiful couples in marriage. Marriage is a covenant made before God and man. It is not to be entered into lightly. Nowadays, vows are not held to the esteem that they should be, but I can tell that you all love one another deeply. Continue to love one another, honestly, openly, and unconditionally as God loves us, his children. Add to it a devotion that cannot be penetrated by these women and men who think that breaking up this covenant is something to be proud of, clinging to one another, and you'll have the formula for successful marriages." He paused, looking at all four of us seriously, making sure his words sank in. "Take one another's hands," he instructed.

Maine took my free hand as I cradled Arkino in the other, and Daddy took Marissa's. Meeting eyes with my soon-to-be husband, I felt tears running down my cheeks. He used his free hand to wipe them away, but there was no use. Every one that he wiped was replaced with another. But they were tears of joy.

"Please repeat after me," he turned to Daddy and Marissa first. "Do you, Alonzo King, take Marissa Hervey to be your wife? To have and to hold from this day forward, for better or for worse, for richer, for poorer, in sickness and in health; from this day forward until death do you part?"

"I do," Daddy said, kissing the back of Rissa's hand.

"And do you, Marissa Hervey, take Alonzo King to be our husband? To have and to hold from this day forward, for better or for worse, for richer, for poorer, in sickness and in health; from this day forward until death do you part?"

"Yes. Yes, I do!" Marissa cheered loudly.

Turning to Maine and me, I felt my stomach start churning. I was nervous. Not because I didn't want to marry Maine, but because this was a big deal. We were about to be married and parents before we were old enough to drink.

"We got this," Maine leaned down and whispered in my ear, calming my fears just like that. When the minister turned to us, he mixed it up a little bit.

"Do you, Arkino Shane, take Sa'Mia King to be your wife and share a life with her, equal in love, embraced as a mirror for your true self, loving her as you would love yourself, promising to honor and cherish her through good times and bad, until death do you part?" he asked, and it was like he knew our history because those vows were customized just for us.

"Hell yeah!" Maine's voice boomed through the room, and everybody laughed. All but the baby, who shifted in his sleep, balling his face up like he was about to start crying. I shot Maine a look and he smiled and shrugged at me.

"Happy to see a young man so willing to take such a big step." The minister chuckled. "And do you, Sa'Mia King, take Arkino Shane to be your husband and share a life with him, equal in love, embraced as a mirror for your true self, loving him as you would love yourself, promising to honor and cherish him through good times and bad, until death do you part?"

"I guess," I teased with a shrug, and it was his turn to side eye me. "Yes. Yes, I do," I laughed softly, making Daddy shake his head and Rissa smile at me being a smart ass, even now.

"Do we have rings?" he asked, acknowledging the situation that we were in, being here at the hospital. To our surprise, Daddy and Maine both pulled out rings.

"We just got ours sized," Daddy explained.

"And I been carrying this one here 'round, waiting for you to find your damn mind," Maine shot shade at me. "Even got it sized up to fit when K2 swole them sausage fingers of yours up," he finished, and I stuck my tongue out at him.

"God is good," the minister said, clapping his hands, impressed at their preparedness before continuing the double ceremony. "Let's keep it going. Men, repeat after me. I give you this ring, as a symbol of my love. As it encircles your finger, may it remind you always that you are surrounded by my endearing love. With this ring, I thee wed."

Daddy and Maine repeated in unison, putting the rings on my and Rissa's fingers.

"And ladies, repeat after me," he said, looking at me and Rissa. We both nodded that we were ready, even though our faces were soaking wet. "With my body, I thee worship. With my heart, I thee cherish. All that I am, I give unto you. All that I have, I share with you. From this day until forever done. With this ring, I thee wed."

We repeated after him, putting the rings on our men's fingers.

"Those rings symbolize your commitment and were exchanged today as a sign of the desires of your hearts. Wear them gladly. Whenever you look at them, remember this joyous day of new life, new beginnings, and the vows and commitments that were made. And now, by the power vested in me by the State of Texas, I hereby pronounce y'all husband and wife. Husbands, kiss your brides!"

Daddy leaned down to kiss Rissa and Maine kissed me with so much love and passion that I felt like he'd sucked the breath out of me. I couldn't breathe and when he let me go, I couldn't take my eyes off of him. Until our son started to whine.

"Lil' nigga's a hater already." Maine smiled, looking down at his firstborn.

"He's probably wet," the nurse that brought him in offered, and Maine grabbed a diaper and wipes from the inside of the rollaway crib. Laying my son in my lap, I took his diaper off and looked up at the nurses like I was about to kill their asses.

"What the fuck happened to him?" I yelled, looking at him and back up at them.

"He was circumcised," Maine offered, putting his hand on my shoulder to calm me down. He knew me, and I was about to get up, stitches and all, and beat somebody's ass.

"Oh, aight," I conceded, finishing the diaper change and passing Arkino to Daddy, who reached for him.

"It was a pleasure meeting y'all. Congratulations on your marriage. Ladies, let's give them some privacy," the minister said, ushering the nurses out of the room with him.

When the door closed behind them, I took in the room, and my heart swelled with joy. Daddy and Marissa were sitting on the couch on the opposite side of the room, cooing at their grandson. Maine was in the chair beside me, looking back and forth between me and them. Everything felt perfect. Well, almost.

I'd be lying if I said it didn't bother me that Trouble wasn't here. *Fuck him*, I said to myself, trying to convince myself that it wasn't eating me up inside. As if he felt my pain, Arkino Alonzo Shane, my son, started to cry louder this time. Daddy brought him to me, and I pulled out my breast to feed him. Seeing something was wrong with me, Maine rubbed his hand down my cheek, turning my face toward him by my chin so that he could look me directly in the face.

"Thank you for my son. Thank you for being my wife."

I gave him a weak smile, and nodded before looking back down at our son, helping him latch on.

"It's okay, baby," I cooed to him, choking back the tears. "I promise it's gonna be okay."

I was talking to myself more than my son. Taking in his perfect little face and all the ones who loved me that were in my presence in this special time in my life, I knew that I had to let Trouble go. Maine may have to deal with him for business. But other than that, his ass was dead to me.

"I love you, Mrs. Shane," Kino said, leaning down and kissing my lips.

"I know."

MAINE

*N*igga, I'm a daddy. Who the fuck would've thought that was how this shit would turn out? I always knew I was gon' marry Mia. But have a baby, yeah, that was way down the line. I don't regret shit about what happened. As a matter of fact, I wouldn't have it any other way. Staring at my wife feeding my son, I promised myself, them, and God, that I would protect them with my life. And I meant that shit. Sa'Mia had been my life and the pain in my ass for so long. But without her, and now, without Arkino Alonzo Shane, or K2, a nigga would be out here lost. I'd never felt so complete in my life.

A thought crossed my mind and I leaned in to kiss Mia and K2 on the forehead. "I'll be right back," I whispered to her.

She looked at me curiously but didn't object. I left the room and went to the elevator, pushing the down arrow. I heard the ding and the door opened.

"I swear you like a virus or some shit, mane." I gritted, looking at Artina.

"I just wanna meet my grandson," she said, holding a teddy bear out to me like that was gon' make any difference. I grabbed her arm and pulled her into the elevator with me. When the door closed, I pushed her, making her stumble into the back of the elevator and hit her back on it. She dropped the bear on the ground, and it took everything in me not to stomp on that bitch.

"You'll never meet my son, Artina. Why the fuck do you keep trying me?"

"I'm so sorry, Arkino. I've been in therapy for years. I'm better. I would never—"

"Never what? Never molest my son like you did me? Never let other niggas do fucked up shit to him for a hit? Fuck you, Artina. When this door opens, you better leave this ghatdamned hospital, and if I ever see you again, I'm ending ya life. This is ya second strike. Don't try me again."

I turned my back to her and pushed the button for the lobby. I heard her sniffling, but that shit ain't move me. She was good with them damn tears and guilt trips. I'd only taken care of her to keep her the fuck away from me, and because I respected her for not aborting a nigga when she had the chance. But she was testing me. She wasn't getting anywhere near my wife, and sure the fuck not my son. This was one secret that Mia ain't know about me, and I'd rather keep it that way. Even if I had to kill this bitch to make it happen.

The elevator doors opened, and I walked straight ahead toward the gift shop. Out of my peripheral, I saw her leave the hospital. If she knew what was best for her, she would keep walking and never cross my path again. As a matter of fact, I was gon' send a team over to her crib to help her... relocate. Walking through the gift shop, I picked up as many bears and balloons and stuffed animals as my arms could hold. Then I grabbed a couple dozen flowers from by the counter when I'd put the other stuff down.

"I can get a cart so you can wheel all this stuff," the cashier offered while she rang me up.

"'Preciate that," I said, paying the $357.89 total I owed.

She gave me my receipt and walked from around the counter with a cart and loaded everything on it.

"Congratulations!" She beamed at my back while I headed back to the elevator and to my family. I didn't respond or look back, just in case she was testing waters that her ass would no doubt drown in.

Getting back on the elevator, I took in breaths, hoping that Mia liked *something* that I'd just bought. When I walked into the room, she was singing to K2, and I stopped to look at her being a mother. *Sa'Mia King is my wife and the mother of my child. Soon to be children. Mrs. Sa'Mia Shane,* I thought. I was the happiest nigga on the planet right now and felt like I was floating, my feet not even touching the ground.

Wheeling the cart to the side of the bed, I saw King asleep on the pull-out couch with Marissa sleep on top of him. I wanted that to be Mia and me when K2 had his first child. With that thought, I smiled so big my cheeks hurt as I listened to her beautiful voice when she sang to our son. I kissed her forehead, and she looked at the cart, tears brimming her eyes. I smiled as our son rested peacefully in his mother's arms and joined in, harmonizing with her.

"Maybe it's your love, it's too good to be true. Baby boy, your love got me trippin' on you. You know your love is big enough, make me trip up on you. Yeah, it's big enough, got me trippin' on you, trip-trippin' on you…"

The End… For Real This Time!

AUTHOR'S NOTE

I'm so grateful to have completed my first three-part series as a member of the Royalty Family. This was the book that caught their interest in me, so there's a special, special meaning for me. I hope you enjoyed meeting Maine and Mia and all the characters that brought them together and almost tore them apart as much as I enjoyed writing them! Check out the backstory of how King met Danielle, and why there was so much beef with him and Kellz in my most recently released short *King and Dani: A Feelings on Safety Valentine's Day Prequel.*

If you like these stories, please stay tuned, because I have so many more to share with y'all.

Thank y'all so much for rockin' wit' Tha Kidd! I promise to keep 'em comin'! Stay tuned!

Always,
Joi Miner

ABOUT THE AUTHOR

Joi Miner, 36, is a mother of two beautiful daughters from Montgomery, AL (currently residing in Birmingham, AL). She is a full-time author, editor, performance poet, storyteller, sexual assault and domestic violence activist, and entrepreneur, who loves spending time with her family, hosting shows, and listening to good music. She loves writing engaging stories, with plot twists that keep readers on their seats! As a freelance non-fiction contributor, for Negus Who Read and I Am The F-Bomb, she shares her insights into this crazy world we live in.

Stay Connected:

Email: authorjoiminer@gmail.com

Facebook Overflow Profile: Author Join Miner
Author Page: https://www.facebook.com/joiminer2

Subscribe to my Newsletter: http://eepurl.com/cKJ7bf
**Join The Official Reading Group: Love, Life, and Joi: The Joi Miner
Reading Group
[My Blog] My Life Is A Joi Miner Novel:**
www.mylifeisajoiminernovel.com

facebook.com/joiminer

twitter.com/joiminer

instagram.com/joiminer

LIKE OUR PAGE!

Be sure to <u>LIKE</u> our Royalty Publishing House page on Facebook!

CPSIA information can be obtained
at www.ICGtesting.com
Printed in the USA
LVHW111752120319
610380LV00004B/457/P

9 781798 462126